The
Whirligig of Time

The
Whirligig of Time

LLOYD BIGGLE, JR.

DOUBLEDAY & COMPANY, INC.

GARDEN CITY, NEW YORK

1979

Library of Congress Cataloging in Publication Data

Biggle, Lloyd, 1923–
The whirligig of time.

I. Title.
PZ4.B593Wh   [PS3552.I43]   813'.5'4
ISBN: 0-385-13211-5
Library of Congress Catalog Card Number 78–1179

First Edition

And thus the whirligig of time brings in his revenges.
—Shakespeare, Twelfth-Night

The
Whirligig of Time

1

19430

Captain Bn Ffallo, of the fifth-grade cargo ship *Esarq,* possessed in abundance a short temper, the vast experience that only a lifetime in space could endow, and all of the superstitions of his profession. When Volp, his third officer, who served as navigator and cargo supervisor, abruptly developed water bloat in all six of his legs—a condition to which his kind was unusually susceptible when subjected to long periods of low gravity—Captain Ffallo stoically accepted this as an evil omen.

He put the unfortunate Volp aground on the world of Wanazk and signed on the only substitute available, a rank apprentice and native of Wanazk named Mkim. Since a change of crew in mid-voyage was viewed universally as certain invitation to disaster, Captain Ffallo resumed his journey and waited with resignation for the catastrophe to strike.

He did not have to wait long. A mere three periods out of Wanazk, the new junior officer presented himself at the captain's quarters, his purple-tinged features fraught with dramatic perplexity. Ffallo immediately suspected the worst: a leaking liquid compartment, a malfunctioning heater on a compartment of perishable goods, or a disastrous cargo shift.

Mkim groped sputteringly for words and finally managed to say, "Sire, there's a double star."

Captain Ffallo relaxed. His new officer was not reporting to him in his role of cargo supervisor, but as the ship's navigator—and the position of navigator on a lightly crewed cargo vessel was a perfunctory assignment, passed out as an afterthought to the most junior officer. The fact was that the ship's drive mechanism contained its own navigational computer; and if, for some unlikely reason, that computer failed, there was a supplementary computer in the control room whose operation was so simple that any ship's officer and most of its crew could quickly plot a position, lay on a course, or calculate an arrival time. Such safeguards multiplied with a ship's size and importance, and even the largest passenger carriers possessed an official navigator only as insurance against an unthinkable emergency.

Since there was nothing wrong with the cargo, and the captain couldn't conceive of any navigational problem that wasn't easily and quickly correctable, he invited Mkim into his quarters, got him seated comfortably, and even offered him a bowl of vrampf, bits of pastry containing a fiery liquor much favored by spacers, to munch on.

Mkim, his purple complexion deepening with pleasure, inhaled a large mouthful of vrampf and began to ruminate with three sets of gums. Watching him, it occurred to Ffallo that Mkim had been spending an inordinate amount of time in taking navigational sightings; but it had been Mkim's free time, and the captain had thought that the youngster was merely practicing. If an apprentice wanted to perfect his navigational skills, or any other skills, on his free time, no captain in the galaxy would object. There always was the one-in-a-billion chance that the additional experience might prove useful.

But now it was evident that this particular apprentice and non-functional navigator needed basic education rather than practice. The captain decided to be kindly about it. "A double star," he repeated. "Are you positive about that?"

"Yes, sire."

"Discovering it must have been quite a thrill for you."

Mkim missed the captain's sarcastic tone. Speaking around another mouthful of vrampf, he mumbled, "Sire?"

"More than half the stars of the galaxy are multiple systems," the captain went on, still speaking sarcastically. "Is it possible to study navigation without noticing this?"

"Sire, on the chart it's a single star."

The captain paused. A statement, even by an apprentice navigator, that their observed position did not match the position their charts indicated was one no captain could take lightly. He demanded incredulously, "Are you trying to tell me we're lost?"

"No, sire. Everything else checks. But there's this one star that has a companion. And according to the chart, it shouldn't."

"Then you're saying there's an error on the chart."

"Yes, sire."

"This," Captain Ffallo announced firmly, "I've got to see for myself."

He strode away, and Mkim meekly followed him.

On the control room chart, Mkim pointed out the star. Unquestionably it was a single, with seven planets. Then Mkim focused the viewing screen to reveal a double star. Captain Ffallo grunted skeptically and took over the screen's controls himself. If there was an error on the chart—and he'd never heard of such a thing—it would have to be reported, and he wasn't about to sign a declaration based on an inexperienced navigator's pointing a screen in the wrong direction.

He oriented himself with care, refocused the screen, looked again. He saw the double star.

But still he hesitated. Was it a true binary? The smaller of the two stars might be a distant one, freakishly placed at this particular moment so as to produce a binary illusion.

On the other hand, the survey ship that charted this sector—space knew how long ago—could have been the victim of the same kind of freakish coincidence in reverse: the smaller star could have been in line with one more distant and mistaken for it. Or it could have been in eclipse at the moment the survey ship made its sighting.

The captain turned to the supplemental navigational computer and satisfied himself that they were properly on course. He examined the chart again, and then he reset the viewing screen. The star system was still binary. Their screen wasn't powerful enough to pick up any of the planets.

"The chart seems to be wrong," the captain admitted grudgingly. "Suppose you draw up a report, and I'll enter it in the log and file a copy with the Galactic Survey. Record the complete data—distance of observation, time, positions of other stars observed." Mkim was assenting eagerly. Too eagerly. "But be sure to say 'apparent,'" the captain cautioned him grimly. "It apparently is a binary, and if so the chart is incorrect, and you recommend an investigation."

"Yes, sire. If we could delay the next jump for a short time, then—"

"Not worth it," the captain snapped. "Correcting charts isn't our business. We'll have done our duty, and more, by bringing it to the Survey's attention. Our business is delivering cargo, and delay costs solvency. Don't ever forget that!"

Mkim looked so crestfallen that the captain felt a flash of sympathy for him. No doubt one of the star's planets had been a protostar, and they had happened onto the scene shortly after it exploded into stellar incandescence. Few apprentice navigators had the opportunity or luck to make such a discovery, and the captain couldn't blame him for wanting to produce a report that was a model of completeness and scientific accuracy.

He grinned and clapped the youngster's shoulder with a friendly tentacle. "Write your report. I'll let you enter it in the log yourself, and I'll message it ahead of us just in case some faster ship makes the same sighting and tries to get its report in first. If you're right, the Survey might even name that second sun after you. Mkim. You'll be immortal."

Mkim beamed a purpling smile at him. "Yes, sire!" He turned and hurried away.

"But don't forget to say 'apparent!'" the captain bellowed after him.

It was a brief, informal ceremony, and the audience that gathered to witness it was a small one. Naz Forlan was being pledged as Mas of Science and Technology of the world of Vezpro. Had Forlan been appointed mas of any other department, the ceremony would have taken place in the Palace of Government, with a vast audience and an appropriate blast of publicity. But few people except those of the department concerned cared who the Mas of Science and Technology was, and although the masfiln himself generously took time off from his multitudinous duties to attend in person and administer the pledge, he was the only high official present. The audience consisted of Forlan's own associates.

The ceremony was quickly completed, with Masfiln Min Kallof smiling and fumbling words—for some obscure reason the Mas of Science and Technology took a different pledge from that imposed on other mases—and Forlan repeating them clearly, as though they meant something, and several times correcting the masfiln.

Then the masfiln dashed off, Forlan spoke briefly to the assembled department about the honor of service, and they all adjourned to the dining hall for a wholly unexpected round of refreshments that the new mas had provided for them at his own expense.

"And who is better qualified to talk about the honor of service than he?" Eld Wolndur remarked to his fiancée, Melris Angoz, as they munched contentedly on a frozen dessert of fruit and sazk juice.

She answered absently, "He's spent virtually his entire career in the department, hasn't he?"

"If he wasn't an alien, he would have been mas years ago."

"That's not true," she protested. "He turned it down several times."

"He did?" Wolndur's expression was incredulous. "Why would anyone refuse an appointment—"

Melris flashed a superior smile. It was the one fault he'd ever been able to find in her. Computer tecs became so accustomed to holding the knowledge of the universe at their finger tips that they tended to confuse knowledge with wisdom and their own mental capacities with those of their computers.

"Politics," she said. "He told me so himself. Some masfilns even try to involve the Mas of Science and Technology in politics. He wouldn't have any of that, so he respectfully declined. I don't know how many times. He doesn't think the department should be involved in politics, and he refuses to pretend he's a politician. Masfiln Kallof promised to let him do the job in his own way."

"He's certainly the best-qualified person," Wolndur said. "He has been for years."

Wolndur glanced at the head table, where Forlan was carrying on a spirited discussion with a section supervisor of nuclear installations. The new mas was small and wiry-looking, with two short legs, an elongated body, and four stubby arms. His flesh had a slightly greenish tint, and—since that obviously disconcerted natives who had business with him—he'd devised an office lighting system that made him look normal. Here in the dining hall, the green tint was obvious.

The only aspect of his appearance that was not completely ridiculous was his oversized head—large for his body, large even for a native of Vezpro—and its disproportion was further distorted because of his bristling head growth.

His subordinates found him kindly, considerate, and brilliant.

Wolndur watched the animated conversation for a moment: the new mas looking grotesque beside his native assistants, who were tall and slender, with handsomely gleaming heads and triple, multidigited legs and arms. Wolndur still thought Forlan had been the victim of a career-long prejudice merely because he was an alien. Even people who liked and admired him were given to poking fun at his appearance.

He said to Melris, "Let's hope he has a peaceful administration."

She shrugged her agreement. "If only they'll let him work without interference, if only there aren't any petty, irrelevant crises, he'll transform this world. He has the plans. He knows how to do it."

"If only," Wolndur agreed bitterly. "It rarely happens, but if only—"

"A year ago they were going to name the new Yengloz power plant after him," Melris said. "He wouldn't let them. He said the department was monument enough for him. He built it from nothing, you know. And with political opposition all the way."

"But now he's mas himself, so at least he won't have a stupid superior harassing him," Wolndur pointed out. "The world of Vezpro will be his monument."

"If only they'll let him work without interference."

"Yes. Let's pray for no political crises, no economic collapses, no stupid social upheavals. Give him a couple of cycles to get started, and no one will be able to stop him. Even a new administration wouldn't dare appoint a replacement."

Wolndur spoke hopefully, but he felt certain that there would be a concerted effort to get the new mas dismissed merely because he was an alien. And if anyone could find the slightest pretext, it would succeed.

A farmer discovered the body. It was lying in a weed-cluttered ditch by a lonely country road, and he saw it only by accident—the setting sun's rays for a moment reflected off something dully red, and the farmer, a thrifty creature in the manner of good farmers anywhere in the galaxy, immediately suspected that an article had been lost or discarded. It might even be worth stopping for. He brought his chugging tractor to a steam-snorting halt and stepped down. Eagerly he leaped into the ditch. There was a saying on this world of Skarnaf that a salvageable discard could be worth a day of good weather—either was the gift of providence.

One look, and the farmer scrambled back to the tractor and drove it at top speed toward the village. There he panted out his story, which brought to his farm a young apprentice medic and the local provost deputy; and then, after the body had been removed, they were followed by a thickening stream of provost investigators, medic specialists, and distinguished scientists with titles the farmer could not pronounce. Finally the worthy farmer and his mate and family were whisked far away to the nearest metropolis that possessed the medical facilities essential for certain mysterious tests.

At every step of the way there were perplexing questions to which no one had answers—especially the farmer. For the body had, in fact, been alive; and whether it continued to live or not, what was wrong with it so baffled medics and provosts and scientists and—finally—politicians, that experts continued to prowl the countryside with strange instruments, and they returned again and again with their plague of questions for the farmer and all of his neighbors.

In a rural area of the world of Skarnaf, an individual had been found suffering the most severe nuclear radiation burns that medical history had recorded. How he managed to survive the experience, no one could guess.

Neither could anyone guess how such a catastrophe could have occurred. Skarnaf was an agricultural world. Its factories, where they existed, were hydropowered, and the world had no nuclear installations, not even experimental ones. The victim certainly had not fallen from space. Neither could he have arrived from another world on a spaceship, for Skarnaf was an important space transfer station, and its approaches were carefully monitored. Further, the victim was a native of Skarnaf.

The experts went away, finally, having concluded that there was no possible way the victim could have received such an overdose of radiation; no possible way he could have survived it; no conceivable method by which he could have arrived where he was found, with or without his injuries. The farmers were left in peace.

The victim remained hospitalized, totally incoherent and likely to die at any moment. His condition shrieked of gross negligence or malfunctioning equipment, and his abandonment suggested an unimaginable callousness, but the authorities, after the most thorough investigation they were capable of, could not understand how either could have happened on Skarnaf. There simply was no place on the planet where the victim could have been exposed to any measure of radiation, let alone such a massive overdose, and there was no indication of where he had come from or how.

But such an untoward event had to be reported to the central government of the Galactic Synthesis, and that report had to make sense. Therefore the authorities decided that the victim of a nuclear disaster on another world had been surreptitiously abandoned in a rural area of Skarnaf, despite the fact that no spaceship could have left him there. They much preferred an unaccountable spaceship to an unaccountable nuclear explosion.

2

Periodically Jan Darzek longed for a crisis. As First Councilor of the Council of Supreme—chairman of the ruling body of the Galactic Synthesis and therefore of the galaxy—he was constantly beset with picayune details that any bright fifth assistant administrator should have been able to handle.

Now he sat disgustedly contemplating an unending strip of computer printout that Supreme was piling onto his desk. Supreme was the world-sized computer that made the government of a galaxy possible, and Darzek had come to regard it as his foremost antagonist. The Council of Supreme met regularly, made decisions, and formulated plans, but it could act only on the basis of information furnished by Supreme. There was no way to determine whether that information was complete or selective; and if the information was not complete, no one knew whether or how Supreme decided what information was to be supplied or withheld.

It seemed to Darzek that when he had a serious problem, Supreme told him as little about it as possible, couched in terms that made the pronouncements of a Delphic oracle a model of clarity. When the problem was trivial, the information came in a continuously unrolling flood.

Darzek picked up a section of the printout, glanced at one item, and grimaced. The world of Cwafcwa was planning a new industrial complex that would, unquestionably, pollute its air. Was there already a pollution problem on Cwafcwa, or would this pollution constitute an unnoticeable blight on an otherwise pure atmosphere? Should the Galactic Synthesis take action to protect the world from its own stupidity or congratulate it on its economic foresight? Supreme's announcement was noncommittal. Darzek's staff would have to perform a reference search, which meant asking Supreme for information that Supreme probably wouldn't have. Remarkable as a world-size computer could be, it suffered the disadvantages of any jerry-built pocket model. It knew only what it was told.

"Computers," Darzek muttered, "are never any smarter than the people using them."

In the end he probably would have to send someone to Cwafcwa, and when that person rendered a report the problem would land on Darzek's desk again and he would have to make a decision—and by that time the industrial complex on Cwafcwa already would be built. It might even have aged to a state of obsolescence.

Such were the complications of governing a galaxy. Darzek pushed the pile of printout aside and longed again for a crisis.

A gong sounded.

Hopefully Darzek stepped to the communications screen and pressed a button. The gong meant that another member of the council was calling, and that member's crisis, if he, she, or it had one, could be as satisfactory as one of Darzek's own. At the very least it would give him an excuse for ignoring Supreme's outpouring of trivia.

But the figure that greeted him was a disappointment. FOUR, the Fourth Councilor, was charged with matters of science and scientific development, but insofar as Darzek was aware, he did nothing at all. He was the council's nonentity, a faceless life form with a row of sensory humps located across his shoulders. When he was alert, the humps were constantly twitching and jerking as he focused and refocused his organs of sight and hearing, but he rarely was alert. He dozed through most council meetings, and when he did speak it was in echoing platitudes, because his vocal apparatus was located in his stomach, near his brain, and his every remark seemed to arrive from an enormous distance, as though he were his own ventriloquist.

Darzek began the politely formal greeting that tradition demanded, and FOUR interrupted him impatiently. "May we call on you at once, Gul Darr?"

"Of course," Darzek responded.

The screen went blank.

So it was a crisis, from a most unpromising source. Not only had FOUR omitted the traditional amenities, but he hadn't bothered to tell Darzek whom he was bringing. Frowning, Darzek pressed another button. FOUR of course knew the transmitter code for Darzek's official residence; but a councilor admitted visitors to his official residence, which was equipped with direct links to Supreme, with care. As First Councilor, Darzek possessed unusual powers and prerogatives, and he had reason to be especially wary. He received unknown visitors only in his private residence, and his pressing of the button automatically directed them there.

He touched off the proper code on his personal transmitter and stepped through.

FOUR already was waiting for him with two strangers. They were natives of the world of Primores, the artificial world that was at the same time the computer Supreme and the capital of the galaxy. This meant almost inevitably that they were civil servants. Darzek greeted them with grave politeness as FOUR performed introductions: UrsWannl, director of the Galactic Survey; and UrsNollf, head of the Department of Astrophysics.

Darzek escorted them into his study and offered chairs. As was customary in the home of anyone who frequently entertained a variety of life forms, there were seating devices of various shapes and functions available. Darzek's visitors ignored them. Darzek faced them, waiting expectantly to be informed of some looming catastrophe that might add interest to his life for a few days or even a term or two.

Finally UrsWannl took a step toward the galaxy's First Councilor and blurted, "There is a new star!"

Darzek looked from one solemn face to the other and then to FOUR, who had no face. He managed to conceal his disappointment. "I'm no astronomer," he said lightly. "Nor am I an astrophysicist. But I distinctly recall reading or hearing that stars are in the process of formation all the time. If that's true, a new star shouldn't be a surprising event. Is the Galactic Synthesis expected to sponsor a christening ceremony?"

UrsNollf blurted, "This new star should not exist. And yet it does."

Darzek asked politely, "Are there scientific rules about a star being born?"

"Call them rules, or laws, or precepts, or scientific principles or whatever you choose," UrsNollf answered tartly. "Certain conditions are absolutely essential. In any event, when a known planet turns into a star—"

Darzek interrupted politely. "Perhaps we should sit down and consider this unexplained birth from the beginning."

They selected chairs for themselves, and Darzek perched himself on the edge of the one nearest to them. Primorian natives were almost as strange-looking as FOUR, but the bulging hump set atop their shoulders contained their brains, and they had faces, on heads that protruded from their chests. As civil servants they were fanatically loyal and extremely intelligent. They also possessed a fondness for red tape that was endemic in every bureaucracy Darzek had ever encountered.

They waited politely until Darzek prompted them. "About this star—"

"We received a report," UrsWannl said, "of a double-star system where the official chart showed a single star with seven planets. The sun is called Nifron. Have you a projector?"

"Coordinates?" Darzek asked.

UrsWannl told him, and Darzek quickly transferred the numbers to a keyboard. Instantly a slice of the galaxy was projected just above their heads. UrsWannl indicated one of the specks of light. "Focus, please." Darzek did so, zooming in on that sun until it had enlarged enormously and its seven planets were visible.

UrsWannl said, "There are occasional reports of this kind, and invariably, for one reason or another, they prove to be in error. The fact is that by this late date the galaxy has been surveyed and resurveyed, and the official charts have been in use long enough to have had even the most subtle of errors detected. Even so, as a matter of policy, any challenge to a chart is investigated at once."

"Naturally," Darzek said. "So of course you investigated this one."

"Expecting to find that a simple error of observation had occasioned the complaint. Usually the observer happens to see two stars in such an alignment that they can be mistaken for a double star. It's occurred often. Instead, we found that the report was correct. The fourth planet, known as Nifron D, has inexplicably turned into a sun."

"Inexplicably?" Darzek repeated. The very word made him feel skeptical. Too often the inexplicable merely meant that someone was inobservant, uninformed, misinformed, or stupid. "In all of the galaxy is there no precedence? It seems to me that I've heard of protostars—bodies that are in the process of becoming stars. In my own solar system, the largest planet has been called a protostar or a dark star."

"A gaseous planet of the proper chemical composition might contract to the point of turning into a star," UrsNollf said. "But this planet was not gaseous. The system was surveyed carefully. We have detailed descriptions and even surface specimens of each of the planets."

"Are you saying that the fourth planet was ordinary dirt and rock and so on?" Darzek demanded.

"It was."

"That doesn't sound like very promising stuff for star material."

"Not very," UrsNollf agreed dryly.

"Has such a thing been known to occur before?"

"Never."

"The world was unpopulated?"

"A barren planet in an excessively barren system."

"Then no damage has been done."

UrsNollf heaved a sigh. "Only to our carefully established knowledge of physical processes. I refuse to believe that such a thing could happen naturally."

"If it didn't happen naturally, then an intelligent agency was involved—accidentally or intentionally."

UrsNollf grunted his assent. "But we can hardly consider it an accident. No one could accidentally turn such a planet into a sun. It would have to be done deliberately, and it would involve enormously complicated preparations and expenses. Why would anyone go to that much trouble with a barren planet in a remote and insignificant system? And who would know how to do such a thing? As far as we know, no one."

Darzek said thoughtfully, "There may be some natural process, something perfectly simple and understandable, that science knows nothing about."

"There may be." UrsNollf hunched his hump forward. "That is how progress is made in science. We keep discovering new phenomena, and we have to devise explanations for them—and then we keep revising the explanations as more phenomena are discovered and eventually we arrive at the truth—or at what seems to be the truth. But it'll require a great deal of convincing to make any scientist accept this particular phenomenon as a natural occurrence. Turning that planet into a sun had to be a deliberate act. If so, the implications fall outside the realm of the scientist. This is why we came to you."

"We're going to investigate the phenomenon in person," UrsWannl said. "We'd like you to accompany us."

"Thank you, but no," Darzek said firmly. "I'm not any kind of scientist. There's no possible assistance I could give to such an expedition. If I went with you, I'd be a mere passenger. You should take the best experts available."

After some discussion, the two civil servants agreed. "But we may never find out what happened," FOUR said glumly. "We can hardly land on a sun and look for evidence."

Darzek saw them to the transmitter. Then he returned to his official residence and the accumulating roll of reports from Supreme. "The problem with acquiring the reputation as a miracle worker," he told himself ruefully, "is that the audience is never satisfied. It's like eating one potato chip. They even begin to expect a miracle where none is called for. They'll probably find a simple scientific explanation and return home wishing they hadn't mentioned Nifron D."

His gong rang.

He pressed the answer button. This time it was FIVE's bright multiplicity of eyes that faced him. The Fifth Councilor was a conical head and a twig of a body surrounded by multifingered tentacles. A brilliant surgeon—her numerous limbs and fingers gave her advantages no human doctor could approach—she was the council's medical authority. Her weak natural voice had to be amplified drastically to be heard, and it had a metallic static about it.

She said cheerfully, "A mystery for you, Gul Darr."

Darzek chuckled. He was extremely fond of FIVE, and he admired her competence without reservation. "Another one?" he asked. "FOUR was just here with the director of the Galactic Survey and the head of the Department of Astrophysics. They found a sun where there isn't supposed to be one."

"This is a much smaller problem," FIVE said. "I've found a patient where there isn't supposed to be one."

Darzek seated himself and said, "Tell me about it." The Fifth Councilor would not bother him with anything less than a truly unusual mystery.

"The world is called Skarnaf," FIVE said. Darzek punched the reference and gazed blankly at the sector of the galaxy that was projected in tiny lights above his head.

"Anything remarkable about the location?" he asked.

"Nothing," FIVE answered. "And that's what's so remarkable. A youth—a native of the planet—has been discovered there suffering from radiation burns."

Darzek waited politely.

"He was hideously burned from a massive overdose of radiation—and yet there is no place on the planet where he could have received it."

"A hospital?" Darzek suggested. "X rays?"

"Impossible. There is no form of medical radiology that could begin to account for such an overdose."

"A nuclear power planet?"

"It's a primitive world. It hasn't progressed as far as anything that old-fashioned. A careful investigation has turned up no place on the planet where he could have been exposed to any kind of radiation."

"Then he must have suffered it somewhere else," Darzek said. "An accident in space?"

"That must be the answer. But in that case, how did he come to be found lying by the road in a rural area of Skarnaf? A ship could have put him down by point transmission, but no ship could have approached the planet that closely without detection. Anyway, why would one bother? If it wanted him to receive medical attention, it would have delivered him to a transfer station for transmission to a hospital on the surface. If it merely wished to get rid of a crew member with an embarrassing fatal injury, it would have jettisoned him in space. There's simply no way he could have received his injuries, no way he could have reached the place where he was found, and to further complicate matters the burns were fresh. They happened not long before he was found."

"You said 'fatal injury.' Was he able to supply any information about himself before he died, or was he found dead?"

"He was still alive at the time of my report, but of course he was in no condition to communicate anything to his doctors. With the injuries described to me, he couldn't possibly survive. He's probably dead by now."

"A most intriguing mystery," Darzek agreed.

"I'm about to go to Skarnaf to see this remarkable victim myself," FIVE announced. "Would you care to accompany me?"

"Only for the pleasure of your company," Darzek said. "If the victim is already dead, not even your skill can help him. If he's alive, there's no possible function I could perform to help him. The one thing that would interest me is whether he was able to describe what happened to him before he died. If he was not, then the person who solves this mystery will have to possess powers that elude me."

"I doubt that, Gul Darr. But it's my duty to investigate medical mysteries, wherever they occur, and I want to make certain that a mystery such as this one can't happen twice—on Skarnaf or anywhere else."

"Of course," Darzek agreed. "And if you discover illuminative details that might bring the mystery into my limited sphere of understanding, please let me have them immediately."

FIVE chuckled. "If I discover anything at all, I'll send a report a once."

Her image faded.

Darzek resignedly turned to the pile of printouts. For the moment, at least, Supreme's outpouring had ceased. Darzek cut the strip and slipped the end onto a spindle, for winding. He would give it to his staff, which would winnow the chaff and hand the really difficult or important problems back to him.

The trouble was that his staff, too, would expect miracles.

Suddenly he frowned and returned to his desk.

A planet had turned into a sun. The galaxy's leading astrophysicist thought it had been done deliberately. In any event, some kind of nuclear process had to be responsible.

And an individual had been found suffering from a massive dose of nuclear radiation.

Darzek punched references on his projector, set two suns blinking for identification, and leaned back to study the large slice of the galaxy that had formed above his head. The planets Skarnaf and Nifron D were at least a quarter of a galaxy apart.

He relaxed and turned off the projector. For a suspenseful moment he thought he'd happened onto a coincidence with frightening implications; but a victim with fresh radiation burns couldn't possibly have acquired them a quarter of a galaxy away.

"Darzek's Law," he muttered. "Simultaneous events can't be coincidental when the distance between them has to be measured in light-years."

The two expeditions departed: FIVE and a few members of her staff for Skarnaf; FOUR, with UrsNollf, UrsWannl, and a large scientific contingent, for the Nifron system. Darzek saw both parties off, re-' turned to his contemplation of Darzek's Law, found its logic unassailable, and again directed his attention at Supreme's outpouring of trivia.

He had been working on it for six days and had all of the more serious problems solved and most of the lesser ones delegated to staff members capable of handling them, and he was actually considering treating himself to a vacation if he could think of a place where he wanted to take one, when Miss Effie Schlupe walked into his office and plopped herself onto a strangely shaped chair. She was a little older and grayer than he remembered, but despite her seventy-plus years she seemed as vigorously alert as ever.

Darzek greeted her with amazed delight. "Schluppy! And you haven't even forgotten my transmitter code. How's the fast-food business?"

Miss Schlupe had been building a conglomerate of food enterprises in the Greater Galaxy, known on Earth as the Large Magellanic Cloud. "Sensational," she said. "I had submarine sandwich and cider franchises going on four hundred worlds, the hamburger chain was doing nicely, and my frozen yogurt line really took off once I found a milk substitute that would work. But I got bored being a business tycoon, so I sold out."

Darzek chuckled. "I'm afraid to ask, but—what'd you sell out for?"

"Spaceships," Miss Schlupe said. "I got myself a fleet. Twenty, in fact. There's a world named Wezzen—know it?"

He shook his head.

"They have a fossil fuel that leaves a peculiar slag when it's burned. It's a little like amber, except that it has startlingly beautiful colors. It isn't biodegradable, so they have a disposal problem with it. I agreed to take some off their hands for a very modest price, and I loaded my twenty ships with it."

Darzek was chuckling louder. "What kind of a price?"

"Grain. I traded the grain for fuel, and it financed the run back to this galaxy."

"What'd you do with the slag?"

"I sold it to worlds where jewelry is popular. Jewelers go wild over it. I rationed it off, just enough to each world to make it seem rare and keep the price up. And whenever I emptied a ship, I sold the ship. You should see my solvency rating."

"So you got rid of all the slag and all the ships, and now you're a multibillionaire."

"Something like that. Except that I kept one ship—the newest and best one. Then I stopped at the world of Yestrux—they specialize in textiles. Know it?"

Darzek shook his head.

"I bought a shipload of remnants." She unfolded a square of brilliantly patterned cloth.

"A bit gaudy," Darzek observed. "You bought an entire shipload of that stuff? What did you do with it?"

"I brought it with me. I'm going to sell it to the Primorians."

Darzek stared at her. "The Primorians are the most sedate and conservative specimens in fifty sectors. They even prefer black hand-kerchiefs. What would they want with bright pieces of cloth?"

"They'll use them for babushkas," Miss Schlupe said confidently.

"Schluppy. You've been away too long. The Primorians have that peculiar head structure that protrudes from their chests. Remember? It would take a contortionist to get a piece of cloth wrapped around it."

"It isn't for their heads. It's for that big hump on their shoulders where their brains are. They're fortunate to have such large brains, but all that bare skin sticking up is unaesthetic. I'm going to start a fad and beautify Primorian society." She got to her feet. "Where's my rocking chair? I can't imagine what kind of sitting apparatus your chairs are made for."

"Every kind," Darzek said. "I'm sure you wore your rocking chair out the last time you were here. Even the best rocking chair has a limit to the amount of mileage—"

"What are *you* doing these days?" Miss Schlupe demanded.

"Making up natural laws. How does this sound? 'Simultaneous

events can't be coincidental when the distance between them has to be measured in light-years.' "

"Sounds great. Does it mean anything?"

"I hope so. If you haven't anything better to do, why don't you take over my Trans-Star Trading Company and stir things up a bit? I'm supposed to be a trader, but Supreme keeps piling trivialities on me, and I haven't pulled off a trading coup for so long my competitors will be getting suspicious."

"Gud Baxak?" Miss Schlupe asked, refering to Darzek's trading assistant.

"Solidly competent and very pedestrian."

"All right. As soon as I get my babushka fad going, I'll shake things up for you. In fact, I'll have Trans-Star handle the babushkas."

"Good idea."

She regarded him narrowly. "You *have* got something on your mind. What was that natural law again?"

"The question is how far apart things can happen and still belong to the same coincidence."

"And that's got you worried?"

Darzek nodded.

"There can't be much going on around here if you have time to make up laws about a thing like that. Never mind. I'll show you some action."

Within days she had her babushka fad launched; within a term, no self-respecting Primorian would be seen in public without one of her gaudy remnants covering his or her hump, and Miss Schlupe was importing more remnants and promoting special colors for festive occasions. Darzek's fellow traders were consumed with envy, and his reputation was saved.

Darzek continued his attempts to define coincidence and cursed Supreme, which began spewing out another accumulation of trivia just as Darzek got his desk cleared.

Then FIVE returned. She had looked into the matter of the unfortunate radiation victim on Skarnaf and prolonged her trip by making a series of unannounced medical inspections along the way, as was her custom. This time she came to Darzek's official residence, and he placed a stand by her chair so she could position her vocal amplifier.

"Did you solve the mystery?" he asked with a smile, seating himself beside her.

She answered seriously, "If this mystery has a solution, it will require talents at least equal to yours to discover it."

"Did the victim die?"

"He hadn't at the time I left. That's a mystery in itself—how he could be exposed to such a measure of radiation and live." She waved a multifingered tentacle wearily. "He should be dead. He should have died within hours of his exposure if not immediately. I have no solution for that mystery, either."

"And—the other mystery?"

"Mysteries. Where and how he was exposed to such intense radiation and how he got to where he was found. The chief proctor of Skarnaf is a superbly competent person, and he has investigated the matter thoroughly. The accident couldn't have happened on Skarnaf, and if it had, he couldn't have traveled unnoticed to where he was found. It's doubtful that he could have moved without help."

"A secret underground research lab," Darzek suggested. "Located close to where he was found."

"Preposterous. It would have had to be built. It's lovely, rich agricultural land, divided into family holdings, and each farmer knows every finger length of his property. You can't excavate an underground lab, and equip it, and conduct experiments that make bangs and probably vent pollutants that would affect crops, under those circumstances."

"It happened elsewhere on Skarnaf—there must be *some* wasteland on the planet—and the victim was transported to where he was found."

"Equally preposterous. Even on wasteland I doubt that anyone could construct a secret underground laboratory on Skarnaf. It would have to have its own power source, for one thing, or it wouldn't be secret, and there are plenty of other objections. But even if there were one, there's no way the victim could have been transported. There is a primitive transmitter network, with a terminal in the nearest village, but anyone bringing a hideously burned person through it would have attracted attention. Once he reached the village, he could only travel by steam tractor or animal-drawn wagon, and either way a local resident would have had to cooperate. And there was no freight shipment that could have contained the victim. No, all that was thoroughly investigated. It couldn't have happened. And he couldn't have arrived by spaceship. Skarnaf has a complete network of orbiting transfer stations, and the movements of every approaching ship are monitored. There was no ship in position to transmit the victim to the surface, and if the accident had happened in space or on another planet, no ship could have got him there that quickly. His burns were *fresh*. He must have arrived where he was found only moments before the farmer saw him.

"In other words," Darzek mused, "he couldn't have been exposed to any kind of radiation, but he was. He couldn't have survived the exposure he received, but he's still alive. And he couldn't have got to the place where he was found, but he did. That's an impressive series of contradictions."

She silently gestured her agreement.

"The best approach would seem to be to identify the victim and trace his recent activities."

"As I told you, the chief proctor is a highly competent person. He's prepared a dossier on the victim, and I brought you a copy." She opened a folder. "The victim's name is Qwasrolk. He's a native of Skarnaf. He was born and grew up virtually at the place where he was found. His parents were farmers. The identification was made through a scar on his back that surviving friends of his family remembered—his back wasn't burned. His hands were so badly burned that his solvency credential is illegible."

"It may be significant that he was found where he once lived," Darzek observed. "He was fatally injured, and his instinct was to go home."

"Except that his home is no longer there. The family sold the land a number of cycles ago, and the buildings were demolished."

"Where has he been lately?" Darzek asked.

"He attended the University of Skarnaf. He was considered a brilliant student—withdrawn, but brilliant. On graduation he accepted a position on the world of Vezpro, which is a highly industrialized planet in a neighboring solar system. He worked there for a cycle and was regarded with high favor and thought to have a promising future. Suddenly he resigned. After that, he simply disappeared."

"How long ago was that?"

"In Vezpronian time, three cycles. In our time, closer to four."

"Interesting," Darzek observed. "What was his specialization?"

FIVE smiled. "That's the most intriguing fact of all. He was a nuclear engineer."

Darzek said slowly, "Is it possible that he was conducting his own nuclear experiments on his old homestead?"

"Absolutely impossible," FIVE said. "That kind of explosion would have left traces, even underground, and the equipment and materials would have required an enormous amount of solvency. Beginning engineers are paid well on Vezpro, but not munificently, and his family wasn't wealthy. It's out of the question. And the explosion couldn't have happened on Vezpro, which specializes in nuclear-powered manufactured goods and therefore has every kind of safeguard and detection device. And if it had, no ship could have got him to Skarnaf that quickly." She got to her feet and handed Darzek the dossier. "Now it's your mystery, Gul Darr. I wish you the pleasure of it."

"Thank you," Darzek said dryly. "At least it'll be a contrast to these piddling problems Supreme keeps dumping onto me."

She took her leave of him, and he read through the dossier, pondered the implications of what had been learned, and decided to leave this particular mystery in the hands of the Skarnaf authorities. The world's chief proctor obviously was a highly competent individual and seemed to be handling the case at least as well as Darzek could. For the next few days he kept his attention on Supreme's trivialities, while Miss Schlupe regaled him each evening with her accounts of trading activities.

Then FOUR returned from Nifron, along with UrsWannl and UrsNollf. They asked Darzek for a conference shortly after they arrived, and Darzek met the three of them in his private residence.

UrsNollf, the astrophysicist, wasted no time on preliminaries. "We have no proof," he announced, "but we suspect that someone has discovered a method for turning a planet into a sun—and has done so."

Darzek got the three of them seated. He remained standing—he'd found it easier to gauge the confidence of this natives of Primores in what they were discussing if he looked down on their queer anatomy and forced them to look up at him. He noted with amusement that the two civil servants, though they were calling on him almost immediately after their arrival, already had succumbed to Miss Schlupe's babushka fad. Their humps sported gaudy coverings.

"Someone has discovered a method for turning a planet into a sun—and has done so," Darzek repeated. "To what purpose?"

FOUR spoke up. "To a scientist, an experiment may need no higher purpose. If it advances knowledge—"

"What knowledge does it advance if it's done in secret?" Darzek demanded.

"The scientist's own knowledge," FOUR replied.

"Why are you so positive that this was not a natural event?"

"There is no natural way that the planet Nifron D could have turned into a sun," UrsNollf said. "None whatsoever. And on the third planet of the system, Nifron C, we discovered—indications."

"Indications of what?"

"A small scientific encampment of some sort. Marks where portable domes and scientific equipment had been emplaced. The planet is sufficiently distant so that the—ignition—could have taken place without harm to those performing the experiment, since the planets weren't in conjunction. Of course they could have left when their preparations were completed and touched off the experiment from space."

Darzek asked bluntly, "Have you found anyone who knows how to turn an ordinary world into a sun?"

"No," UrsNollf answered. "And I have consulted Supreme. I asked for the names of scientists who might have that competence. Supreme knows of none."

"And yet you consider it scientifically possible."

"Since it has been done, yes."

"But you don't know that it has been done," Darzek said patiently "You merely speculate that it has been done because you can't think of any other explanation for what happened."

The three of them were silent.

"Have you thought of submitting the problem to the leading astrophysicists of the galaxy and asking for their opinions?"

"I did that before we left," UrsNollf said stiffly. "I now have their replies. They're as baffled as I am."

"Did this supposed scientific expedition leave any clues other than the fact of its presence?"

UrsWannl spoke. "It left some debris behind. All of it originated on one world. That may mean that the expedition came from there, or it may mean only that the supplies were acquired there—or on a world that imported them."

"What is the world?" Darzek asked.

"It's a quarter of the way across the galaxy, and as far as we know, it has no connection with this event other than the debris. It isn't noted for astrophysical research. It's called Vezpro."

"Vezpro," Darzek murmured. "That's interesting. I thank you for your efforts. I'll give your findings my most careful consideration."

"Have you any suggestions for us?" FOUR demanded.

"I recommend that you summon the best scientists available and try to figure out how it was done. Whatever ramifications this problem may have, that part of the investigation will have to be conducted by scientists."

"Very well," FOUR said, his echoing voice conveying relief that he could do *something*. "I'll call a conference."

The three of them left. A moment later Miss Schlupe entered. By special arrangement she observed meetings secretly, eavesdropped whenever she felt like it, and read reports on any subject that interested her.

Now she remarked cheerfully, "I think we can scratch Darzek's Law. A coincidence can have a much longer measurement than you thought."

"Do three impossibilities add up to a coincidence?" Darzek asked.

"Three?"

"A planet turning into a sun, which all the scientists say is impossible. A radiation victim where there's no radiation, which obviously is impossible. And a connection between the two events when they're a quarter of a galaxy apart, which is both impossible and inconceivable."

"It's the fulcrum that provides a connection."

"The world of Vezpro?"

"Yes."

"It sounds feasible," Darzek conceded. "The radiation victim worked there. The debris found on Nifron C came from there. But the radiation victim must have been one of thousands of nuclear engineers employed on Vezpro, and he disappeared from there more than three cycles ago. As for the debris—"

He turned to his communications console and punched out a question for Supreme. And as was Supreme's custom, he was immediately told far more about Vezpro than he wanted to know. He cut the strip into sheets and read them, passing each one to Miss Schlupe as he finished.

Finally he leaned back. "It's a flourishing industrial world. It spreads its products across half the galaxy, at least. The members of that mysterious expedition could have picked them up anywhere. They probably bought them somewhere close to Nifron."

"Then you don't think Vezpro has any connection with either mystery?"

"I don't see how it could have."

"Has it occurred to you that the ability to turn a world into a sun has a tremendous potential for both good and evil?"

"It has," Darzek said. "It's also occurred to me that the only evil we've ever encountered on member worlds of the Galactic Synthesis originated outside the Synthesis. Vezpro is a member world. If those who turned Nifron D into a sun wanted to keep their identity a secret, would they leave debris about that advertised the world they came from?"

"You wouldn't," Miss Schlupe said. "I wouldn't. Who can say how an alien mind works?"

"You think we should go to Vezpro?"

"I think," Miss Schlupe said firmly, "that Vezpro is the only real clue you have."

4

The world of Vezpro lay below them—a beautiful swirl of colors and white, wispy clouds. Most worlds looked beautiful from space, and Jan Darzek had begun to wonder if this one were like a deceptively luscious-looking fruit—bursting with appetizing ripeness and rotten inside.

"I haven't got a penny," Miss Schlupe said dryly.

"It'd be an exorbitant price for any thought I've had since we arrived here," Darzek answered. Then he remarked, in a voice that was more reflective than accusing, "You said Vezpro was the only real clue I had."

"It was. It is."

Darzek nodded absently. He had found no hint of a clue to either of his mysteries on this world, and yet he could understand Miss Schlupe's stubborn suspicion that something was drastically wrong here. Perhaps it was only because everything seemed so irreproachably correct.

They were eating in a transfer station restaurant. Each member world of the Galactic Synthesis was surrounded by such stations, the number varying with the amount of interstellar trade the world engaged in, and Vezpro's multitude of stations suggested the rings of Saturn. Ships docked at the stations; passengers and cargo reached the world's surface by transmitter.

The restaurants that were operated on many of the stations were a profitable sideline. Arriving or embarking passengers often paused to eat there and enjoy their first or last look at Vezpro. Citizens often came up to partake of the uniquely spectacular view, either of the planet or of the sweep of richly starred sky, that each transfer station restaurant offered. The food, unfortunately, was much the same everywhere.

But Darzek and Miss Schlupe had found several dishes that any gourmet from Earth would have appreciated, thanks to a crinkly, paper-thin fungus that Miss Schlupe called mushrooms. She was already experimenting with methods of preserving it so they could take a supply back to Primores, and Darzek had to firmly scuttle her notion of a new chain of fast-food franchises featuring mushroom burgers or pizza.

Darzek took another bite of the sautéed fungus and sighed. "If it weren't for these mushrooms, I'd call this trip a total waste of time."

"You were considering a vacation anyway," she pointed out.

"As someone once remarked, it was a long way to come to eat. We've been here for more than a term, and we know almost exactly what we knew when we arrived."

"Qwasrolk's radiation burns suggest an atomic bomb," Miss Schlupe said.

"Atomic bombs have been banned in the Galactic Synthesis for so long that only Supreme would have memory of them. Anyway, this is a crimeless society."

"All it takes to ruin the record of a crimeless society is one criminal," Miss Schlupe observed.

"Schluppy, we're not talking about purse snatching. Making atomic bombs might be a hobby for some perverted scientist, but he couldn't set one off on Skarnaf without it being noticed. As for the Nifron D matter, there's still no proof that it wasn't a natural event, still no possible connection with Qwasrolk, and certainly no evidence that a crime was committed there."

Miss Schlupe said dryly, "It may not be illegal, but turning worthless planets into suns certainly is a peculiar hobby. It also provides a basis for villainy on a scale I'd rather not contemplate."

"True, but you can't have villainy without a villain, and we haven't found any. In fact, we haven't found anything. So why don't we go home?"

"Because," Miss Schlupe said firmly, "we don't dare take a chance on being wrong."

To give credence to his presence on Vezpro, Darzek had opened a branch office of the Trans-Star Trading Company. While Gud Baxak, in his thorough but pedestrian way, developed a respectable volume of trade, Darzek and Miss Schlupe went their separate ways every morning, each searching for a trail that was nonexistent or had long since faded. They met again at night, in a large apartment adjoining the Trans-Star office—for such was the common business and living arrangement on Vezpro.

Darzek undertook to investigate the Nifron C debris, and he actually identified the manufacturer of some discarded containers and even established which manufacturing lot they had come from. That lot had, alas, been shipped across a large chunk of the galaxy, and the scientific expedition very easily could have acquired those particular containers on some world close to the Nifron system or on any of a thousand worlds in between—because they were bought by food-processing companies that filled them and shipped them along to their own customers. Taking another approach, Darzek had a computer study made to determine what food-processing companies used containers and film-packing materials of the types that originated on Vezpro and were abandoned on Nifron C. When the total passed one hundred and forty-seven thousand, with wholesale traders in the millions and retail outlets utterly beyond count, he cancelled the project.

Miss Schlupe undertook to extend the investigation of the unfortunate Qwasrolk, who miraculously was still alive on Skarnaf, though comatose and expected to die at any moment. She began by hiring and training her own investigative force of natives, and with their help she managed to dig somewhat deeper into Qwasrolk's past. She talked with his fellow workers, found three places where he'd lived during his stay on Vezpro, interviewed landlords and neighbors. He had been ordinary and completely colorless—almost antisocial—in his private life, but his fellow workers thought him brilliant. He had moved away suddenly with his tenancy paid a full two terms in advance, something unheard of, at the time he resigned his job. No one knew where he had gone.

Thus both their trails ended. Miss Schlupe kept her investigators tenaciously digging, however unpromising the results, but she and Darzek turned their attention to the only other possible source of a clue on Vezpro, the Vezpronians themselves. These were a serious, hard-working people: tall, distortedly human-looking (if one could overlook their triple arms and legs, their multifingered arms without hands, and the complete absence of body hair). They dressed in such flamboyant colors that Darzek slyly suggested to Miss Schlupe that she start importing brightly patterned remnants to cover the gleaming baldness that met their gazes everywhere.

Darzek, returning late to the rather Spartan rooms that constituted a luxury apartment on Vezpro, halted in the doorway and stared. Miss Schlupe sat in the center of the windowless pentagon that served as their living room, rocking vigorously in a gleaming white rocking chair. She had been at it for some time, because the thick, gaudily colored floor piece—as the Vezpronians called rugs—was rucked up, and her rocking had become bumpy.

"Where did you get it?" Darzek demanded.

"I found the strangest little street of shops in a tunnel under the city," she said. "I suppose it's kind of a museum piece, and the natives visit it to gloat over the primitive ways of their remote ancestors. There are all kinds of handicrafts made and sold there, and I saw this character making things by hand out of plastic, so I drew the design for this and stood over him until he got it right. He did a good job. How was the theater?"

Darzek dropped onto a freakishly shaped lounge and kicked his shoes off. A fellow trader had generously invited him to a theater party, and he had thought a glimpse of Vezpronian night life might be amusing. He had been wrong. "I needed a laugh or two," he said. "I didn't get any."

"What did you think of Vezpronian culture?"

"I wouldn't call their theater 'culture.' There's some moral objection to live actors, so they use robots. Or androids. Or maybe 'dummies' would be a better term—the whole thing reminded me of a ventriloquist show without the ventriloquists. They were offstage using radios, I suppose. The presentation was a morality play based on an incomprehensible religion."

"You didn't go to a theater," Miss Schlupe said. "You went to church."

"Impossible. There was no offering."

"You went to church," Miss Schlupe repeated firmly. "Vezpro has quite good theaters, if you can put up with the wailing they call music. What you saw is the Zarstamb, which is a kind of evangelical show run by the Zarstans, who hail from the world of Zarst."

"That's this system's sixth planet, isn't it?" Darzek asked. "I didn't know it was habitable. It shouldn't be habitable. It's too far from the sun."

"Habitable or not, that's where they come from. The Zarstans are a religious sect of scientists and technologists."

Darzek shrugged. "Why not? There are religious sects of everything else."

"I thought their robots were amazing."

"Probably they were," Darzek said. "'Amazing' and 'entertaining' are two entirely different concepts. As for the religion—"

He broke off as Gud Baxak entered excitedly from the office area of their quarters. Darzek's chief trading assistant was enjoying himself on Vezpro—being triple limbed himself, he seemed to have a curious affinity for the Vezpronians, even though his native planet was on the other side of the galaxy and his thick body and strangely shaped head made him look fully as alien as Darzek did. "Visitors!" he whispered.

"At this time of night?" Darzek said resentfully. "What are they— nocturnal aliens?"

"One is a Vezpronian," Gud Baxak said, his voice vibrant with awe. "The other is an alien of some sort but not a nocturnal." He paused. "The Vezpronian says he is the masfiln!"

Darzek got to his feet and retrieved his shoes. That seemed the least he could do, since the masfiln was the premier or president of Vezpro. The world had a highly democratic society; the masfiln was frequently seen in public, mingling freely with the masses, and Vezpronian society seemed to function with commendably informal etiquette. But Darzek's hunch was that one ought to receive the masfiln at home while wearing shoes.

"Probably he wants to buy a babushka," Darzek told Miss Schlupe. "Would you like to be introduced to high society, or would you rather snoop?"

"I'll snoop," Miss Schlupe said. "I may want to meet these characters when they won't know me."

"Use the panel, then."

Darzek had installed a one-way panel that looked into the trading office. He waited until Miss Schlupe had made herself comfortable there, and then he followed Gud Baxak into the presence of the visitors.

They got to their feet to greet Darzek. The Vezpronian was elderly —as indicated by the mass of wrinkles on his bald head—and conservatively dressed in pale lavender. Darzek had seen the masfiln several times at a distance, and he recognized him at once.

But Darzek had never seen his companion, and the life form was new to him. An enormous head sported a tremendous shock of orange hair, or something like hair. The skin possessed a peculiar, deathlike tint of green. There were six limbs, but they obviously functioned as two short legs and four stubby arms, whereas the much larger Vezpronians had three lengthy specimens of each. Finally, this alien's limbs were attached to a ridiculously small body.

Gud Baxak, with much ceremony, introduced Gul Darr, trader of Primores. Then he discreetly slipped away to his own quarters.

"I am Min Kallof, Masfiln of Vezpro," the Vezpronian announced. "This is Naz Forlan, my Mas of Science and Technology. We apologize for disturbing you so late."

Darzek bowed. "Such an honor rarely comes the way of an ordinary trader. It is hardly to be called a disturbance, at any time. All of the hospitality this humble office affords is yours." He got the two of them seated again, this time maneuvering them into chairs where Miss Schlupe would have an unobstructed view of them. He seated himself nearby.

The masfiln waited politely until Darzek had managed to position himself on a chair designed for occupants with more and differently arranged legs. Then he leaned forward. "Gul Darr, trader you may be, but we know that you are not ordinary. We have been referred to you by Supreme itself. Why this is we have no idea, but when the message arrived we sought for you at once."

Darzek assumed his most modest mien. "Many of us whose central offices are located on the capital world are occasionally asked to perform small services for the Council of Supreme or the various governmental departments of the Synthesis."

"It is not a service that we require," the masfiln said. "Supreme has referred us to you for counsel."

"You are welcome to any I am capable of offering."

"To begin with, the government of Vezpro received a message that informed us—"

The Mas of Science and Technology spoke for the first time. His voice was the softest Darzek had ever heard. Every word was a caress and yet uttered with a precision rarely experienced with the more complex form of galactic speech. And that soft, precise voice filled the room. "Perhaps it would be well to determine first if this really is the trader Gul Darr."

The masfiln gestured apologetically. "To be sure. With an issue as critically important and confidential as this one—"

"Your caution does both of you credit," Darzek murmured. "But I, too, like to be certain of whom I am counseling. Naturally a poor trader does not move in social circles where the masfiln and his delegates are known to him personally."

The two exchanged uncomfortable glances. Darzek, secretly amused, let them make it their own problem. They had come to see him. Finally they both produced identification credentials that were the strangest of their kind that Darzek had ever seen. They were small rectangles of transparent material, and when Darzek looked at its owner through one of them, the moment he had the face properly framed it appeared on the transparency along with a printed identification in both the Vezpronian and the galactic scripts.

Having identified his visitors, Darzek produced a credential he had prepared for himself before he left Primores. In impressive language it identified him as a special emissary of Supreme. His was a blank sheet until he impressed it with his solvency credential, the invisible palm tattoo that served as a universal identification in galactic society. Immediately it became alight with his photo and a statement of his authority.

The two of them read it with an awe that approached Gud Baxak's. "Supreme does indeed have confidence in you," the masfiln remarked. "Now I understand why we were referred to an unknown trader named Gul Darr."

Darzek said politely, "The Council of Supreme needs many eyes and ears to govern a galaxy, and it may be that I can serve both the council and yourselves better if the world of Vezpro knows me only as Gul Darr, the trader. I ask, therefore, that you keep my official status secret."

The Mas of Science and Technology rubbed his bushy head fretfully. "These matters are beyond our experience. So is this communication, concerning which Supreme has referred us to you for counsel."

He passed an indited sheet to Darzek. The material was an unusual, ultrathin metal with a weave like cloth. The writing, in the common galactic script, had been produced by a mechanical inditer, probably a voice dictator. *HAVE YOU HEARD WHAT HAPPENED TO NIFRON D? VEZPRO, TOO, WILL BE TURNED INTO A SUN ON THE FIRST DAY OF THE NEW CYCLE UNLESS MY ORDERS ARE FULFILLED. I WILL PRESENT THEM LATER, AFTER YOU HAVE HAD TIME TO INVESTIGATE THE NIFRON SYSTEM AND CONTEMPLATE THE FATE OF ITS FOURTH PLANET. FOR FUTURE COMMUNICATIONS, CODE XRT.*

"What attempts have you made to trace this letter?" Darzek asked.

They regarded him blankly. In a society that had no crime, scientific police work was virtually unknown. The world's proctors would be concerned almost exclusively with accidents, crowd movement, matters of industrial safety, and the like. The proctors on Skarnaf who had investigated the radiation victim so effectively obviously had unusual talents.

They could tell him nothing about the letter except that it had arrived in an intergovernmental mail distribution addressed to the masfiln. It could have originated in any governmental department on Vezpro, or even on the satellites or the colony worlds. They had conducted a discreet inquiry, but it turned up no one who remembered the communication, even though its material was distinctive.

"Then it could have been slipped into the mail by anyone," Darzek observed. "What's the population of Vezpro?"

"About five billion," the masfiln said. "Why do you ask?"

"I was considering the problem of identifying the sender. If he's one of five billion, it'll be rather complex."

Actually, he was considering the problem of evacuating a world. Removing five billion people to safety might prove impossible.

"Should we investigate the Nifron system?" the masfiln asked.

"Since you have brought this letter to the attention of Supreme, I am sure that the appropriate governmental department already is doing so. You should file an official request for a report of its findings. Otherwise, there would seem to be nothing you can do until you receive the next communication. You'll have a better understanding of the problem when you know what the writer's 'orders' consist of. Have you kept the contents of this communication confidential?"

"Only the two of us and our representative on Primores know about it."

"Good. My counsel, then, is that you give the letter to me and take no further action. It might be disastrous to make the matter public or even discuss it in official circles."

"Ah!" The masfiln seemed vastly relieved. "Then we are to leave the problem in your hands?"

"For the present. At least until you receive another communication. I ask only that you instruct your chief proctor to give me his full cooperation whenever I request it—and ask no questions."

Naz Forlan's soft voice filled the room again. "If you will pardon a suggestion, sire—the chief proctor is not the most brilliant member of your delegates. Since a scientific question is involved, I suggest that it should be my department that cooperates with Gul Darr."

"An excellent suggestion," Darzek agreed. He had intended to ask for such cooperation in any event, and Miss Schlupe's native detective force would certainly be more effective than any personnel the chief proctor could supply. "Since it might arouse curiosity if an unknown trader were to call on the masfiln frequently, perhaps I should communicate with you through your Mas of Science and Technology." He turned to Forlan. "Can you receive a trader without causing comment?"

"Of course," Forlan answered. "I have a section that makes direct purchases of raw materials that are in short supply."

"Then I'll call on you when I need to and discuss raw materials."

He escorted the two officials to the office transmitter.

Miss Schlupe already had settled herself in her rocking chair when Darzek returned to their living quarters, but she was not rocking. She sat tilted back with her eyes closed.

Darzek dropped into his own favorite chair and kicked his shoes off again. It seemed impossible, anywhere except on Earth, to acquire shoes that were comfortable for human feet. "How would you describe our visitors?" he asked.

"Puzzled," Miss Schlupe said without opening her eyes. "And puzzling."

"Strange the way individuals who have no experience of crime react when they encounter it. These didn't hare off to Nifron D to find out if the threat had any substance, as we uncivilized types from Earth might have done. They asked their representative on Primores to ask Supreme what they should do."

"Our crimeless society has suddenly produced a criminal," Miss Schlupe said. "That's much more interesting than their reaction to it."

"Or a practical joker?"

"Baloney. It's a transparent case of blackmail. Pay up, or your world goes poof."

"Or maybe it's a crank letter from someone who found out about a peculiar natural event in the Nifron system and is trying to cash in on it."

Miss Schlupe began rocking vigorously. "When the new year approaches, and Vezpro has the option of paying off or calling what might be a bluff—could we afford to take a chance that it's a crank letter?"

"That may depend on what the blackmail consists of. With five billion lives at stake, I'd say—no."

5

Darzek sat at his desk with the masfiln's mysterious letter before him, but he was moodily studying his desk calendar. It was a product of Vezpro's ingenious technology: circular in shape, with the galactic standard calendar arranged about its outer circumference. On an inner circle the Vezpronian year appeared, and around the center—in constant motion—were all of the planets of Vezpro's solar system along with their satellites. The day's date was illuminated: a softly glowing, green glyph. The central sun glowed brightly enough to serve as a night light, and the entire structure was almost a meter tall.

Darzek found it irritating. One glance gave him such a complexity of information that it made him feel ignorant.

Darzek had extracted as many details as he could from the physical evidence of the letter. These were unfortunately few. The unique-looking substance it was written on turned out to be a common type of luxury stationery, manufactured on Vezpro but probably available all over the galaxy. The machine on which it was written had been mass-produced—also on Vezpro—in the billions and exported just as widely. Darzek had read the message at least five hundred times, pondering phraseology and choice of words, and he knew while he did so that the sender would have been intelligent enough to disguise any distinctive habits of expression that would identify him or his world of origin.

That left only two angles to work on: The science of turning a world into a sun, which already had the experts stumped; and criminal psychology, which had no experts—or even amateurs—in a society that had never produced a criminal.

"Why the new cycle?" Darzek demanded. "When the message was sent, that was almost a cycle in the future."

"Gives the government plenty of time to worry," Miss Schlupe suggested.

"Nonsense. No one can worry for a cycle—especially a Vezpronian cycle, which is almost eighteen months of Earth time and a quarter longer than the standard galactic year. It allows too much time for accidents to happen to the best laid plans, or minds to change, or governments to be voted out of office, or even to have someone figure out how it'll be done and by whom. Is our blackmailing scientist merely a bad psychologist, or does he have some sinister purpose I can't fathom? Or is he some kind of nut? The letter sounds nutty."

"Maybe it takes time to arrange to blow up a world," Miss Schlupe said.

"Very likely it does. In that case, why not wait until you're ready? Then you can threaten to do it next term, or tomorrow, instead of in the remote future. This makes no sense at all. Also, it's very bad theater and lacks the artistic touch. The timing isn't so good, either. It's been more than two terms since that letter arrived. Why make a threat and then wait so long to follow it up?"

"Is the new cycle a holiday?"

Darzek turned to her. "It is. Does that have some special significance? Do what I say, or I'll turn your world into a sun and spoil your holiday? Besides, I count seven other major holidays that come first."

"Maybe the delay is to give the government time to send someone to Nifron D. I have a different question. Why did they stage the demonstration on the other side of the galaxy? Why not use an uninhabited planet or statellite in this sector? Then the Vezpronians would be dramatically reminded of the threat every time they looked up."

"I've already asked myself that," Darzek said. "The only logical answer is that turning a world into a sun requires some rather ostentatious preparations that are best carried out in a remote and unpopulated part of space—supplies delivered, conspicuous ground installations, maybe a large work force. But if that's the case, how does our blackmailer expect to get away with such preparations on a populous world like Vezpro? Especially if the government is alerted and starts looking suspiciously at anything that suggests a nuclear happening?"

"Which brings us back to the possibility that the whole thing is a bluff," Miss Schlupe observed.

Darzek was scrutinizing his desk calendar again. "Why the new cycle? Could there be some scientific reason for that? Vezpro's position in space, or the alignment of the planets, or some such thing?"

"You're thinking of a natural cause," Miss Schlupe said.

"No. I'm thinking of a catastrophe to which natural events contribute and which couldn't occur without them. Here's a job for you. I want to know how good Vezpro's scientists are—especially our esteemed Mas of Science and Technology, Naz Forlan. He may be a political hack."

"I'll find out."

"Do that. You quietly find out whether he knows anything, and I'll call on him and ask him."

A distinguished emissary of Supreme, Darzek thought, even when incognito, should not run his own errands. He sent Gud Baxak to inquire as to when it would be convenient for Gul Darr to call on the Mas of Science and Technology. Naz Forlan responded that he was at Gul Darr's service, day or night, and invited him to come at once. Darzek donned the dark cloak that most traders affected on Vezpro and stepped through Gud Baxak's office transmitter to the government complex.

Naz Forlan, looking like a grotesquely misconstructed greenish dwarf, stood waiting for Darzek in the reception hall. He murmured formal greetings in his soft, musical voice, ceremoniously escorted Darzek to his private office, and got him seated. Then he vanished behind a massive desk and a moment later was lifted into view by an elevating chair that compensated for his diminutive stature. His green complexion had abruptly changed to a normal Vezpronian pink. Darzek did not think to attribute this to the room's strange lighting until the interview was almost over.

"Since you're officially a trader, perhaps it would be best if you sold me something," Forlan said.

"What do you need?"

"This world always is in short supply of certain rare metals."

"Give me a list. Trans-Star will supply them in any quantities you want."

Forlan studied him perplexedly. "Then you really are a trader?"

"But of course. The fact that Supreme entrusts me with missions from time to time in no way interferes with my business. Give me your list of shortages, and I'll supply any item on it at five per cent below the minimum bid."

Now Forlan was staring at him. "You make that offer without even knowing what the minimum bids are?"

Darzek smiled. He felt like the city slicker lecturing a small-town merchant. "The reason you have shortages is because you're dealing with traders who can't see beyond the third sector. And you're being overcharged because they think in shipload quantities. My associates and I have connections throughout this galaxy—and even, in special circumstances, the next. We're accustomed to supplying entire worlds. One can safely discount the minimum bid when handling such quantities."

"I fear that I'm rather naive in such matters," Forlan said apologetically. "Until I was appointed mas, my concern was with the use of things, not with the procuring of them. Very well. I'll give you a statement of quantities and minimum bids. Now—as for this other matter—"

"This other matter concerns a scientific problem, and I'm not a scientist. I'd like two confidential assistants—an expert nuclear engineer and a computer technician—and a secure place for them to work."

Forlan thought for a moment. Then he flipped a switch on his desk. "Wolndur and Angoz, please. Immediately."

A short time later a male and a female Vezpronian entered the room. They wore identical clothing—baggy, gaudy triple-legged trousers in a smear of bright colors, and similarly colored, smock-like triple-armed coats. Both looked extremely young. Darzek was about to protest that the problem already had baffled the best experts in the galaxy and wasn't about to be solved by kindergartners, but Forlan anticipated him.

"We're confronted with the impossible, Gul Darr, but youth is not afraid of new ideas and sometimes takes impossibilities in stride. This may be an instance where imagination counts more than experience. May I present Eld Wolndur, of my nuclear engineering staff, and Melris Angoz, a highly competent computer technician."

He turned to them. "Gul Darr is a trader. He also is a special emissary of Supreme, but no one except yourselves is to know that. Understand?" They both gazed awesomely at Darzek. Forlan continued, "We'll set up a special office for you. Officially, you're working with Gul Darr to develop new procurement methods for rare metals. Unofficially, you'll be working on a highly secret problem. Gul Darr will tell you what he wants you to do, or what line of research he wants you to follow. From this moment he is your superior, and you are answerable only to him. You will discuss your work with no one except him. He will report progress through myself to the masfiln when he considers that advisable." He turned to Darzek. "Is that satisfactory? I'll leave it to you to tell them what you think they should know."

Darzek regarded his new assistants doubtfully. As Vezpronians, they probably were attractive youngsters—Melris Angoz bright-eyed and alert; Wolndur sturdy and highly serious-looking. No doubt they would approach any task he gave them with enthusiasm and perhaps even with as much imagination as Forlan claimed, but Darzek would have preferred a generous measure of knowledge and experience.

He reminded himself that a message to UrsNollf would bring him a delegation of the best scientists in the galaxy, and he should have no difficulty in finding routine tasks for these two in case their imaginations flagged. "Make certain that your office has a direct link to the world's computer," he told them. "When you're ready to start work, a message to the Trans-Star Trading Company will reach me immediately."

Back in the Trans-Star office, Darzek gave Gud Baxak the memorandum Forlan had prepared for him on rare metals, quantities needed, and minimum bids, and told him what was required. Then he retired to the pentagon living room. Miss Schlupe was out, so he appropriated her rocking chair.

He was still rocking and meditating when she returned. She seated herself opposite him and announced, "Your mas is a paragon. He's been in the national service all of his professional life, he's held high rank for years, and everyone speaks admiringly of him. He also acts as consultant to various private companies, which is customary and proper, and he's probably the local equivalent of a multimillionaire. In other words, he doesn't need a government job, and he'd acquire a lot more solvency as a full-time private consultant, but he's loyal. Our term would be 'patriotic.' Any questions?"

"Yes. What's his specialization?"

"Metallurgy and several related fields. He's considered brilliant."

"Anything connected with nuclear science or engineering?"

"Nothing. Why—is there something suspicious about him?"

"There's always something suspicious about paragons," Darzek said.

"Did he refuse to cooperate?"

"No. He was fully cooperative. The only oddity was that he gave me a couple of youngsters for assistants. He said that a problem like this requires imagination rather than experience, and youth is less likely to be baffled by impossibilities."

"He may be right," Miss Schlupe said. "UrsNollf's committee got nowhere, and he picked the most experienced people available. What

are you moping about? If they don't perform, you can either fire
them or ignore them."

"I made the mistake of asking for assistants. Now I have to think
of something for them to do."

With the full of authority of the mas behind them, it did not take
Darzek's new assistants long to establish themselves in a suitable
office. They sent for him the following morning, and he went to see
them at once.

At one end of the long room, Melris had installed her banks of
computer keyboards—they looked like a massive jumble of organ
and piano parts. At the other end, Wolndur had set up his workscreens for scientific calculations. Three long work tables filled the
center of the room, though what sort of activities his assistants expected to perform on them Darzek could not guess and did not
bother to ask.

He sat down with them at one of the tables and first impressed
them with the critical need for secrecy. Then he graphically described the threat to the world of Vezpro. When finally they grasped
the fact that he was serious, they were staggered.

"To begin with, I want two things from you," Darzek told them.
"I want a complete scientific and computer study comparing the
worlds Nifron D and Vezpro—Nifron D as it was at the approximate
time that it turned into a sun, since we don't know the exact moment, and Vezpro as it will be on the new cycle. I want to know if
there are any natural phenomena that are the same or similar. I also
want a check made of individuals who might have a grievance, real
or imagined, against the world of Vezpro. Include all kinds of scientists and anyone wealthy enough to hire scientists. Any questions?"

They stared at him mutely. Darzek wondered whether they were
overwhelmed at the notion of their world being turned into a sun or
because a stupid emissary of Supreme seemed to think it was possible. "This is the kind of problem that gets solved by a lucky guess,
not by brilliant reasoning," he said. "Don't feel disappointed when
the results you get are negative. That just means that we'll have to
guess again."

Once they had recovered, the prospect of investigating wrong
guesses did not seem to discourage them. They went to work energet-
ically, and Darzek returned to his pentagon-shaped living room for
further meditation.

He told Miss Schulpe what he had done, and she said, "I don't think much of your natural phenomena search, but the grievance one ought to cut across a lot of territory."

"What are you working on?" Darzek asked.

"I'll tell you if I find anything."

She went off to check reports from her investigators, who used an office in a seedy part of the capital city, and Darzek resumed his meditating. He spent the day at it, and when he finished he could not remember another occasion when he had thought so long and accomplished so little. He had turned the problem over and over without finding anything suggesting a handle with which it could be picked up or even grasped. He hadn't even been able to think of another angle that his assistants could investigate.

Miss Schlupe returned late, and before they'd had a chance to talk, Eld Wolndur arrived. Gud Baxak, who was working tirelessly on the problem of rare metals for Vezpro, announced him, and Darzek went to the office to talk with him.

Wolndur presented him with two studies. The first demonstrated convincingly that there was no physical similarity between Nifron D at the time of its conversion into a sun and Vezpro on the new cycle. Positions of sister planets and satellites, seasons, tidal factors, alignment of the sun and planetary masses—if there was a common denominator anywhere, Wolndur was unable to find it.

The second study contained a list of names with information about them.

Darzek, without mentioning that the energy of his new assistants was exceeding his most optimistic expectations, presented both his congratulations and his thanks.

"And—what shall we work on next?" Wolndur asked.

"Anything you think appropriate," Darzek said, gesturing grandly. The mas had said youthful imagination might be more valuable than experience. Darzek, since he had nothing else for them to do, was more than willing to give their imaginations complete latitude.

He took the studies to the living room and handed the list of names to Miss Schlupe. "Any of this in your territory?" he asked.

Persons who for one reason or another had a grievance against Vezpro: a millionaire manufacturer who had closed his Vezpro plant because of—he said—silly harassment about safety regulations; government employees who had lost their jobs because of incompetence or politics and were nourishing lifelong grudges; individuals who had been assessed tax penalties and resented it; alien traders who disliked Vezpro's regulations and said so, both vocally and vehemently. It was a long list. Miss Schlupe glanced at it for a few minutes.

Then she pushed it aside. "Garbage. Do you want me to check on all these people?"

"Do you have the staff to do it?"

"No. I'm adding people as fast as I can, but I have more important things for them to do. I can take the millionaires right away. Otherwise, there's just one name that looks interesting."

Darzek nodded. "Raf Lolln. An astrophysicist with a grievance against Vezpro. It's almost too obvious. I'm going to see him myself."

"When?"

Darzek got to his feet. "Now. He lives on the other side of the planet. It'll be morning, there."

It took Darzek three transmitter jumps from the terminal of Klinoz, the capital city: one to Hornitx, the major city on the eastern continent; one to Gglarr, a once charming rural city that had been devastatingly improved by the addition of light industries; and, finally, one to the residence of Raf Lolln, an astrophysicist whose differences with the University of Vezpro twenty years before had led to his dismissal.

To Darzek's disappointment, he found an extremely elderly Vezpronian with a cherubic, mischievous smile, living in luxurious surroundings on a lovely country estate. Darzek presented his credential as emissary of Supreme. Lolln's eyes widened, but his face lost none of its puckish expression.

"I'm afraid you're lost," he said. "Supreme is a computer; computers are slaves of dogma. This is the one point in the universe where dogma is not worshipped. How did you happen to come here?"

"In search of an astrophysicist who has nothing to do with dogma," Darzek answered.

Lolln uttered a cackling laugh. "That's what the University of Vezpro said when it hired me. It failed to add that it also expected me to keep quiet about it. However—" He gestured disdainfully. "The lack of an opportunity to corrupt the youth of this planet by making it think also brings freedom from responsibility. My mate and I both inherited solvency, I do some industrial consulting, we live comfortably in delightful surroundings, and I'm able to enlarge on my nonconformity in private. Why do you need an astrophysicist? Sit down, sit down. One of those chairs ought to fit."

Darzek seated himself, and the old scientist perched on a chair nearby and composed himself to listen. After a moment's reflection, Darzek told him—without mentioning Vezpro's connection—about the mysterious conversion of the planet Nifron D.

When he finished, Lolln's face was wreathed in ecstasy. "And they all said it was impossible!" he exclaimed. "What a triumph for dogma! They went, they saw it, they studied it, and they concluded that it couldn't be done. According to dogma, the universe doesn't exist. I can prove it. As for your Nifron D—"

He sprang to his feet. There was an enormous workscreen at one side of the room, and Lolln perched at the keyboard and began to fill it with mathematical and scientific symbols. One line followed another. Finally, almost at the bottom of the screen, he brought the procession to a halt.

He turned. "There. Proven."

"What's proven?" Darzek asked.

"That Nifron D couldn't be turned into a sun. You're not a scientist?"

"Not even remotely."

"Pity." Lolln got to his feet and slowly backed away from the screen, studying his creation. "It's a thing of beauty. It's exciting. It's magnificent. And it proves conclusively that what you have just told me isn't so. Do you know why? Each mathematical or scientific symbol represents an assumption. Conventional science considers them fixed entities, cast in imperishable alloys and forever changeless, but they're nothing but assumptions. Their only value is as tools we can use until we find better ones. If just one of those assumptions is incorrect, then my proof is incorrect. Conversely, if my proof is incorrect, and I believe you when you tell me it is, then one or more of my assumptions is wrong."

"How would you go about finding out which one?"

"Ah! That's why it's so much easier to be a dogmatist. Each one of all those symbols must be studied, analyzed, tested, experimented with—it could take a lifetime, and mine is almost over. Unless—I'm an outcast, you know—unless you could obtain access to the world computer for me. Could you?"

"Certainly. This world's computer, or that of any other world—or Supreme itself."

"In that case, I'll do it. I can't guarantee success, but I can guarantee that this road is the only one."

Darzek thanked him, and Lolln waved the thanks aside with his puckish grin. "The thanks are mine. I've been saying for years that the galaxy's leading astrophysicists are nitwits. I never thought I'd have the opportunity to prove it."

"If you'll work in Klinoz, I can furnish you with a computer tec and also a young assistant."

Lolln reflected for a moment. "I'd have to make some arrangements here. I could come in three days."

Darzek gave him the transmitter code of the Trans-Star office and promised to find living quarters for him and have any equipment he wanted waiting for him if he would send a list.

Then he returned to Klinoz. Miss Schlupe was exercising her rocking chair. She said, "Well?"

"He may be a find," Darzek said. "He's the first astrophysicist I've met who didn't say the thing was impossible and proceed to prove it. He said that things that happen are possible, and if the proof contradicts reality, then the proof is wrong. He's going to try to find out where it's wrong."

"Then I can cross him off the list?"

"Unfortunately, no. He jokes about his being dismissed from the university, but obviously that hurt. Also, he's independently wealthy. He's a natural suspect."

Miss Schlupe arched her eyebrows. "Is there anyone in this case who isn't a suspect?"

Darzek said meditatively, "I'll tell Wolndur and Melris to cooperate fully with Lolln but also to keep an eye on him. I want to know whether his research is aimed at solving the problem or confusing the issue. Wolndur should know enough science to recognize an obvious fraud. And then I'll tell Lolln—confidentially—that I suspect Wolndur and Melris of being in collusion with the blackmailer and ask him to keep an eye on them."

Miss Schlupe scowled at him. "Nonsense! Those youngsters aren't expert enough or experienced enough to be involved in a crime as scientifically complicated as this one. I also think they're too loyal."

"Loyalty is no commendation until we find out what—or whom—they're loyal to. Telling Lolln to watch them will make him think I trust him. You were right. At this point, we have to suspect everyone."

Gud Baxak climaxed a ceaseless whirlwind of day and night activity by tottering off to the Mas of Science and Technology with contracts to supply Vezpro's annual needs for several rare metals at a price 5 per cent lower than the minimum bids offered by other traders. Forlan was delighted—he was saving his world money and at the same time obtaining a guaranteed source of essential, hard-to-obtain items. Gud Baxak was delighted at having consummated the largest transaction of his career.

Jan Darzek saw no need to inform either of them that Trans-Star would lose solvency on half the orders and barely break even on the rest. He had a reputation to make. By the time the contracts were reviewed, approved, and executed, everyone of importance in the Vezpronian government would have heard of Gul Darr and his Trans-Star Trading Company; and Darzek, invested with the glow of his expensive new status, could get on with his real work just as soon as he figured out what that might be.

Raf Lolln arrived on schedule, and Darzek got him settled in his living quarters—which like Darzek's adjoined the Trans-Star office —and then introduced him to Wolndur and Melris, who were expecting him. He told Wolndur to have Lolln's solvency credential registered, so he could enter their office whenever he wished. When Darzek left them, Lolln had commenced his lecture on dogma, and Wolndur was listening politely.

Darzek looked in on them again two days later and found the lecture still in progress. Lolln seemed to have made a convert. The two scientists, old and young, were staring in aesthetic fascination at an endless formula on the largest screen, and fragments—bits swept away and piled up for reconsideration later—cluttered the other screens. At the far end of the room, Melris sat surrounded by her keyboards, doodling absently on some project of her own while she waited for their next request.

The scientists were too engrossed to notice Darzek. Melris motioned to him, and he circled the tables and crossed the room to her. She looked cautiously in the direction of Raf Lolln, and then she whispered, "I want to talk to you."

"Trans-Star office," Darzek whispered back.

"This evening?"

Darzek gave her the Vezpronian shrug of assent, turned, and made his way out again. Lolln had commenced a lecture on one of the jumble of symbols, and the scientists remained oblivious of his presence. Darzek closed the door quietly.

Melris arrived late, bringing Wolndur with her, and he was carrying a large box of computer printouts and trodding on her three heels as though he were quite as mystified as Darzek was. The box reminded Darzek of the mountain of trivia that Supreme periodically dumped on him. He greeted them resignedly, showed Wolndur where he could set the box, and said, without enthusiasm, "Yes? You've discovered something?"

"She hasn't told me," Wolndur said, glancing resentfully at her. "Lolln has been there all the time, and you asked us—but I think you're wrong about him."

"I'm frequently wrong," Darzek said cheerfully. "In some instances, it's much better to be wrong until proven right than right until proven wrong."

Wolndur pondered this with obvious skepticism. Darzek had the impression that the young scientist would have preferred to convert it to a scientific formula and spread it over a screen where he could test it properly.

Melris interrupted. "I've run a computer check on any nuclear irregularities that have occurred in this sector of the galaxy," she said. "The world of Skarnaf has a radiation victim for whom there is no possible accounting."

Darzek frowned. He would have preferred to keep information about the unfortunate Qwasrolk to himself, but he could hardly reprimand his computer technician for effectively exercising her imagination.

Before he could comment, Wolndur had refocused his thinking from Darzek's unscientific postulate to Melris's discovery. "How does that affect our problem?" he demanded.

"It suggests illegal nuclear experimentation," Melris said.

"So it does," Wolndur agreed. "But why Skarnaf? The slightest radiation leakage there would bring the authorities down on one immediately. Skarnaf has no nuclear facilities. No one would attempt illegal research there."

"The victim once worked on Vezpro," Melris said. "His name is Qwasrolk."

"I don't recognize it," Wolndur said. "Should I?"

"I don't know."

"Tell us what you've learned," Darzek suggested.

"Very little is known about him," she said. "He was found in a rural area of Skarnaf, badly burned and obviously the victim of a massive dose of radiation. He should have died immediately, but he was still alive at the date of this report. The chief proctor of Skarnaf managed to identify him—he's a native of that world—and traced him to Vezpro. Our own proctors cooperated in an investigation here. He worked for a Vezpronian firm as a nuclear engineer for a time, and then he disappeared."

Wolndur turned to Darzek. "Vezpro hires tens of thousands of nuclear engineers from all over this sector. Many of them serve apprenticeships here and acquire experience that enables them to obtain superior employment elsewhere. The fact that he once worked here wouldn't necessarily connect him with Vezpro—or with our problem."

"But his accident might," Melris objected. "I've never heard of anyone being injured in a nuclear accident. It suggests illegal if not amateurish experimentation."

"It does," Wolndur agreed. "But turning a world into a sun isn't an amateurish experiment, and his accident would have had to occur on Skarnaf, wouldn't it, since that's where he was found?"

"I asked for a check on his solvency credential," Melris said. "He continued to use it here on Vezpro for almost two cycles after he disappeared."

Darzek was regarding her with increasing respect. He hadn't thought of checking Qwasrolk's use of his solvency credential. He wondered if Miss Schlupe had. It opened up to them a detailed history of Qwasrolk's existence on Vezpro. His every purchase, his every movement through the world's transmitter network had been recorded in the central computer.

"He may have found employment under another name—which would be illegal and suggests illegal activity," Melris went on. She turned to Darzek. "I suggest, sire, that we inform the mas and ask him to take some nuclear personnel experts to Skarnaf and see if any of them recognize this Qwasrolk."

From the descriptions of Qwasrolk Darzek had been supplied with, no one was likely to recognize him; but there seemed no harm in trying, and Melris already had discovered useful and intriguing information that the previous investigation had overlooked. She deserved to have her suggestions respected. "Where is the mas likely to be?" Darzek asked.

They told him, and Darzek sent Gud Baxak with a message.

The Mas of Science and Technology showed no displeasure or even surprise at being summoned away from his evening meal or whatever recreation he might have been engaged in, but the moment he entered the room Darzek realized that he had been guilty of an act of gross discourtesy. They should have met the mas in his own office. Here there were no chairs that compensated for his ridiculously small stature, and the luminescent wall panels accentuated the mas's vividly green complexion.

But he seemed completely at ease. He listened attentively to Melris's discovery and when she had finished he echoed Wolndur's skepticism. "Skarnaf? What could that have to do with our problem?"

Melris did not answer. Darzek was her chief. If the mas had to be convinced, clearly that was Darzek's task.

"Do you have any recollection of a Qwasrolk?" the mas asked Wolndur. Wolndur gestured negatively. "I don't," Forlan said. "Of course my contacts with nuclear personnel have been limited." He turned to Darzek. "What do you think, Gul Darr?"

"I think that any information at all about this Qwasrolk is likely to be useful," Darzek said. "Certainly let's have some personnel experts try to identify him. Even if he has nothing to do with our problem, we have an obligation to help Skarnaf. Illegal nuclear research is a serious matter."

Forlan shrugged his agreement. "We'll go in the morning. I'll arrange for a ship and invite the nuclear personnel experts most likely to recognize him."

When they reached Skarnaf, a high government official was waiting for them at the transfer station where their ship docked. The visit of a mas from a neighboring world required an elaborate and unfortunately prolonged ceremony. While it proceeded, Darzek slipped aside, made a few quiet inquiries of station personnel, and succeeded in identifying the planet's chief proctor, a pleasant-looking individual of Darzek's own stature—for the natives of Skarnaf were approximately human in appearance except for a rather disconcerting rearrangement of their organs of sight, smell, and hearing. He introduced himself as an emissary of Supreme and asked for a private conference.

The chief proctor immediately led him to the transfer station manager's office, evicted the manager, and made the two of them comfortable. Darzek began by offering congratulations on the Qwasrolk investigation, and then—emphasizing the need for secrecy—he related the entire story, from the discovery of the planet turned into a sun to the delivery of a blackmail letter on Vezpro.

"Do you think this Qwasrolk had something to do with the Nifron D matter?" the chief asked bluntly.

"Because of his connection with Vezpro, and the nature of his accident, I think it possible that he did."

"But the Nifron D matter could have had nothing to do with his accident. We've established positively that no ship could have placed him where he was found, and he could not have got from Nifron D to Skarnaf by any means according to the timing you've established. The accident had to occur here."

"Probably a staff of scientists and engineers would be required to perfect the method of turning a world into a sun," Darzek said. "Some would remain at work in a secret laboratory while others went to Nifron."

"Then you think the secret laboratory is on Skarnaf?"

"If the accident couldn't have happened anywhere else, then the secret laboratory is here."

"I agree," the chief proctor said. "That's why we're still looking for it."

"Have you got any information from Qwasrolk?"

"Unfortunately, no. You'll understand that when you see him. The doctors can't believe the evidence of their own science. They say he should be dead. He certainly looks dead, but occasionally he mutters something almost intelligible. Of course we're recording every sound, but thus far no one has been able to comprehend anything, in any language." He paused. "To be frank, I don't like this mass intrusion. I tried to prevent it, but high diplomacy is involved. From what you've told me, I suppose it's justified. If my world were threatened, I'd want every clue investigated."

"I don't like it, either," Darzek said. "You've handled the investigation with a rare competence, and I'm confident that you'll continue to do so. But I don't want to assume the role of an obstructionist, and I suppose there is a remote chance of a useful identification."

"No one," the chief proctor said firmly, "is going to identify Qwasrolk by looking at him. You'll understand that the moment you see him. I'm grateful for this information. I'll double the teams looking for the secret laboratory, since that situation obviously is much more serious than we'd thought. Now we'd better join the others—the ceremonies should be over." He led Darzek to the nearest transmitter.

They caught up with Forlan's party in the lobby of a building Darzek identified as a governmental administration unit. It was only when they had passed through an office complex that he recognized it as a hospital.

They moved along a wide corridor, and on either side were tiers of healing capsules, three high, set in the walls. In each lay a patient, sealed against the outside world, visible through a transparent, bulging, sliding door. The natives of Skarnaf were sufficiently human in appearance to make Darzek feel homesick, but those in the hospital affected him differently. The sick, of any life form, were pathetic.

A doctor had joined them, distinctive in his blue one-piece suit. Like the chief proctor, he resented this mass intrusion; unlike the proctor, he felt no diplomatic compulsion to be polite about it. He spoke petulantly to the official in the native language, and then he turned to the visiting party and spoke in Galactic.

"I have advised against this," he said. "The patient remains in a state of crisis. He is so horribly disfigured that any kind of identification is out of the question. He suffered exposure to a radiation so intense we have no way of measuring it or even guessing what it was. He should have died. Nevertheless, he survived and is surviving, and if he is left undisturbed, he may eventually be able to tell us what happened."

"Is there any chance at all that he'll recover?" Darzek asked.

"Since he has lived this long when he should have died at once, anything is possible. He may recover. He is much more likely to die before you see him."

"Have you been able to question him?" Naz Forlan asked.

"He has not yet been conscious—not rationally so. Sometimes in his delirium he seems to be trying to talk, and we record what he says, but no one has been able to understand it."

Forlan thought for a moment. "And you say he is disfigured beyond recognition?"

"I would say so. Of course no one in this hospital knew him previously, but I very much doubt that anyone who did would recognize him."

"How was he identified as Qwasrolk?"

"I don't know," the doctor said shortly. "The proctors identified him before he arrived here."

"We have no intention of disturbing your patient," Forlan said. "No effort will be made to talk with him. All we request is that our party be permitted to look at him. It's extremely important. We may be able to help your chief proctor learn something about his accident."

The doctor gestured resignedly. "Before you do so, do any of the rest of you have questions?"

"Have you been able to make any kind of a medical deduction concerning what happened to him?" Darzek asked.

"He was exposed to radiation of an unbelievable intensity," the doctor said, "but only for an instant, I think. A fraction of an instant. More than that fraction would have incinerated him. It's as though some safety device momentarily failed to function. Say a shield dropped into place a mere fraction of a fraction too late. An instant sooner, and he would have been safe; an instant later, and there would have been no remains to survive."

"Then you deduce that some kind of nuclear experiment was involved?"

"I do, since no other explanation accounts for such an accident on Skarnaf. You'll have to ask the nuclear scientists what kind of experiment would produce radiation of that intensity. I can only say that it was beyond my ability to calculate it, and the exposure time was immeasurably brief."

"Thank you."

They moved further along the corridor. Then, at the doctor's request, they stepped onto the black walkway adjacent to the healing capsules. It rose slowly, lifting them to the level of the upper tier. The doctor opened one of the capsules, and the nuclear personnel experts began filing past, each taking one brief look at the patient.

Darzek knew long before he reached the capsule that there would be no identification. Each expert glanced quickly and jerked his head away, sickened. When finally Darzek came close enough to see for himself, he understood why. He had seen war photos of atomic or firebomb victims. This was their epitome. What once had been a human-type head was a seared skull covered with a burned parchment of flesh. Ears were gone. Hair, nose, even the lips and eyelids were missing, leaving the grinning, toothy face of a death mask. Clothing had slightly protected the body, which was merely burned and looked like one monstrous scab. The scent of dead and decaying flesh was nauseous.

Naz Forlan came at the end of the line, along with Wolndur, Melris, Darzek, and the doctor. He called ahead to the personnel experts, "Did any of you recognize him?"

No response was necessary. This gruesomely burned body would be unrecognizable no matter how well one had known it.

The doctor asked bluntly, "Well—are you satisfied?"

Before Forlan could answer, Qwasrolk's lidless eyes turned toward them. They moved slowly, studying each of the party in turn. Darzek had to fight to control his nausea as the glazed vision rested momentarily on him. Then the eyes moved on, leaving him with the feeling that he'd been stabbed with revulsion. They rested briefly on Forlan, on Wolndur, on Melris, on the doctor. Jerkily they returned, focusing vacantly on one gaping observer after another.

Suddenly Qwasrolk vanished, leaving all of them staring disbelievingly at an empty capsule.

7

Miss Schlupe had discovered a new restaurant. There was nothing special about the food except the fungus garnishing that all of the transfer station restaurants offered; but this station had an extremely low orbit and featured a magnification viewer in its dining room. Darzek watched, fascinated, while the terrain unrolled below him.

Fascinated and horrified.

Traveling about by transmitter, one got the impression that an industrial world was paved with industries and cities; but Vezpro, although its industrial cities were huge complexes, produced a high percentage of its own food, and land suitable for cultivation was intensely developed. It reminded him of Earth, seen from a low plane flight, and the idea that somewhere in the galaxy lurked a malignant intelligence that would deliberately incinerate all of that beauty was frightening.

Finally a long bank of clouds drifted beneath them. The viewer, a moment later, focused on outer space and its dazzling panorama of stars, and Darzek nibbled his food and turned to Miss Schlupe.

"You were talking about ESP," she reminded him.

"So I was," Darzek agreed pensively. "Extrasensory perception. Ever since we first learned that the galaxy is inhabited by vast numbers of intelligent life forms, I've been anticipating a meeting with one that had a portfolio of unnatural powers. Thus far I've found only highly exceptional supertalented individuals that can occur in any life form, including our own. I've encountered unmistakable, startling instances of prognostication or telepathy, but this is my first experience with a genuine teleport."

"Are you certain it wasn't a trick?" Miss Schlupe asked.

Darzek nibbled again and swallowed. "I don't see how it could have been, unless you want to call all of parapsychology a trick. The doctor was at least as amazed as the rest of us—he proceeded to pull the capsule apart looking for his patient, and then what he had to say in his native tongue was certainly better left untranslated, which the diplomat wisely did. The chief proctor's anger was just as genuine. He thought he was well on the way to solving the case, and then we showed up and deprived him of his only witness. I pointed out to him that an individual with the ability to teleport was likely to vanish at any time and our being there was merely a coincidence, but I don't think he believed me. He's no fool, by the way, but we knew that already. The first thing he did was send a platoon of proctors to the place in the country where this Qwasrolk had been found."

Darzek paused for another nibble. "They found him again. But the moment he saw them he vanished a second time, and he hasn't been seen since—at least, he hadn't been seen again up to the time we left Skarnaf."

"Did you point out to him that it was his own proctors who were responsible for the second disappearance?" Miss Schulpe asked.

"As a matter of fact, I did. And he pointed out in turn that without the first disappearance, his proctors wouldn't have caused the second. He understands our problem, though. He has a rare competence. I like him."

"And how did our esteemed Mas of Science and Technology react to the whole business?"

"He thought it a wasted trip. He'd hoped one of his personnel specialists would recognize Qwasrolk as a scientist who'd worked here under another name after that mysterious disappearance three cycles ago. That would have been a valuable lead. But with those hideous burns, Qwasrolk isn't recognizable under any name, and Forlan realized that the moment he saw him."

"It was hardly a wasted trip," Miss Schlupe observed thoughtfully. "Now you know—maybe—how he got where they found him."

"Right. I pointed that out to the chief proctor, too. It solves the most knotty problem about the whole business. We had a long discussion, mostly speculating on the possibility of teleporting across space. If this is possible, Qwasrolk's secret research may have been performed on another planet, perhaps even a remote planet—which is a cheerful thought, since it widens the area of search from a mere world to maybe the whole galaxy. It also raises another question. If teleporting through space is possible, Qwasrolk may have passed near or through a sun—if a teleport actually 'passes.' He may simply leave one place and arrive at another. There aren't any experts on the subject. If that happened, then there was no secret laboratory or illegal nuclear experiment, and Qwasrolk had nothing to do with

Nifron D or the blackmail threat to Vezpro. He's only a teleport who got his navigation slightly confused."

"What it amounts to," Miss Schlupe said, getting out her knitting, "is that you've made the Qwasrolk problem much more complicated without contributing a thing to the solution of your other problem."

Darzek looked at her irritably. The sly smile that she had been directing at him from time to time was becoming irksome. "All right," he said. "Out with it. What nefarious activities have you been engaged in while I was away?"

The smile broadened. "I got to wondering if Qwasrolk was the only nuclear engineer or physicist who'd disappeared from Vezpro."

"Good thought. Was he?"

"No. Thus far I've identified more than forty others." She paused. "You're taking the news calmly. I thought you'd flip. What are *you* thinking about?"

"The blackmailer," Darzek said. "Why would anyone send a letter like that one and then not follow it up? What's he waiting for?"

After a few attempts to make use of Vezpro's proctors, Miss Schlupe had concentrated on expanding her own investigative agency, and she now had a growing force of more than three hundred agents. She agreed with Darzek that Vezpro's chief proctor—in contrast to the one on Skarnaf—was a twirp, and his entire staff was better qualified to function as garbage collectors than as police.

"But remember—none of them has ever had to function as police," Darzek observed.

"Neither have those on Skarnaf," Miss Schlupe said, "but the ones they sent here were able to ask questions and find out things. I wouldn't send a Vezpro proctor to track down the date of New Year's Day."

She had begun by hiring people in lower-paid occupations to make routine investigations for her in their spare time. They were delighted to acquire extra solvency in such an easy manner. If they performed adequately, she gave them more work to do. Those who possessed genuine talent were given full-time jobs with good pay. She also recruited children, who were equally delighted to earn solvency during their frequent vacation periods. The Vezpro system of education seemed to function in fits and starts, and Darzek, after one attempt, decided not to take the time to figure it out.

On a traders' tour of manufacturing installations, Darzek happened onto one of Miss Schlupe's urchins, wistfully seeking information about her cousin-uncle Xaniff, and he reflected, not for the first time, that Miss Schlupe was a genius. She understood that the true investigator had to be an actor, and she probably had rehearsed this youngster's performance as carefully as though it were to be done on the stage—but only after first doing her own meticulous investigation so as to fully understand all family ties and relationships of the multilimbed Vezpronians.

Darzek was occupying himself with a series of communications with UrsNollf, prodding him to pose scientific questions of Supreme. Some of the questions had been suggested by Raf Lolln when the Vezpro computer found them indigestible. But Supreme, the world-sized computer, remained subject to its own vagaries and limitations. It found the questions equally indigestible.

Days passed. The mysteriously missing Qwasrolk remained missing, whether alive or dead. The doctors on Skarnaf were doubtful that he could survive long outside his healing capsule. Melris Angoz, after her brilliant coup in tracking down a radiation victim Darzek already knew about, had produced nothing further. Raf Lolln continued to dissect scientific formulae with Wolndur's assistance, searching vainly for the fatal error imposed by scientific dogma.

Darzek sat at his desk and moodily contemplated the automated calendar of Vezpro and its sister planets. In front of him lay Miss Schlupe's updated list of missing nuclear physicists and engineers. The total now stood at slightly more than one hundred, which was ridiculous. Had some secret organization hired enormous numbers of nuclear specialists, used them to bring a fantastically complicated research project to a successful conclusion, tested the results on Nifron D, and then threatened the world of Vezpro?

The cost would have been enormous. That effectively ruled out crackpots and terrorist groups, and terrorist groups didn't exist in galactic society anyway.

But neither did the blackmailing of governments and threats of world destruction.

Studying his calendar, Darzek began to wonder about Vezpro's colonies on its sister planets. Some of them might be wealthy; some might be dissatisfied with their colonial status and want independence. Even in galactic society that kind of thing happened, but there were far too many peaceful ways of resolving such differences for either party to think of resorting to violence.

It looked like an unpromising line of investigation, but Darzek had nothing else to work on. He sent for Gud Baxak and said to him, "Tell me about Vezpro's colonies on the other planets."

Gud Baxak cheerfully obliged, and Darzek's idea was torpedoed by his first sentences. Like so many industrial worlds with the good fortune of being the only habitable planet in their solar systems, Vezpro had systematically stripped its sister planets of their resources. The "colonies" planted there had functioned only to mine whatever could be grabbed profitably. One smaller planet, whose mineral resources had long since been exhausted, served as a dump for nuclear wastes. Its population consisted of a few caretaker scientists who lived in an insulated dome behind many layers of lead-reinforced concrete.

Colonists on the other worlds were in fact employees who signed on for limited periods to work in those mines that were still marginally profitable. They were well paid; their working conditions were considered excellent. Such colonists were unlikely to revolt, and in any case they wouldn't have the capital to finance nuclear experimentation.

Darzek pushed the calendar—and his bright idea—aside. Then he picked it up again. "Just a moment. This seventh planet. Zarst. I dimly remember Gula Schlu mentioning that the Zarstans are a religious sect of scientists and technologists. You didn't mention Zarst."

Gud Baxak gestured indifferently. "What is there to tell? The secrets of a religion are known only to its initiates."

"Is it considered a colony of Vezpro?"

"I think it is independent."

"What's its population?"

Gud Baxak punched a question on his reference computer and waved a hand futilely. "It is not given. Only the Zarstans know."

Darzek punched out a few questions of his own and turned to the large wall screen. The world of Zarst suddenly had become interesting.

The screen showed him a frozen cinder without atmosphere. The few surface installations obviously related to mining operations. The only available statistics concerned mining production of a hundred cycles previously.

Darzek said slowly, "If Zarst is an independent world, then it must be Certified and a member of the Galactic Synthesis. Otherwise, neither Vezpro nor any other member of the Synthesis can legally be in contact with it, and it wouldn't be sending religious robot shows to Vezpro. And if it's a member, certain statistical information has to be furnished regularly to Supreme and is public property."

"Supreme may know," Gud Baxak observed.

"If Supreme has that kind of information, then every world has it. On the other hand, if Zarst is officially a colony world of Vezpro and in practice has merely been granted an unusual degree of independence, Vezpro must have statistical information and furnish it regularly to Supreme. Either way, the world's population figures and other information should be readily available."

Gud Baxak tried his computer again. "Nothing."

"A religion of scientists," Darzek mused. "With their own world, yet. What better place for secret nuclear research?" Gud Baxak did not answer. "Where do these religious scientists get their education?" Darzek asked. "Do they have their own university? Or do they send their novices to Vezpro to study science? For that matter, where do they get their solvency? The robot show I attended had no admission charge, and those robots must be expensive to build. Supporting a community on a barren planet like Zarst must be expensive. What sort of a solvency rating does this religious order have?"

Gud Baxak punched his computer. "Nothing."

"Go ask questions," Darzek told him. "The Vezpronian traders should know *something* about Zarst."

Gud Baxak obediently headed for the transmitter.

He evidently received a thorough briefing from the first person he asked, because he returned almost at once. "It's a religious scientific community," he said. "Zarst was once a colony of Vezpro, but when the ores could no longer be removed profitably, the combine that owned mineral rights and installations sold them—sold the world— to the religious community. And Vezpro, wanting to retain the community's good will—and because the world had no value anyway— granted it a cooperative independence."

"What's a cooperative independence?" Darzek asked.

"Vezpro pledged not to interfere in the affairs of the religious community as long as they were not contrary to the welfare of Vezpro's citizens."

"Interesting. In fact, fascinating. Where'd the Zarstans get the solvency to buy a world?"

"It is thought to be an immensely weathy community. It sells scientific and technological services."

"Mmm—yes. That could make it wealthy. Where does it train its scientists and technicians? On Zarst?"

"They are converted," Gud Baxak said, sounding apologetic.

Darzek stared at him. "Do you mean that they only recruit scientists to their religion—people who are already trained?"

"Competent scientists, engineers, and technologists who have no mundane attachments, who are males—or male-like, depending on their species, and all species are welcome—these are invited to become Zarstans."

"No wonder they can sell scientific and technological services!"

"I believe they still work the mines on Zarst," Gud Baxak said. "That isn't known for certain, but it is thought that they could do it profitably because they would have no labor costs."

"Is there a direct transmitter link between Vezpro and Zarst?"

"When they occupy the same quadrant. Otherwise, one goes by way of one of the other planets."

"So transportation is cheap," Darzek mused. "But the members of the community have to eat. They need clothing. They finance their robot shows, and no doubt they maintain recruiting stations on other worlds. All of that has to be an enormously expensive operation. What sort of services do they sell?"

"Industrial design, fabrication design and layout, the solving of fabrication and design problems, marketing consultation—" Gud Baxak made an all-encompassing gesture. "Any kind of problem related to planning the fabrication and marketing of goods can be taken to the Zarstans, and they guarantee to solve it or they do not charge. Their services are indispensable to Vezpro's industry."

"But when they do charge, no doubt their services are expensive," Darzek suggested.

"In some instances, it's an agreed fee. More often it's a royalty on each item sold."

Darzek leaned back meditatively. "I suppose this is cheaper for fabricators than hiring their own staffs."

"The Zarstans are said to be highly competent. They work for virtually all fabrication concerns on Vezpro and for those on other worlds as well."

"Then they must be enormously wealthy. That explains why they can offer free robot shows to recruit new members."

"The shows also demonstrate their robots," Gud Baxak said. "Their skill in designing robots is famous."

"No doubt. I think I'd like to know more about it. In fact, I'd like to know everything about the Zarstans, including what they know about themselves."

Gud Baxak said patiently, "The secrets of a religion—"

"Gud Baxak," Darzek said firmly, "I'm about to frighten a world government silly and shake a few cracks in the foundation of that religious community. And when I finish, you'll be able to punch your computer and get all the statistics you want about Zarst."

"Yes, sire."

"As for secrets, anything known to an entire community can be found out by anyone who wants to take the trouble. It's possible, though, that there are secrets within secrets, and maybe secrets within those known only to a favored few. As I said, I'd like to know *everything* about the Zarstans."

"Yes, sire."

Darzek thought for a moment. "Cracking foundations is a good act, but I've got to be certain that they aren't holding anything back. I'd better have a look at Zarst myself."

"But sire—"

"How does one go about buying a factory?"

Gud Baxak blinked. He had been with Darzek long enough to accustom himself to the unusual, if not the inexplicable, but totally unexpected questions inevitably caused him acute mental distress. He answered hesitantly, "One would first have to find a factory that's for sale."

"Do so," Darzek said. "If possible, a small factory."

"Yes, sire."

"One capable of making a single consumer item would be preferable. And the item should have something to do with nucleonics."

"Yes, sire."

"I don't really want to buy one. I just want to find one that's known to be for sale. If necessary, you can take an option, but don't pay much for it. I only want it for a few days, ten at the most, and there's no point in squandering solvency. Get it free if you can. And bring back a few samples of the product."

"Yes, sire."

Gud Baxak, seething with curiosity, strode to the transmitter. He had a quality that enhanced his value to Darzek. No matter how curious he was, no matter how inexplicable his instructions seemed to him, he could do what he was told without asking a single question.

Darzek turned to his desk and picked up Miss Schlupe's list of a hundred-plus missing nuclear physicists and engineers. He wondered if he had accidentally discovered what had happened to them.

8

When Darzek had attended the Zarstans' theater—or church—he had not been aware that he was taking part in a religious ceremony. He'd thought he was attending the most confusing dramatic presentation that intelligence could contrive. The audience surrounded the play, but this arrangement had none of the direct logic of theater-in-the-round. Instead, it was theater-in-all-directions. The seating was on a level, and the room was crossed and crisscrossed by wide aisles. Wherever two aisles intersected, there was an oval, and in these ovals the play took place. The members of the audience watched the nearest oval. The performance was almost completed before Darzek realized that the various segments of the play were moving from oval to oval and repeating themselves, so that the dramatic presentation consisted of a multitude of parts that each area of the audience was seeing in a different sequence.

The effect on a member of the audience—since he heard the dialog in several ovals simultaneously and had to strain to follow that of the oval nearest to him—was visual pandemonium and aural consternation. The surroundings were as stark as those of a summer barn theater on the verge of bankruptcy, with oddly contoured, un-cushioned, backless seats that were the most uncomfortable Darzek had experienced since he'd attended a small rural church as a child. Perhaps this should have furnished a clue for him, but he had not even suspected that he was watching the proselytizing efforts of a major religion.

The robots, of course, were spectacular in their simulations of genuine actors.

On this, his second visit to the building, Darzek found the theater closed. The tall, slanting entranceways with strangely scalloped openings were filled with shimmering luminescence. The effect looked so odd that he stepped closer, was tempted to touch, and decided not to. It was a barricade of light waves, and it looked like woven strands of color.

He turned to the left, to a door he had not noticed on the previous occasion, and entered the Zarstans' religious headquarters on Vezpro.

It was as Spartan as the theater had been. The problem with a totally industrialized society, Darzek thought, was that more and more buildings and rooms and even the contents of rooms came to be designed for machines. This one was the natural habitat of automated cleaners, sterilizing robots that snooped out the last wispy trace of bacteria, transmitting cabinets for ordering food or anything else, mechanical messengers, reference computers with their bulging viewing screens. There was no need for closets except those custom-designed for machines; no need for storage space because anything wanted could be ordered at once by transmitter; no need for filing cabinets when machines digested everything and spewed it out on request.

This barren Zarstan headquarters would never pose a problem for any cleaning machine. In the walls, like a row of displays at an aquarium, were miniature theaters where fantastically ingenious miniature robots enacted scenes of religious import over and over. Probably the entire sequence told a story or preached a sermon. Darzek moved slowly from display to display; the tiny robots presented their histrionics; the sonorous message of the Zarstans' religion boomed at him from each display's concealed audiocation. Those watching were an incongruous assortment of life forms who wandered about in desultory fashion with more of an air of killing time than of experiencing a religious revelation.

At the center of the room, on an enclosed dais that looked like a large box, sat a white-robed Zarstan. "Questions answered, sermons delivered on request," Darzek murmured. The priest was an alien type Darzek could not immediately identify, and he had an air of profound meditation and total obliviousness to his surroundings. His countenance, with its saucer-sized eyes and noseless, scaly face and head, amply endorsed the Zarstans' democratic principles, at least as concerned males of all species.

A Skarnaffian entered the room, and Darzek turned and followed him toward the central dais. The Skarnaffian was an undersecretary from the Skarnaffian Embassy, armed with impeccable credentials, and his visit here had been effected on the strength of Darzek's own impeccable credentials as a special emissary of Supreme. Darzek had obtained the ambassador's cooperation and also a guarantee that this small errand by one of his staff would remain confidential.

Darzek's hunch was that no questions about a missing cousin-uncle from one of Miss Schlupe's urchins would be treated seriously by this order of scientific priests. He wanted an inquiry with the greatest possible impact, and an official call from a world embassy concerning one of its citizens would have to be accorded respect, if not ceremony.

The undersecretary was in formal black diplomatic robes; Darzek had insisted on that. Obviously such formal visits were uncommon here, and the white-robed priest looked down at him in amazement. Darzek noticed for the first time that the priest's chest was ornamented with lines of ribbed material set with jewels—a design that looked vaguely familiar until Darzek experienced a revelation that left him feeling silly: the priest was wearing the diagram of an atom; the jewels were electrons. The priest himself was, presumably, the nucleus and proton. Darzek stood behind the undersecretary in the patient attitude of one awaiting his turn and listened to the conversation.

Darzek's hunch proved correct. The priest examined the undersecretary's credentials with care, and, when he had returned them, his voice was deferential. "How may the prime forces of the universe serve you?"

"I seek information," the Skarnaffian said. "Official information, for the use of my government."

"This nameless particle is at your service."

"Some three Vezpronian cycles ago, a citizen of Skarnaf disappeared on this planet. It now becomes imperative to learn what happened to him. His name is Qwasrolk. A nuclear engineer."

The priest had his head cocked, listening politely, but his scaly face was expressionless.

"It is possible that he became a Zarstan," the undersecretary went on. "We would be most appreciative of a record check."

"Regretfully, I cannot assist you."

"But why not? We only need to know—"

"The Order of Prime Forces maintains no such records."

The undersecretary regarded him perplexedly. "Do you mean to say that when a person joins your order you don't even record who he is?"

"Once transmutation occurs, the particle loses its identity and becomes a nameless but transcending force. What it was before has no significance. What it is, is all. No, the Order maintains no record of what its particles have been—only of what they have become. So I cannot assist you."

"If you refuse to assist, we shall have no choice but to have the ambassador himself take the question to your Order's Prime Number."

"He is of course welcome to do so. Please convey to him the Prime Number's invitation. Also the Order's regret that there are no records to assist him in his quest."

The priest's jerk of his scaly head was a dismissal. The undersecretary turned away with a shrug; the priest directed his gaze inquiringly at Darzek, who stepped forward.

Darzek spoke in a manner unfamiliarly humble to him. "This worthless one seeks knowledge. Is the road to transmutation a long one?"

"Long," the priest agreed. "And difficult—as is true of all goals worthy of attainment. But the meritorious often have traveled it unknowingly and are much closer to their goal than they realize. Are you free of family obligations?"

"Completely."

"Are you a male of your own species?"

"I am."

"And—your specialization?"

"The mentalities of intelligent life forms."

The priest gazed at him blankly. Then he said, sounding genuinely regretful, "The road would indeed be long for you. You would first have to qualify yourself in some aspect of science or technology."

"Surely your Order has a need for those who specialize in the sciences of living beings," Darzek protested.

"A limited need," the priest conceded. "But the Order provides its own training for such specialists—who must be knowledgeable in science or technology as well. And we do not accept novices according to any particular need, but in accordance with their qualifications, which must include mastery of some aspect of science or technology."

"I understand. As you said, the road will be a long one. Does not your Order provide assistance for those who seek the most worthy of goals?"

The scaly face scowled negatively. "Those who come to us in good faith already have set their feet upon the road."

"Then I must find the road myself and travel it alone?"

"Until you are deemed qualified and worthy," the priest said.

"Thank you."

The priest intoned something that may have been a blessing and wished him good fortune in his search, and Darzek thanked him again and left. Using the public transmitter in the theater lobby, he went directly to the government complex and the office where his scientific assistants were at work.

He found Wolndur and Lolln gathered around Melris Angoz and a pile of computer effluence that looked as though the machine had been stuck and running for a week. He did not ask if there'd been any progress. All three of them wore the thick gloom that descends suddenly when a promising assumption remains promising until the ten-millionth test.

Lolln growled, "We think we've found *where* the fallacy is, but we can't find *what* it is."

"Sorry to interrupt," Darzek said, "but I need your assistant for another line of research." He spoke to Wolndur. "I want you to go down to the Zarstan headquarters and try to enlist."

Melris looked up blankly. *"What?"*

Darzek grinned—he was aware that the two of them were, as it was put on Earth, going steady. "Pretend you want to enlist. Be truthful about everything else. There's a fellow worker, female, you're attracted to, but you wonder if you aren't destined for higher things. Find out as much as you can."

"Well—all right."

He went out. Lolln, perplexedly scratching his wrinkled bald head, was staring at Darzek. Melris was looking concernedly after Wolndur. "Don't worry," Darzek told the two of them. "I'm about to take the Zarstans and their religion apart. If they grab him, I'll get him back for you."

At the office of the Masfiln of Vezpro, Darzek sent in his name and was admitted at once. Min Kallof seemed to have acquired a few more wrinkles since the night he called at Darzek's office with his Mas of Science and Technology. He regarded Darzek with puzzlement.

"I thought it was agreed that we would communicate through Naz Forlan."

"Only on matters that concern him," Darzek said. "My call is an official one in behalf of the Council of Supreme, and it concerns your office. Why is the government of Vezpro maintaining relations with an Uncertified World?"

Kallof stared at him. He finally managed to say, *"Uncertified—"*

"Members of the Galactic Synthesis," Darzek went on, "of which Vezpro of course is one, or any of its citizens, are forbidden to have contact with a nonmember, an Uncertified World, or with any of its citizens. The penalties are severe. I have just learned that Vezpro has been maintaining relations with an Uncertified World for many years."

"But that is not true!"

"The world is Zarst."

"But Zarst—" Kallof paused. "Zarst is—was—a colony of Vezpro."

"And when Vezpro gave Zarst its independence, was it certified for membership in the Galactic Synthesis?"

Kallof did not answer. His initial reaction of indignation over a preposterous accusation had dissolved into one of stark consternation.

Darzek seated himself. "This," he said, in a tone of voice that admitted no argument, "is what I want you to do."

When Darzek left the masfiln, he looked in again on his scientific assistants. This time all of the gloom was focused on Wolndur; the others were laughing at him.

"He turned me down!" Wolndur said indignantly. "He said I would have to return to the university for at least two years of advanced study!"

"That's what I wanted to know," Darzek said. He asked Lolln, "Do you know anything about nuclear research conducted by the Zarstans?"

"I know nothing about them except what pertains to their mundane nuclear technology," Lolln said. "They are highly competent in that."

"And if they are competent in that, is there anything that would prevent their going beyond the mundane into the area of pure research?"

"I suppose not, if they wanted to invest the time and solvency."

"Obviously they limit their membership to highly qualified scientists. They're reputed to be immensely wealthy. Are there any individuals, or organizations, or governments you know of who would be better qualified either as to scientific personnel or solvency to figure out a method for turning a planet into a sun?"

Lolln thought for a moment. "Strange it never occurred to me," he said. "It must be the Zarstans. As you say, no one else would have either the scientific resources or the solvency. It would cost them only for materials, since their priests are unpaid. I wouldn't say that they have the best scientific brains in this sector of the galaxy, but they certainly have a concentration of highly qualified scientists that's not available anywhere else."

"Thank you," Darzek said. "Now all of you can go back to work." He dropped his hand on Wolndur's shoulder and grinned consolingly. "Don't feel bad. He turned me down, too. And it wasn't for a lack of advanced study. He told me I wasn't even ready for kindergarten."

At the Trans-Star office, Darzek found Gud Baxak there ahead of him with a strange assortment of weird-looking articles, each complete with design drawings and specifications. Gud Baxak said, "Sire, factories making these things are available."

"Did you spend any solvency?" Darzek asked.

"No, sire. I had no difficulties in obtaining ten-day options. Apparently it is understood that the buying of factories requires study and calculation, and that there will be considerable negotiations."

"There certainly will before I buy one."

"Do you wish information regarding these—" Gud Baxak's hand swept over the incongruous miscellany he had spread out in the corner of the office. "—these items?"

"Later. Is Gula Schlu in?"

"I don't know, sire. I just returned with these—these—"

"Right. I'll check."

Miss Schlupe was in. She took one look at Darzek's face and announced, "You're going to start a war."

"That's one way to put it," Darzek said. "I'm tired of sitting around meditating imponderables and waiting for someone else to act. And I'm tired of being put off when I want to know something."

"Do you think the answer's on Zarst?"

"It's a secret religion. It accepts only people with a great deal of scientific education and expertise—and I do mean a great deal. I sent Wolndur to apply, and he was turned down. If there are scientists in the neighborhood capable of turning a world into a sun, Zarst is as likely to have them as anyone. Also, Zarst is almost certainly responsible for a good number of your missing scientists and technologists. Qwasrolk may have been a convert."

"So what are you going to do?"

"Invade the place."

"Want me to come?"

"No. I'm leaving you in charge of reinforcements. This has to be timed just right. Problem is, I don't know what I'm going to do until I get there. I'm going as a legitimate businessman. I'll take Gud Baxak with me. Also Raf Lolln. How many members of your detective force could masquerade as businessmen?"

"Not many. Five or six. Maybe ten if you aren't too particular."

"I'll take all ten if I can figure angles for them. Too bad Vezpro's chief proctor is a nincompoop, but he is, so we'll have to arrange everything ourselves. The government of Vezpro will cooperate fully. Maybe I can borrow some proctors from Skarnaf."

"You're kidding," Miss Schlupe said. "Do you mean we're really doing something legal?"

"We certainly are. When Zarst was granted its independence, it neglected to apply to the Galactic Synthesis for certification."

"Ah!"

"So all the worlds doing business with Zarst are engaged in illegal traffic with an Uncertified World—which fact hasn't occurred to any of them because they were doing business with Zarst when it was a colony, and they overlooked the significance of its change of status. Some may not know about it. But the penalties are severe if anyone wants to make a galactic case of it, and I'm mad enough to do that. Yes, Vezpro will cooperate fully. So will any other world we ask."

"And so will Zarst, when it finds it's about to be completely isolated," Miss Schlupe observed.

Darzek frowned. "That part's tricky. They can say, 'We have no secrets from you. Come and look at whatever you like.' But a world is a large place, and who can say how many miles of underground tunnels have concealed entrances and illegal nuclear research? So the cooperation of other worlds may not help at all. We've got to get loose on Zarst and see as much as we can before the Zarstans know we're looking."

9

It took five days to get the operation organized. While Darzek shifted assignments and argued with Miss Schlupe over the planning, he learned what he could about the world of Zarst and its inhabitants. By the time he finally stepped through the last of a series of transmitters and set foot on—rather, in—the planet owned by the Order of Prime Forces, he was somewhat better informed than he had been, but he couldn't call himself enlightened. The fact was that the only people who knew much about Zarst were the Zarstans, and the one thing that Darzek had established with certainty was that all the priests were sworn to secrecy concerning every aspect of their world and Order except the qualifications for joining.

Somewhere above, on the surface of the seventh planet, was the bleak, airless, frozen landscape. From the mining combine that owned it, the Zarstans had purchased a barren planet that for uncounted cycles had been gradually stripped of its mineral wealth. Its surface was uninhabited except for stations in the invisible guidance network that regulated the enormous spaceship traffic to Vezpro—maintained there by the Vezpronian government with the Zarstans' permission. The world did not have a transfer station, so no ships called there. Its supplies and anything else its population needed were imported from Vezpro by transmitter. If its exploited veins of ore still yielded minerals, or if the Zarstans had found new deposits, they were exported the same way. It was much cheaper than space transport and far more convenient. When the planets were properly positioned, a flow of ore could be sent directly to a smelter on Vezpro.

The Zarstans lived, worked, and supposedly worshipped in the networks of tunnels that originally were mining excavations, extensively modified to suit their needs. What Darzek had been unable to find out—and what he desperately needed to know—was what he would encounter once he slipped past the public areas where the Zarstans performed and transacted business.

Every informant had failed him. He had even visited another mineral-exhausted planet in the Vezpro system whose tunnels had been turned into a tourist attraction. It featured artificial stalagmites and stalactites, frozen waterfalls in rainbow colors, and other simulated wonders that never existed in nature. The gullible admired them through the transparent walls of a heated tunnel that led through the mine to an enormous underground excavation, famous for its echo effects, where weird musical concerts were given. Darzek found that establishment somehow reassuring—it proved that humans had no monopoly on the bad taste in the universe—but he knew there would be no such nonsense on Zarst.

There wasn't. When he stepped through the final transmitter it was neither a tourist trap nor a cathedral that he emerged in, but a business office; and he saw immediately that the amount of business transacted there was huge. The reception hall was an enormous, vaulted room, and throngs of diversified life forms were coming and going constantly. Probably 80 per cent of the customers were Vezpronians, which only confirmed what both rumor and logic had indicated, that Vezpro was the Zarstans' best customer.

Darzek marched confidently toward the reception desk, with Raf Lolln trailing after him and trying valiantly to look like an industrialist. They both wore revoltingly colored garments of the type affected by the more affluent Vezpronians, and Darzek felt absolutely like an ass and was trying hard not to show it. He had never had on pink, purple, and green trousers before.

A multilimbed, white-robed, electron-ornamented priest politely inquired as to their business, took the firm name Darzek supplied, glanced briefly at one of the rolls of drawings that Gud Baxak had collected, and imperiously ordered them to wait. There were comfortable lounge groupings, with chairs, recliners, stools of various sizes and designs—every type of sitting or resting device that could be devised for the comfort of an unpredictable variety of life forms.

Darzek seated himself, and Raf Lolln, after poking about the furniture, picked a chair for himself nearby. The plan now was in operation. Miss Schlupe, with Vezpronian officials, was controlling all transmitter traffic to Zarst, and a company of Skarnaffian proctors, with the chief proctor himself in charge, was standing by and ready for action. Darzek tried to relax. The flow of traffic had ceased abruptly with Darzek's entrance. Customers were leaving, but none were arriving. The priest at the reception desk seemed not to have noticed.

Then Gud Baxak stepped from the transmitter. He looked about, saw Darzek, and found a seat for himself near the transmitter. After him, at intervals, Miss Schlupe's investigators arrived one at a time to simulate an influx of customers. Each reported at the reception desk, talked with the priest, displayed a roll of design drawings while spouting a carefully rehearsed story, and was waved to the lounge area.

With nothing to do but wait, Darzek studied his surroundings. The hall's walls and vaulted ceiling were smooth as plaster and a gleaming white. The lighting came from large colored jewels representing atoms, some of them exceedingly strange-looking to Darzek. Had it not been for the spectacular lights and the cleanliness of the place, Darzek would have been reminded of a transportation waiting room. The only object that interested him was at the remote end of the hall: the transmitter station to on-planet locations. At intervals the receptionist pronounced a name—usually Vezpronian but sometimes a gargle of syllables—and a young priest stepped forward to guide the summoned customer to the transmitter and his destination.

The room's waiting population gradually diminished, since no customers had arrived after the last of Miss Schlupe's investigators. Those who had finished their business emerged from the transmitter at the far end of the room, crossed to the interworld transmitter, and left. Darzek turned to watch Raf Lolln, wondering how the old scientist was reacting to the fact that he was about to commit a crime. Any kind of an illegal act should have been incomprehensible to him.

It was. He still hadn't grasped what it was he was about to do. He said suddenly to Darzek, "I think you're wrong about your assistants. I've been watching both of them carefully, and I'm sure they could not be involved in activity against their own world. They're splendid workers, too."

Darzek smiled and said politely, "You may be right." The previous day, Wolndur and Melris had told him the same thing about Raf Lolln.

Finally only Darzek, Raf Lolln, Gud Baxak, and the ten investigators were left in the waiting room. The receptionist was becoming puzzled. No doubt the priests were accustomed to slack periods and rush periods, but a virtually empty waiting room was unusual. The receptionist called Darzek's name, stood up and looked around, and then sat down with an alien equivalent of a shrug. Darzek, with Raf

Lolln hurrying after him, followed the young priest and guide to the far transmitter.

"Nuclear design," the guide said politely, punching buttons on the transmitter's destination board. "Follow me, please." The priest stepped through. Darzek immediately punched another number: 3939392839. He motioned to Raf Lolln and stepped through, and the old scientist followed him.

Behind them, a sequence of events was set in motion. The transmitter's destination number, since Darzek had set it for two passages, returned to zero. The guide, who certainly would return to the reception hall at once in search of his lost customers, would not be able to discover where they had gone unless the transmitter was equipped with a recording device, and consulting it would take time. His search would be interrupted before he could get the machine apart.

The moment Darzek and Raf Lolln entered the transmitter, Gud Baxak would have got to his feet, leisurely strolled to the interworld transmitter, and departed. His arrival at his destination would be the signal for action. The waiting Skarnaffian proctors would pour into the Zarstan waiting room and seize the astonished priest and the guide. They and any other priests entering the reception hall would be hustled off the planet before they could sound an alarm.

In the meantime, Miss Schlupe's ten investigators would hurry to the interior transmitter, punch destination numbers they had been supplied with in advance, and step through. Their assignments were to use their ears and eyes, cover as much territory as they could, and learn as much as possible about the Zarstan establishment before they were physically restrained. In the meantime, more proctors would be arriving, and when it became obvious that Darzek, Raf Lolln, and the investigators had seen as much as they were likely to see or were captives, the proctors would begin their takeover of the world of Zarst.

The numbers, including Darzek's, had been obtained by Miss Schlupe from a renegade priest who had left the Order. Only an emotional appeal to his patriotism had induced him to violate his priestly oath—he was a Vezpronian—and the transmitter numbers, to key points in the establishment, were all that he would divulge.

Darzek, with Raf Lolln stumbling after him, emerged in a broad corridor that was vaulted like the reception room, with gleaming white walls and ceiling. It was dimly lit with colored, jewel-like lights that were placed at intervals high up on the walls. He could see a tremendous sweep of it before it gradually curved out of sight in either direction.

There was no one in sight. Darzek quickly slipped off his cloak and outer garments, and Raf Lolln did the same. Underneath they wore white robes that were as close a facsimile of a priest's clothing as could be produced in the short time they'd had, complete with jeweled electrons. Darzek made a bundle of the discarded garments, tucked it under his robe, mentally flipped a coin, and turned right. On the left side of the corridor, which was the outside of the vast, curving circle it seemed to form, they occasionally passed openings into smaller passageways, some slanting upward or downward. Darzek glanced into each one without breaking his stride. He set a brisk pace, and Lolln had to scramble and huff to keep up with him. He paused only when he found an opening that led into a large shaft with a spiraling ramp leading downward. Leaning over a railing, he dropped the bundle of discarded clothing. It bounced from level to level and finally vanished.

They moved on along the curving corridor, making haste cautiously and as noiselessly as possible. The mystic number seemed to have sent them to a level that was not in use, at least during that time of day. That Darzek had seen nothing of interest did not surprise him—he'd considered the renegade priest's numbers a gamble—but he was puzzled that they'd met no one. He began to wonder how long it would take an arc of that curvature to make a complete circle. Obviously they should have turned the other way.

Then they encountered a door. Double doors.

On their right. All of the other openings had been on the left. And opposite the doors was an alcove with another transmitter. Miss Schlupe's informant had been only slightly in error about the number.

Behind them he heard footsteps. Someone cried out. Darzek did not hesitate. The doors were broad, with typical Vezpronian hinges that ran from floor to ceiling and operated pneumatically, and they would support a door weighing a ton in a manner that made it possible to open it with one finger. Darzek pushed one of the doors open. With Raf Lolln on his heels, he slipped through.

Heat smote them in the face. They were in an enormous room, on a slanting balcony that curved around an abyss. It was a cathedral, with a ceiling that arched to infinity, but that thought occurred to Darzek only much later. What he grasped now was a dim impression of unclothed worshippers about him and, in the center of the abyss, a monstrous, blazing sun, with rays that shot toward him.

Then the intense light and heat blinded him.

He was still clasping his hands to his eyes when the priests seized him.

"A special emissary of Supreme," the Prime Number said heavily. He kept his eyes steadily on Darzek; he was of a life form that Darzek had not seen before, but there was no mistaking his attitude. He was outraged. "If you had presented your credentials honorably, you would have been received as the Order's exalted guest."

"Would you have shown me your place of worship?" Darzek asked politely.

The Prime Number was silent for a moment. Then he said, "In every religion, there are matters that are of no concern to outsiders."

"I have explained to you the threat to the world of Vezpro," Darzek said. "If your Order is not responsible, surely it is in your best interest to cooperate and assist us. If it is responsible, you will understand that you cannot proceed and have your Order survive."

"Why would my Order threaten Vezpro?" the Prime Number demanded. "It is essential to our existence."

"It is also essential to your prosperity," Darzek observed dryly. "Threatening it could be a way to greater prosperity."

The Prime Number had no reply.

"At this moment," Darzek said, "everything concerning your religion is of intense interest to a special emissary of Supreme. Either you cooperate fully with myself and my agents, or this world will be classified Uncertified and you'll be completely isolated. Which will it be?"

"We have no choice," the Prime Number muttered. His anger had not lessened.

"No, you don't. But you need have no concern about your secrets. I, and my agents, and Supreme, keep secrets at least as well as your priests."

The Prime Number got to his feet resignedly. "Very well. What do you want to see?"

"Everything," Darzek answered bluntly.

He conferred privately with Miss Schlupe's investigators, all of whom had been taken prisoner in forbidden places. Some had managed to roam about much longer than others, but none of them had seen anything of interest.

The only worthwhile clue, then, was the cathedral of the miniature sun that Darzek and Raf Lolln had happened onto. Darzek first presented the chief proctor of Skarnaf to the Prime Number and told him that the proctors were to be permitted to search everywhere and see everything. The Prime Number gestured resignedly and gave the order.

Then Darzek sent for Raf Lolln and asked that the Order's leading astrophysicist explain to him the miniature sun that they had seen. The Prime Number hesitated—clearly that secret was the key to the Order's holy of holies—but soon Raf Lolln was in conference with an elderly priest, who was filling a workscreen with formulae.

Darzek found Miss Schlupe waiting patiently in the reception hall. "This is Gula Schlu," he told the Prime Number. "She also is an emissary of Supreme. She seeks information concerning an individual from Skarnaf whom your order recruited some three cycles ago."

"Regretfully, we have no records," the Prime Number said.

"Regretfully, you had better find some records," Miss Schlupe said firmly. "The recruit's name was Qwasrolk."

The Prime Number gestured bewilderedly. "Once a transmutation has taken place, an individual's past has no significance for us. It should have none for you. Why keep records if there is no need for them?"

"That's your problem," Miss Schlupe said. "I refuse to believe that there are no records of any kind about the members of your Order. How do you know how many members you have? How would you decide how much food to order? How could you arrange activities? It defies logic, and a scientific religion has got to be logical. Until you produce some records on Qwasrolk, the transmitter embargo remains in effect."

The Prime Number got to his feet wearily. "I will ask."

The spiritual leader of the Order of Prime Forces clearly was no administrator. He had to rummage through departments he probably had never visited before and may not have known existed. Finally he located a secretary-priest who actually was a computer technician and whose department maintained some records. It seemed that it was the Order's custom to notify a priest's next of kin on his death, and that obscure action was not known or thought of by most priests of the Order, including the Prime Number. It necessitated some rudimentary record keeping.

"The name," Miss Schlupe said, "is Qwasrolk. As far as I know, he is not dead."

The secretary-priest worked briefly at a strangely arranged keyboard. "Qwasrolk. From Skarnaf."

"That's the one."

"Joined the Order from Vezpro. A little more than three cycles ago, if you're referring to Vezpronian cycles."

"What can you tell me about him?" Miss Schlupe asked impatiently.

"Nothing."

Miss Schlupe placed both hands on hips. "Listen, Buster, there's a limit to the amount of nonsense I'll take in one afternoon."

The secretary-priest worked his keyboard again, sat back with a negative gesture. "After his novicehood, which takes—in Vezpronian time—a bit more than half a cycle, he was assigned to industrial design. But our records on him end about a half cycle after that."

"Why?" Miss Schlupe demanded.

"He disappeared."

While Miss Schlupe attempted to coax more information from a computer that almost certainly had none, and the Prime Number tried to locate another obscure department that maintained records, Darzek returned to the scientific conference between Raf Lolln and the astrophysicist priest.

The formulae now filled the screen and could be measured in meters, and the two paused to argue occasionally when a new segment was added. Raf Lolln was enjoying himself immensely, and so— Darzek thought—was the priest.

Another argument broke out. The priest moved a segment of formula to a smaller screen and began to dissect it. One component at a time was isolated, enlarged, carried through a series of derivatives, and finally returned to its original position.

Suddenly there was a sharp intake of breath, and Raf Lolln leaned forward excitedly.

One small cluster of symbols had exploded the scientific dogma of a galaxy.

10

Darzek gave his desk calendar a spin and remarked, "Do you realize that we didn't accomplish a thing?"

Miss Schlupe arched her eyebrows. "If the Zarstans can produce a miniature sun, what's to prevent their doing it on a larger scale? And even if they're innocent, knowing how it's done ought to be an enormous help to us. Raf Lolln is in ecstasy."

"I noticed. Unfortunately, their miniature sun is just that—it's only a few centimeters in diameter, and they do the rest with mirrors to make it look maybe thirty or forty meters across. The thing is an optical illusion."

"I didn't know that," Miss Schlupe said. "Illusion or not, it certainly looks impressive."

"It ought to. Producing a sun of any size is a tremendous achievement, and Raf Lolln is right to feel ecstatic. He said it could be done, and dogma said it couldn't. Too bad we have to keep it a secret—he could have a great time laughing at all the galaxy's leading scientists, especially those that got him fired. Unfortunately, taking a small mass of carefully compounded materials and starting a sun-type nuclear reaction with it is not the same thing as starting the same reaction with a large planet. Worlds aren't compounded according to the Zarstans' chemical formula. They would have to use whatever was there, and I have my doubts that their technique would work. They agree with me. They've promised to study the problem, though, and Raf Lolln will work with them, so I suppose we did accomplish that. As for Qwasrolk—"

Miss Schlupe said disgustedly, "We moved his disappearance up one year. I suppose they're telling the truth."

"I think so. They probably lose more recruits than they're willing to admit. Their religion is based on a worship of pure science, but it functions as a commercial enterprise. Talented young scientists wanting to devote their lives to research and the discovery of the secrets of the universe find themselves designing nuclear flowerpots or some such absurdity, which must be disillusioning. Qwasrolk probably got frustrated and bored, and finally he walked out."

"And found someone who was interested in pure research—like how to turn a planet into a sun?"

"Maybe. I've sent for UrsNollf."

Miss Schlupe looked up from her knitting. "What do you need him for? He's just another dogmatist, and he's also a bureaucrat."

"True. But he'll know how to describe the Zarstan experiments to Supreme, after which Supreme might be able to provide some information about turning planets into suns. Which may or may not be helpful. Knowing how it's done doesn't necessarily mean that we could stop it."

Miss Schlupe's knitting needles clicked. "Dratted yarn," she muttered. "I haven't been able to find any decent stuff since I left Earth."

"Only Earth has sheep."

"Maybe I should import a flock. Is there a rule against it?"

"Probably."

"Is there a rule against making miniature suns?"

"There may be after UrsNollf reports to Supreme."

"Did Qwasrolk have anything to do with making the Zarstans' miniature sun?"

"No. The technique must be almost as old as the Order. But he may have learned how it was done."

Miss Schlupe's needles clicked again. "I think you need more than UrsNollf and Raf Lolln keeping an eye on the Zarstans. For fanatics, religion can justify anything, and this lot is both slippery and mercenary. A few fat chunks of blackmail would finance the expansion of their religion across the galaxy. Also, they've got the solvency reserves to conduct scientific research on a large scale, they've got their own world for secret experiments—what'll you bet the Skarnaf proctors didn't find half the tunnels in that place?—and they certainly have plenty of capable scientists. I'd say that makes them the leading suspect."

"The situation is a lot worse than that," Darzek said. "At the moment, they're the only suspect."

A government messenger presented himself at the Trans-Star office to ask if it would be convenient for the distinguished Gul Darr to receive a visit from the Mas of Science and Technology. Darzek had taken some pains to make certain that neither Forlan nor anyone else whose services weren't needed was informed about the Zarstan raid, and he wondered who had talked. He affected the weary posture of an overworked trader, reflected for a moment, and decided that he could spare a few minutes for an interview if the mas arrived promptly.

A few minutes later Naz Forlan stepped through the transmitter. Darzek greeted him warmly and led him to his private quarters, and Forlan, without comment, handed over a letter.

Darzek recognized the woven material at once. The inditing, too, was precisely the same as that of the earlier message. Unlike it, this one consisted of several pages. Darzek waved Forlan to a chair and sat down himself and began to read.

The writer had wasted no time in coming to the point. If Vezpro wished to continue to exist as a world instead of as a sun, the following requirements must be met: First, payment of a billion billion solvency units. The detailed procedure for handling the certificates was so complicated that Darzek skipped it. Second, the transfer of a modern spaceship, capacity at least one thousand cargo compartments, to be left in orbit around an unspecified uninhabited planet and equipped with supply and passenger compartments for an unlimited cruise with three hundred passengers plus crew. Third, the spaceship must contain, each in her own passenger compartment, two hundred young females from the world of Vezpro, aged fourteen to seventeen. Further details would be supplied later. Signed, *CODE XRT*.

Darzek felt delighted and said so. At long last, a ransom note!

Forlan regarded him perplexedly, his green complexion deepening. "It's a list of impossibilities!" he protested. "It cannot possibly be met. I'm not an expert in solvency, but even I can see that a billion billion units are a ridiculous demand, even for such a wealthy world as Vezpro. I suppose the ship is a relatively minor problem, but the two hundred females—you seem pleased!"

"We had very few clues," Darzek said. "This letter gives us several. The two hundred females, for example. That's a suggestive request."

"Suggestive in what way?" Forlan asked.

"It suggests that our villain is a native Vezpronian—or that he has a large staff of cohorts who are Vezpronians. Only a Vezpronian would want Vezpronian females."

Forlan's preplexity—and greenness—deepened. "Has it occurred to you that we're dealing with some kind of perverted genius? If he can do what he threatens, he may be the most brilliant scientist in the galaxy. If he can't, he has a different sort of genius."

"That has occurred to me," Darzek acknowledged.

"Then we must be exceedingly cautious in any deductions we make about him. Such a genius would be quite capable of demanding Vezpronian females just to create the illusion that he's Vezpronian—and send us chasing after a nonexistent native scientist."

Darzek had reached the same conclusion the moment he read the letter, but he hadn't expected such reasoning from Forlan. He said with a grin, "If he's as devious as that, he might be a Vezpronian asking for Vezpronian females because he knows we will reason that he is too brilliant to give himself away in such a simple fashion and therefore we'll conclude that he must be an alien."

Forlan gestured bewilderedly. "I'm a scientist. The psychology of the perverted genius is beyond me. So are solvency dealings in amounts larger than my salary. I have consulted our Mas of Finance, and he thinks it possible to create an illusion of solvency where in fact none exists. This seems like a risky thing to do, but if the solvency isn't available I suppose we have no choice. The fact that further details are to be supplied later suggests that there will be negotiations, or discussions, and someone must be placed in charge of them. If you have no objection, my choice will be Eld Wolndur. His association with you makes him better qualified than anyone else, and I'm sure your assistance and advice will be invaluable to him—and to Vezpro."

Darzek sat back and regarded the mas calculatingly. The time had come, he thought, to be blunt. First Wolndur had been handed a scientific problem far beyond his capacity. Now, with no experience of any kind, he was being expected to take charge of a problem that would make the most experienced diplomat flinch. "I'll be glad to assist him in any way I can," Darzek said. "He's a personable youngster, and no doubt he has a promising future as a scientist. But isn't it foolish to entrust the handling of any aspect of a problem of this complexity, scientific or otherwise, to one whose experience is so limited? I shouldn't have to remind you that the fate of a world may be involved."

It was the mas's turn to regard Darzek calculatingly. Then he smiled. "Please understand—I, too, am capable of subtleties. This secret is known only to those concerned with it, and I ask you to tell it to no one. When the first letter arrived, I assembled a special committee of scientists from a dozen worlds. They are the most competent available in five sectors, and they have been at work on the scientific problem ever since. They are attempting to determine whether it really is possible to turn Vezpro into a sun; and, even if they decide that it is not, as a precautionary measure they are considering all of the ways in which it might be done if it were possible —the equipment needed, the necessary installations, and how they could be detected. While this committee works in secret, Eld Wolndur is the person officially in charge of investigating the scientific threat and handling the demands made in this letter. Do you think I am wrong in assuming that the writer of the letter may be in a position to know what is happening on Vezpro?"

"I think you'd be foolish if you didn't," Darzek said.

"Only I—and now you—know that my committee is supporting Wolndur scientifically. You will be supporting him in the negotiations or discussions. But the fact that he has only a youth to deal with just might make the letter writer overconfident. If you'd like to meet with my committee—"

"It would waste their time and mine," Darzek said. "They couldn't explain what they're doing in terms simple enough for me to understand. I'm a trader, not a scientist. I'll be glad to assist Wolndur."

He did not think it necessary to add that Wolndur's problem was one that he understood far better than Forlan could have imagined. From his detective experience on Earth, there was little that he didn't know about ransom drops. That was the moment when the criminal was the most vulnerable. If this perverted genius thought they would timidly accede to his demands and leave a spaceship parked somewhere in orbit for the taking, he was singularly naive.

So Darzek would assist Wolndur, with pleasure. He also would make some private arrangements of his own.

"I didn't think he'd be stupid enough to ask for anything like that," Miss Schlupe announced, when Darzek told her about the letter. "We've got him."

"That was my first reaction," Darzek said. "Now I'm not so sure. How do you inconspicuously stake out a planet?"

"A ship on the opposite side?"

"If he approaches cautiously, as he certainly would, he couldn't help detecting it. The stake-out ship would have to be in orbit, too."

"A ship on the planet?"

"A deep-space ship that lands and takes off from a planet doesn't exist. When cargo and passengers can be transmitted to and from the surface, it isn't necessary. Spaceships are built in space and stay there. We'd have to have a special ship designed and constructed, and even if there was time for that, I doubt that a ship could take off from a planet and catch one that's already in space. One jump, and it'd be lost."

"Park the ship in orbit and disable it," Miss Schlupe suggested.

"I've thought of that, too. No doubt it will be taken care of in those details that are to follow. We can't really start planning until we receive them."

"Then there's only one answer," Miss Schlupe said. "Hide an army on board."

"That'll be taken care of, too, unless our mad genius is a complete fool."

Miss Schlupe snapped her fingers. "The females. They can be our own agents. I'll pick them out myself and start training them now."

Darzek nodded. "My thought exactly. We'll work out a plan for them to take over the ship. Of course we'll also try all the other things we think we can get away with."

Eld Wolndur notified Darzek that the government had received a letter labeled FIRST SUPPLEMENTARY INSTRUCTIONS, the implication being that there would be others to follow. He brought it to Darzek.

It consisted of a single line, an order to contact a trader named Kernopplix.

"Know him?" Darzek asked.

"No. No governmental department has ever done business with him."

Darzek sent for Gud Baxak, but he'd never heard of a trader named Kernopplix.

The letter contained a transmitter address. "Will you accompany me?" Wolndur asked Darzek.

"I'll do better than that," Darzek said. "I'll go see him myself."

Wolndur protested that the responsibility was his, and Darzek asked, "Why would a government official—especially one whose function had nothing to do with acquisitions—be calling on an obscure trader? Probably this Kernopplix is newly arrived and unknown to the trading community, and a whisper that the government is interested in him, for any reason, will cause comment. Whereas I, a trader, can make a courtesy call with the utmost propriety, and anyone learning of it will assume that I went there to find out whether he is able to supply anything I can use."

Wolndur brightened. "I understand. It also would arouse curiosity if I called on him frequently and bought nothing, but you are free to associate with a fellow trader as much as you like. You can tell this Kernopplix that you've been secretly appointed to handle all of the demands that involve trade."

"Very good. I'll have to be appropriately greedy and insist on my commission regardless of what arrangements he thinks he's empowered to make. He'll be suspicious if I don't. He'll certainly have things arranged so he can extract his own commission."

Wolndur went his way happily, and Darzek, punching the transmitter address supplied in the letter, went to see Kernopplix.

The mysterious trader had established himself in cramped, shabby quarters that only charitably could have been called a hole-in-the-wall office, and he seemed to be waiting for an official visit. A call by a trader named Gul Darr momentarily disconcerted him until Darzek explained his secret status.

"A very proper thought," Kernopplix observed. "We can deal as one trader with another, and there will be no hint of governmental involvement. That is well thought of. My instructions are to behave as a normal trader, and of course a trader of my standing would have no government contacts. I've been wondering how to cope with that problem."

His voice had a sleek, oily quality that made Darzek think of the more obnoxious type of salesman one occasionally encountered on Earth. He was a spiderlike individual, and he already had adopted clothing in one of the revolting combinations of colors affected by the Vezpronians. Darzek counted thirteen limbs that apparently functioned either as arms or legs, but these were no more disconcerting than the headless body with organs of sight and speech and hearing appended to the stubby termination almost as an afterthought. He introduced himself as a native of the planet Bbran, which Darzek had never heard of, and he announced cheerfully, "As long as the solvency is forthcoming on schedule, it doesn't matter to me who transfers it."

Darzek responded to Kernopplix's offer of a sitting bench by helping himself to a more comfortable-looking chair on the opposite side of the room. He did so only because he deduced that this was Kernopplix's chair, and he knew that walls of moral ascendency could be built with very small bricks. Kernopplix stood looking disconcertedly at Darzek, and then he perched himself on the bench. Except for these two pieces of furniture, the office was a tiny, bare cubicle. What the adjacent living quarters contained, Darzek was not prepared to guess, but he deduced that the Bbranian trader was a marginal operator, the type who would be perpetually on the verge of bankruptcy and willing to do anything for a smidgen of solvency. In this operation he would merely be a messenger, with no authority except to carry out orders precisely and ask for instructions when any problem arose that the orders did not cover.

Kernopplix immediately confirmed Darzek's deduction. "I'll be brief," he said. "I have instructions. I intend to follow them as exactly as I can. First, I am to assure you that I know nothing whatsoever about the reason the Vezpronian government is entering into this transaction. I desire to know nothing about it. It has been made clear to me that it is in the best interests of all parties, including myself, if I continue to know nothing about it, so I shall ask for no confidences and refuse to hear any that are offered. Your position may be the same, but that is no concern of mine.

"My role is simply that of a transfer agent. I am to see that a certain spaceship is purchased by the Vezpronian government. The ship has been selected and an option has been taken on it. I will close the option and have the ship brought to Vezpro the moment solvency for it is transferred to me. I am to have the usual trader's commission on the purchase.

"I then have specific instructions concerning the outfitting of the ship—the compartments, their furnishings, the ship's supplies, and so on. I will arrange this as soon as the ship arrives and sufficient solvency is made available.

"Once the ship is outfitted according to my instructions, I have further instructions concerning its passengers. Two hundred Vezpronian females, ages fourteen to seventeen, are to be examined and certified healthy by doctors of my choice in my presence and personally conducted by me to compartments in the spaceship. Each compartment transmitter is to be disengaged by me personally once the occupant is placed there. In the meantime, I will hire two crews and charter a second spaceship—for which Vezpro will furnish the necessary solvency. The crews of both ships will be handed sealed orders, to be opened only after they have reached their first destination —which I will tell them only at the moment they are ready to depart. I do not now have those sealed orders. They will be supplied to me after the preparations are completed, along with any additional instructions my employer may have. I myself will not know what the sealed orders consist of. I will never know, because I am to travel on the chartered ship and leave it at the first destination.

"Finally, I have been asked to assure you that I have never seen my employer and have no notion of who or what he may be." He paused. "I believe that covers it. Except that of course I am to receive the usual trader's commission on the solvency expended in outfitting the ship, and I am to arrange all purchases myself. However, because I am a trader, I don't believe in forcing a fellow trader to work for nothing. All traders are entitled to their fair commission. Because the Vezpronian government gave you the task of working with me, you probably expect to collect a commission yourself, and I don't see why you shouldn't. I suggest that I add your commission to the invoices you submit to the government. You can then remit net solvency, and both of us will have a handsome profit."

"That's very kind of you," Darzek murmured.

"Not at all. I understand that you would expect to handle these purchases yourself, and it isn't every day that a trader is able to buy and outfit a spaceship—certainly not a trader from a poor world like mine. It's only fair that you should have a commission, too.

"One more thing. If my mission succeeds in every detail, I am to receive an enormous bonus, so I intend to be exceedingly careful to follow my instructions as precisely as possible. If my mission fails through no fault of mine, I also am to receive a bonus."

Darzek said politely, "In other words, there's no amount of payment that would persuade you to bend your instructions slightly."

"None whatsoever. I also have a strong feeling of loyalty to my employer, whoever he is. He's making me rich."

"Then all we need to do, just for a start, is to persuade Vezpro to provide enough solvency to purchase the ship."

If the spider had possessed a face, it would have been beaming at Darzek. "That certainly is the essential first step. Understand, I have no idea at all as to why the Vezpronian government wants to be a party to this transaction. It all seems very perplexing to me. But the solvency for the ship is certainly the essential first step."

11

Vezpro was hosting its annual trades fair, a gala occasion that lasted eighteen days, filled transient accommodations with traders, manufacturers, designers, engineers, and visitors who simply liked trades fairs, and brought most activities on the world to a temporary halt while everyone either took part in the fair or milled about with the visitors.

Miss Schlupe, who loved fairs of any kind, attended it the first day and returned disappointed. "It's like getting lost in a mammoth appliance store where everything has such an ultramodern design you can't figure out what it is," she said. "And there aren't any refreshments—no samples, not even anything for sale. Which gives me an idea."

"No," Darzek said firmly. "Absolutely not. I will not have you going into the fried chicken, or hamburger, or pizza business. We've got serious work to do here."

"Actually, I was thinking of tacos," Miss Schlupe said. "I told you once—it's frightfully difficult to start a fried chicken business without chickens, and as far as I know there aren't any closer than Earth. As for hamburgers—"

"Never mind. Did the fair suggest anything related to our problem?"

"Not that I noticed. Unless it's possible to hook up a billion nuclear-powered bookends and set off a world."

Darzek arched his eyebrows. "Nuclear-powered . . . bookends?"

"There were things that looked like bookends. I don't know what they were used for. I got the impression that almost everything Vezpro manufactures is nuclear-powered."

"No doubt that's why so many nuclear engineers and scientists come here to study and work."

"I suppose that's also why so many of them disappear here," Miss Schlupe said. "Did I tell you I've added another forty-seven to the list?"

"Did you ask the Zarstans to check it for you?"

"Yes. They only admit to knowing thirty-three of them. The Prime Number has finally grasped the fact that Vezpro has a potentially serious problem that could destroy his Order, and he's cooperating fully—after his fashion."

"How many genuine disappearances have you turned up?" Darzek asked.

"More than fifty."

"Other worlds may be hiring Vezpro's engineers in order to steal its manufacturing secrets. Naturally they'd go about it surreptitiously."

"Do you believe that?"

"It's one more possibility. Look what happens on Earth with industrial espionage."

"This isn't Earth, and these characters are supposed to exist on a moral plane that's light-years above the one occupied by us groveling humans. Are you going to the fair?"

Darzek gestured wearily. "I doubt that I could learn anything from acres of nuclear bookends, but I'm going to the official reception, which of course they call a symposium. It's restricted to ultraimportant visitors, but for some reason the masfiln himself sent me an invitation, so I suppose I've got to go."

"You should feel honored," Miss Schlupe said severely.

"I don't. It isn't me that's ultraimportant, it's the emissary of Supreme, and only the masfiln and the Mas of Science and Technology know who I am. There's no fun in being ultraimportant if no one is aware of it."

"You might learn something."

"Not about our problem. No government official would dare whisper at a trades fair symposium that next year's orders might not be filled because the world is going to blow up. There's just one thing I'm curious about. Is this slippery character Kernopplix considered an ultraimportant person, and if so, by whom?"

Darzek blamed it on his Earth heritage: he never entered a building without wondering what it looked like from the outside. In a transmitterized society, his curiosity was rarely satisfied. One punched an address number on the destination board, stepped through a transmitter, and arrived in a foyer at his destination—or, if the building were a large one, in a reception room or hall. The exterior was not only unseen, but never seen, and—Darzek thought—

probably just as well left to the imagination. Architects were unlikely to take pains with an invisible exterior.

If access to the building were restricted, then the transmitter number was private and known only to the select group whose status, business, employment, membership, or political pull granted admission rights. One also could *personalize* transmitters so that only one's self or a selected list of individuals could use them, and that by way of the invisibly tattooed solvency credential that all galactic citizens wore in some convenient place, usually the palm of a hand, if they had a hand.

The masfiln's reception was open to those who had received invitations, and the invitations stated the transmitter destination number. Darzek, impeccably attired in clashing colors that Vezpro considered proper symp-dress, punched the number, stepped through, and found himself in a milling mass of life forms that filled the Palace of Government's huge reception room.

He gradually maneuvered his way past a blur of misshapen arms, distorted legs, tentacles, bloated or attenuated torsos, and heads that varied from the grotesquely oversized to the apparently nonexistent. Eventually he reached the enormous but equally crowded symposium room beyond. At the far side, on a dais, stood the masfiln and a group of his delegates, none of them familiar to Darzek. There was no reception line, but anyone interested in being "received" mounted the dais and exchanged a few words with each official before moving on.

Darzek managed a complete circuit of the room without seeing anyone he recognized except the masfiln, and he avoided the dais. Apparently few of his trader friends were in the ultraimportant class, and if Kernopplix were present in such a crowd, Darzek knew he would happen onto him only by accident. Finally he maneuvered his way into an alcove, where odd pieces of furniture apparently had been grouped for the use of people who weren't speaking. Darzek seated himself and waited to see whether any mountains would come to him.

When one finally did, it was not the mountain he expected. Naz Forlan, the Mas of Science and Technology, quietly made his way through the throng and, with a nod and a smile, destroyed the furniture arrangement by moving a chair toward Darzek.

He leaned close, to make himself heard over a roomful of unblended communicative noises, and said politely, "Good evening,

Gul Darr. A state occasion such as this one must be singularly unexciting for you."

"It is," Darzek agreed frankly. "I've seen so many, on so many worlds. One circuit of the room, and the jumble of trade statistics I heard gave me a headache."

"I should have thought trade statistics would be important to a trader," Forlan observed. His soft, resonant voice remained distinct even in that jumble of sound.

"Only his own," Darzek said.

Forlan smiled. "Yes. I suppose each of those traders and fabricators is excessively concerned with his own statistics, and those of the governmental representatives have relevance only for each other." He paused. "Have you made any progress?"

"Except for passing along the demands presented by this character Kernopplix, none. By the way, I was wondering if he is here tonight."

"Kernopplix? At a state reception?" The mas seemed horrified at the thought.

"He does seem a bit on the slimy side," Darzek agreed.

"Is there any news of that unfortunate young engineer Qwasrolk?"

"The chief proctor of Skarnaf has informed me that Qwasrolk has been sighted twice since our visit there. Each time he disappeared before he could be apprehended or even spoken to."

"Very strange," Forlan mused. "I have the feeling that he could help us, if only we could communicate. Such an accident as his is so excessively rare that it could not occur in industry without being widely publicized and discussed and investigated. So it must have involved some peculiar form of private research. Coupled with this Nifron D event and the threat to Vezpro—I very much wish that someone could talk with him."

"He's not likely to be of much help as long as he disappears the moment anyone sets eyes on him," Darzek observed.

"True," Forlan agreed. "And that may be more unusual than his injuries. Could there be a connection?"

"Between his injuries and his ability to teleport? I hadn't thought about that. I have no idea. It's an intriguing notion. Unfortunately, cause and effect aren't susceptible to frequent testing when the cause is a nuclear catastrophe."

"All of which leaves us—where?"

"It leaves us with Kernopplix," Darzek said.

"Yes. The masfiln presented his demands to the financial council today. I haven't heard the reaction."

Darzek asked in surprise, "Didn't you attend?"

Forlan gestured indifferently. "I'm a scientist. I don't know what the basis for the allocation of solvency should be called, but it certainly isn't scientific. Obviously a scientist wasn't needed, so I stayed away." He paused. "I'm worried, Gul Darr. I don't understand this thing—every scientist studies basic nucleonics, of course, and my experience goes far beyond that, but when I attend a meeting of my committee, I can't comprehend half of what is said. And then—the decision on the Kernopplix demands is completely out of my hands. I don't understand it, and I have no control over what is done about it—and yet the responsibility is mine."

Darzek turned to him and said frankly, "I've heard that your status as an alien is resented. I've even heard a suggestion that this entire affair was rigged to force you out of office."

Forlan's four arms shaped an emphatic negative. "That couldn't possibly be true. There are so many simpler ways of forcing a mas's resignation. Anyway, in politics everyone has a limited period of usefulness. One has only to let natural events take their course. Why go to any special trouble to get rid of me?"

"Certain irrational emotions seem to be the common denominator of the universe," Darzek said. "They may be mild in one place and harsh in another, but they exist everywhere. People look down upon, or fear, or resent what is strange—and an alien is strange."

Forlan turned a pained expression on him. "Did you ever hear of a world named Hlaswann?"

Darzek thought for a moment. "No. I never did."

"The world of my birth," Forlan said. "Its sun suddenly went nova. Thanks to modern science, this was predicted in time to remove the entire population. The natives of Hlaswann were scattered through a dozen sectors. Vezpro took a million of us. I was only a baby at the time. I have no recollection whatsoever of Hlaswann. Vezpro is the only world I've ever known."

His eyes were fixed on Darzek with intense sincerity. "You call me an alien because of my external shape, but I'm as native as any Vezpronian. This world gave me refuge, a home, education, a career, and prosperity with honors and distinction. I'll serve it in any way I can, whenever I'm asked. Not because I'm indebted to it, though my debt is incalculable, but because I am a Vezpronian. Because it's my world, the only one I've ever known." He got to his feet. "And," he went on, still meeting Darzek's eyes intensely, "though I was a baby, I know, vividly, what happened to Hlaswann. When I became older, I was curious enough to investigate, and I found a detailed record of a world being incinerated. Having had that happen to the world of my birth, I certainly don't want it to happen again, to my adoptive world." He turned with a gesture of farewell, friendly but distant, as though there were experiences that would forever set them apart, and moved away.

A few minutes later, Eld Wolndur appeared at Darzek's side. "I saw you talking with the mas," he said. "Did he give you the news?"

"He told me some things I hadn't known," Darzek said. "What's *the* news?"

"The finance council won't believe that there's any danger. It thinks Kernopplix is a fraud."

"Which he may be."

"It considers his demands so ridiculous that it wouldn't entertain them even if it were convinced that he was genuine. There can be no dealings with him of any kind in the name of the Vezpronian government. That's an order."

"It's an extraordinarily difficult proposition," Darzek said. "The only way he could demonstrate that the threat is a real one is by turning Vezpro into a sun—which of course would make it rather difficult for him to collect his ransom."

"It might make it easier for him to collect from other worlds, though," Wolndur said, a worried frown making ripples across his bald head.

"True. Does Kernopplix know he's been turned down?"

"No. Since the council has ordered that no one connected with the government should have any dealings with him, I thought perhaps that you . . ."

Darzek got to his feet. People were continuing to arrive; the crowd was seeping into the alcove even while they talked, and twice he'd had his feet stepped on. "I'm certainly not accomplishing anything here," he said. "I might as well give him your news now and see how he reacts. Suppose you meet me later at the Trans-Star office, and I'll tell you what happened."

"All right," Wolndur agreed.

Darzek edged his way into the slowly circulating mass and determinedly began to force a passage toward the reception room and the exit transmitter.

Suddenly a scream rang out.

Crowded as the room was, its occupants somehow managed to draw back and clear an open space. In its center stood a horribly burned and disfigured shape, a hideous caricature of a life form: Qwasrolk, clad in a shabby robe salvaged from someone's rag bin. What remained of his hospital bandages were filthy rags. He looked about him; the gaping, seared hole that had been his mouth moved as though to speak. Then, just as abruptly as he had appeared, he vanished.

Darzek resolutely pushed his way through the horrified crowd. There was nothing that could be done there and a great deal that had to be done elsewhere, at once. He finally reached the reception room and its transmitters and returned to the Trans-Star office. There he told Miss Schlupe what had happened and set her and Gud Baxak to work immediately, checking ships Qwasrolk could have stowed away on.

"If only we could talk to him," Miss Schlupe said irritably. "Find out why he came here and what he's looking for."

"At the moment I'm more concerned with how he came here," Darzek said.

"But the 'why' is as important as the 'how,'" Miss Schlupe objected. "Maybe he had a paranoid nostalgia that made him return to the place he worked, just as he returned to his childhood home on Skarnaf."

"Maybe. But I doubt that he did much work at the Palace of Government, or even attended any functions there. I'd like to hear from him why he came here. I'd like to hear anything at all from him."

They went to work on the problem, and Darzek, because he wasn't needed—Gud Baxak had a superb competence in any matter involving ship movements, and Miss Schlupe could supervise an entire investigative staff between knitting stitches—Darzek decided he might as well fulfill his errand to Kernopplix.

The spidery trader was home and pleased to receive a visit from the distinguished Gul Darr. He greeted Darzek with the same oily cordiality he had displayed on Darzek's first visit. "I have been proceeding," he announced cheerfully. "I've renewed my option on the ship, and I have purchase orders ready for the passenger and freight compartments and the necessary supplies. How soon will the solvency be available?"

"It won't be," Darzek said bluntly. "Vezpro's finance council met today and rejected your request. It refuses to provide any solvency."

"Ah!" Kernopplix exclaimed. There was a strange suggestion of exultation in his voice, suggesting that his face, if he'd had one, would have been beaming at Darzek. For an instant Darzek wondered if he'd been misunderstood.

But when Kernopplix spoke again, it was with a note of regret. "It's extraordinarily difficult to function without solvency."

"Virtually impossible," Darzek agreed gravely.

"Indeed it is. It poses enormous difficulties. The council's answer does, in fact, amount to an outright refusal. Am I justified in that conclusion?"

"I do believe that you are entirely justified in that conclusion," Darzek agreed. "Without the finance council's approval, no solvency is available. Therefore, whatever the administration's inclination may be, its only answer can be a refusal."

"Even if the masfiln is favorably disposed?" Kernopplix asked.

"Even if the masfiln is favorably disposed, he can't make solvency available to us without the approval of the finance council. So the net result is a refusal, regardless of what he thinks."

"What does he think?"

"I have no idea," Darzek said. "I'm only a humble messenger, relaying information that has been relayed to me. Even if the masfiln knew me personally, I doubt that he'd confide in me."

"I see. What you want from me, then, is a reply that you can relay to be relayed."

Darzek considered this. "I doubt that the finance council is expecting a reply. Your message didn't sound like the opening of negotiations. It sounded like an ultimatum, and the council rejected it. However, if you have a reply, I'll see that it is relayed."

"Precisely." Kernopplix clucked his approval. "This is a very proper arrangement. There should be no direct contact between the government and my humble self. We agreed on that. Very well. If you will kindly wait a moment, I have been provided with sealed instructions for every contingency."

He darted from the room with startling speed, all thirteen limbs functioning as legs. A few minutes later he returned with a piece of woven parchment like the material the masfiln's letters had been indited on. It was folded and sealed.

"You see the label," he said, waving it under Darzek's nose. " 'Outright refusal of demands.' Does that cover the situation? I have various instructions concerning counterproposals or requests for delay, but none of them would seem to apply. You're saying the world's finance council will provide no solvency and therefore you offer nothing. And that amounts to outright refusal, doesn't it?"

"Quite correct," Darzek assured him.

"Then this is the proper instruction." Kernopplix's voice again gave Darzek the impression he was being beamed at. The spidery appendages broke the seal and unfolded the message.

"Well," Kernopplix said when he'd finished reading. "There's nothing further for me to do. Nor you, I suppose." He sounded bitterly disappointed. "There's no message to relay. We'll simply have to wait."

He handed the parchment to Darzek. It said, "A demonstration will be arranged. Make no further effort in the matter of obtaining the government's cooperation. Wait until the government comes to you."

"So." Kernopplix effected a sweeping gesture with several of his limbs. "I am to wait. When you are ready to come to me, I'll be here."

Darzek performed the ceremonious gesture of farewell. "When—or if—the government changes its mind, or when—or if—the finance council makes the solvency available, I'll know where to find you."

He took his leave and returned to the Trans-Star office, where he found Wolndur waiting with Melris Angoz. He told them what had happened, and Melris frowned apprehensively.

"A demonstration? Of what?"

"The only kind of demonstration that would achieve the desired result would be to turn something into a sun," Darzek said. "One of your moons, perhaps."

"Wouldn't that make Vezpro rather uncomfortably warm?"

"No doubt. But not as warm as if Vezpro were turned into a sun."

"We must do something!" Wolndur exclaimed.

"You might make a thorough check of your moons," Darzek suggested.

"I must talk with the mas," Wolndur said and hurried away.

Melris was studying Darzek thoughtfully. "Gul Darr, would it be possible to get solvency from the Council of Supreme for an emergency such as this one?"

"It's possible to ask," Darzek said. He controlled unlimited solvency himself, as First Councilor, but he did not know whether the term "unlimited" extended to infinity—and a billion billion solvency units sounded like infinity to him. He easily could have provided enough solvency to buy and outfit the spaceship and thus stall Kernopplix for a term or two. Perhaps he should have.

But as long as the blackmailer had promised a demonstration, Darzek thought he might as well wait and see what it was. A demonstration didn't sound threatening.

"Will you ask?" Melris persisted.

"I'll send Supreme a full report at once, but I doubt that anything will happen. Supreme is like your finance council. It doesn't believe there's any danger because it doesn't comprehend what the danger could be."

"I thought Supreme comprehended everything," she said.

"Tsk. And you a computer expert. Supreme is like any other computer, only it's enormously bigger and more complicated. It knows only what it's been told, and no one has told it how to turn a world into a sun."

"But if there's a demonstration?"

"Like your finance council, Supreme needs to be shown. A demonstration might show it."

12

UrsNollf arrived, went immediately to Zarst, and was not seen again for twelve days. He returned dazzled by the Zarstan research. "A most strange organization," he told Darzek. "One part of it is an amazingly successful business—it designs products and consults on production problems for fabricators from several sectors. Another part of it is devoted to advanced research in the sciences. And of course all of its members are devotedly religious."

"I know," Darzek said. "They worship science."

"I would not say so, no. Science is only one of a number of studies. It is a means to the understanding of what they worship—the ultimate essence of the universe. Hence their queer costumes that look like some scientific puzzle involving the atomic structure."

"You seem to have enjoyed yourself," Darzek said. "Did you find out anything?"

"I learned more than you'd care to hear me describe, but as concerns the Nifron D problem—I can assure you, positively, that the experimental research on Zarst has nothing to do with turning worlds into suns. For all their discoveries, the Zarstans are scientifically incapable of that. My personal opinion is that they also would be incapable of it ethically and morally and religiously. Such a thing would deface the universe and be contrary to their most profound beliefs."

"If you say so," Darzek said. "I'll go right on being suspicious of them, because it's my job to be suspicious of everyone. You don't know, for example, how many secret laboratories they failed to show you. And you don't know about Qwasrolk."

"Who—or what—is Qwasrolk?"

"Never mind. The Mas of Science and Technology has set up a secret committee to study the problem of turning a planet into a sun. Let's go see him. I'd like to have you sit in on the committee's meetings and let me know how competent it is."

They went to see Forlan, who was delighted to meet one of the galaxy's leading astrophysicists. He offered the government's hospitality and his own to UrsNollf during his visit and immediately invited the committee members to meet him.

Darzek left UrsNollf in Naz Forlan's obviously capable hands and returned to the Trans-Star office. There he settled himself in his private quarters and spent some time in trying to figure out what, if anything, he had accomplished since his arrival on Vezpro.

Miss Schlupe returned and dropped wearily into her rocking chair. "Well, I've done it," she said. "Wolndur has his moon search organized, and I've got fifty of my people scattered through the search parties. Though it beats me why you want them there—they're unskilled and uneducated and wouldn't know a nuclear bomb from a sewage disposal unit."

"That's irrelevant," Darzek said. "What I really want to know is whether a thorough search is made."

Miss Schlupe said bluntly, *"I* think the whole project is a dratted waste of time and effort."

"You're probably right. UrsNollf says turning any but Vezpro's smallest moon into a sun would make the planet uninhabitable, and even the smallest moon would make the world too hot for comfort, so I rather doubt that a moon would be used. A population or a government wouldn't be disposed to pay ransom to save a world that's too uncomfortable to live on."

"Even if a moon is used, they won't find anything," Miss Schlupe said. "The entire population of Vezpro wouldn't be large enough to search all the moons properly, and we don't know whether we're looking for something the size of a power plant or a match box, or whether it'd be on the surface or buried ten kilometers deep. So I say it's a silly waste of time. Why bother?"

"Because we're too stupid to think of anything better to do. If the blackmailer is laughing hilariously at us, so much the better. Later on, it may make him underestimate us when he shouldn't. So we'll search the moons."

"Can't that committee of nuclear experts tell us what to look for?" Miss Schlupe asked.

"How expert is an expert? UrsNollf has never encountered such a problem, and neither has anyone else on Forlan's committee. Forlan is a metallurgist; he knows a little about nuclear science, but with a problem of this complexity he can only do what I do: ask an expert and hope that he gets a right answer. Wolndur is a very bright youngster and no doubt competent at assembling facts, provided that the facts aren't hidden too deeply. I have the feeling that everyone concerned is as likely to hatch an egg as come up with a solution, and they're all concentrating so hard on the scientific puzzle that they haven't grasped the fact that this is a two-part proposition: figuring out a way to turn a world into a sun doesn't necessarily show us how to keep someone else from doing it. The one real expert I've met is our computer tec."

"Melris Angoz?"

"Right. I'm sorry she's not on Primores. She'd put a strain on all of Supreme's unused think tanks. She's run checks on some highly imaginative ideas."

"But she hasn't found anything."

"She found Qwasrolk. The fact that we already knew about him doesn't distract from her achievement. If there's anything else to find with a computer, she'll do it."

"Qwasrolk," Miss Schlupe muttered. She had been trying to find the radiation victim herself, now that he was known to be on Vezpro —or to have been on Vezpro—but without a whisper of success. There was no clue as to how he got there or where he went. "I suppose there's nothing for us to do but sit around waiting for the demonstration," she said. "I wonder if it'll be announced in advance, admission by invitation only, special bleachers for high-ranking guests. It wouldn't do to have the thing happen when no one's around to admire it."

"A demonstration like this one doesn't require an audience," Darzek told her. "It makes a lasting impression. While we're waiting for it, we ought to do a little detecting. Have you tracked down everything that can be learned about those missing nuclear scientists?"

"I don't know. We keep trying."

Later, Darzek sat alone in the living room gloomily reviewing what he knew. He still had no answers—only questions. What *had* happened to Nifron D? The missing nuclear engineers and scientists Miss Schlupe kept identifying might be involved in the scheme, but none of them seemed to have the qualifications to originate it. If the threat to Vezpro were genuine, the criminal they were looking for had a knowledge of nuclear physics that transcended that of the galaxy's leading experts. And if it were a hoax, Kernopplix's employer still was a very shrewd crook. In a society where neither crime nor criminals were supposed to exist, Darzek was confronted with a monstrous noncrime engineered by a master noncriminal.

He heard a rush of footsteps and thought that Miss Schlupe was returning, perhaps with a bargain she'd picked up in the "mushrooms" she was so fond of, but it was UrsNollf who burst in on him.

"We've done it!" he exclaimed.

It took a moment for Darzek to focus his thoughts. "You mean—the committee has found out how—"

"It has, and we're arranging a demonstration." Darzek winced. "Would you like to watch?"

"Of course," Darzek said, and added, "So it seems that the impossible is no longer impossible."

"So we're about to prove!"

"When will the demonstration take place?" Darzek asked. It amused him that UrsNollf, whose first reaction to the committee's work had been to proclaim it preposterous, now described its success in terms of "we."

"The advance party just left. We'll follow tomorrow."

It was a single sun Darzek had never heard of, with a scattering of ash-heap planets: a slum of a solar system, until this moment of no value to anyone. Now one of those planets was about to be touched into incandescence by a magic wand Darzek refused to try to understand. He politely ignored the drawings spread out on a table in a special observation compartment of the command ship.

The scientists of Naz Forlan's committee were gloating over them, as was UrsNollf. The Mas of Science and Technology was studying them gravely and asking an occasional question. Darzek was much more interested in a three-dimensional photograph of the triggering device. It was actual size, and it stood in the center of the compartment and reached from floor to ceiling. It suggested that the operation of converting a world into a sun was not an inconspicuous one; but Darzek, familiar with the normal processes of technology by which complicated gadgets became progressively smaller, had no doubt that many of the indescribable innards of this monster could be miniaturized.

Even in its present form it would require an excessively thorough search to locate it on a doomed world if its creator took any pains to conceal it. On one of Vezpro's moons, for example, in a cavern or fault with the opening sealed over, it could be found only by pealing off the moon's surface. No wonder Wolndur's search had been futile!

But perhaps, now that the scientists knew what those innards consisted of, they could create detection devices. He fervently hoped so.

He said as much to Forlan, who had left the drawings and joined him to study the photographic model.

Forlan gestured his agreement. "Once one miracle has been achieved, one is justified in expecting more."

"Do you understand the thing?" Darzek asked.

"Frankly, no. I understand the principle, of course. And I understand what they have done, up to a point. But beyond that point we enter a realm of pure nuclear theory that even experts negotiate more by instinct than by reason. There I'm completely lost. I can only congratulate them on their brilliance."

"And—since you can't understand what they've done—hope that they are right?"

"No," Forlan said bluntly. "I hope that they are wrong. I hope that the thing *is* impossible. Then we can stop worrying. If their test succeeds, then we have to go on worrying, and we must also start worrying, as you suggest, about detection devices and how to make use of them. I would much prefer that the making of suns be left to the universe's natural processes."

Darzek dryly agreed.

Their ship was in orbit well beyond the system's scattering of planets. For all their brilliance, the scientists seemed doubtful as to the demarcation of safety in such an experiment. They had placed scanners on the doomed planet, on the orbiting satellites, on nearby planets, and on the ship's exterior, and the ship itself was carefully shielded. Now they drifted, and the scanners nearest the triggering device—which looked like a giant pear with a flat bottom—were transmitting the final preparations to viewing screens in Darzek's compartment.

Since he could not understand what was taking place, he quickly tired of watching. He had another look at the drawings on the table —a massive jumble of lines and cryptic symbols—and then he found a comfortable chair for himself and watched the scientists.

They were a typical cross section of the intelligent life forms of a galaxy—from UrsNollf and his misplaced head and bulging hump of a brain to the four-armed Forlan and the triple-armed and -legged Vezpronians to the multiple-limbed, massive headed, insectlike types that some said were the most brilliant of all. Most of them looked like something one might expect to see under a microscope, but Darzek had no doubt that Naz Forland had assembled the most brilliant team of nuclear scientists available. If they couldn't do the job, no one could.

And they said that they could do it.

Eventually the final tinkering was completed; the scientists responsible for it left the doomed planet by transmitting to a waiting spaceship, which speedily placed itself at an orbital distance slightly beyond Darzek's ship. One small group of scientists was huddled over a bank of instruments, taking readings in several languages. Finally they turned questioningly to Forlan.

"All systems are go," Darzek muttered.

"Proceed whenever you're ready," Forlan said. He seated himself beside Darzek, and the two of them watched the cluster of viewing screens. The largest showed the triggering device from a distance of a kilometer or so, a lonely, white object starkly alien against a barren landscape. Darzek—and the doomed world—waited.

Then Armageddon flashed, and at the same instant the screen went blank. Darzek turned to another screen, fed by a scanner on an orbiting satellite just above the holocaust. The glowing ball spread and seemed about to envelop the planet. Then it faded abruptly, lost in swirling smoke and debris.

Darzek turned to Forlan, who was staring in fascination. The other scientists' attitudes had altered from triumph to dismay. They all continued to watch, but already it was apparent that the doomed planet was no longer doomed; and as the swirling cloud gradually thinned, the satellite scanner revealed what Darzek already had guessed. A small chunk of the planet had been converted to gasses, but all the experiment had accomplished was to blast a gigantic and probably super-radioactive hole in the world's ash-heap surface.

UrsNollf looked crushed. He turned away from Darzek, unable to speak. Nearby, a multiple-segmented scientist muttered, "Something went wrong."

Forlan said quietly, "I think, rather, that something was wrong to begin with." Then he smiled at Darzek. "This means that you can invite that unmentionable character Kernopplix to leave Vezpro on the next ship. If he doesn't, I'll ask our legal department to devise some kind of action against him. Will you call on him the moment we return?"

"Certainly, if you want me to," Darzek said. "But there might be some way to handle this to our advantage. After all, Kernopplix is only an agent. It's his employer that we want."

Forlan subsided and gestures wearily with all four arms. "Of course. It's his employer that we should seek punishment for. Kernopplix is only a messenger." He brightened. "I'll leave Kernopplix to you. My department can return to its normal routine, I can catch up on my work, and the masfiln can sleep soundly. He needs it."

UrsNollf came over to the two of them and began stammering an involved explanation of what might have gone wrong. Forlan silenced him with a multiarmed gesture. "Never mind. You will of course want to land as soon as it can be done safely to investigate and perhaps perform tests. If you think it worthwhile, you can try again. Vezpro will continue to provide any necessary solvency. We want your answer to be definitive and final. Those who wish to continue to work on the project will transfer to the other ship. This one will return to Vezpro immediately."

UrsNollf walked away, shoulders slumped over his oddly placed head.

Forlan leaned back and heaved a sigh. He looked like one for whom a totally unexpected reprieve had just arrived. "A billion billion solvency units," he said. "The finance council wanted my unequivocal endorsement that the safety of Vezpro and its population of five billion required that payment. All I could answer was that I didn't know. Either way the blame would have been mine—and deservedly so. The Mas of Science and Technology is supposed to know. It'll be a pleasure to go back and assure the council that its decision was the correct one."

Darzek nodded absently. He was thinking about Kernopplix. He understood Forlan's impulse—it would have been a pleasure to order the slimy creature to leave. But it would be a much greater pleasure to make use of him. There should be some way to bait a trap with him.

Suddenly the compartment was empty except for themselves. All of the scientists had transferred to the other ship. Darzek took his leave of Forlan, and, with a final glance at the no longer doomed world and its giant cavity, he went to his private compartment and sprawled on the thick sleeping mat without bothering to remove his clothes. It had been a long, suspenseful ordeal, and he felt exhausted.

Drifting off to sleep, he felt the vibration of their first jump through space.

Forlan shook him awake. His face was ashen, and he seemed incapable of speech. He gestured and vanished into the transmitter. Darzek leaped to his feet and followed.

In the control room, Forlan, the captain, and the ship's navigator stood looking at the large viewing screen. It showed a double star.

Darzek, not yet fully awake, gazed at it incomprehensibly. "What is it?" he asked.

"Vezpro," Forlan said hoarsely.

"*Vezpro?* You mean—Vezpro is . . ."

The navigator stammered an explanation. The system's eleventh planet, a small, unspeakably remote rock heap, had inexplicably turned into a sun. The world of Vezpro was now a part of a double star system.

Darzek rubbed his eyes and looked again. "So that's the demonstration."

Forlan said nothing.

"For an operation that can't be done," Darzek said, "it looks highly effective."

13

It was night in Klinoz, the capital of Vezpro. Darzek, who had slept away his return journey, was wide awake. He settled himself in the room he and Miss Schlupe used as a combination living room and private study, parked his feet on a nearby chair, and—he'd had no tobacco for years—reflected that if he'd owned a cigar, this was the time to smoke it.

Miss Schlupe, wearing a brightly patterned robe over a long night-gown and with her hair down—one of the few times he'd ever seen her without the neat bun that had been the fashion with her since she was a girl—walked in and stood over him. "Did you see it?" she demanded.

Darzek nodded. "A most convincing demonstration. I wish I understood it."

"You mean—understood how it was done?"

"Why would I want to clutter my mind with that? I wish I understood our mad scientist's reasoning. The eleventh planet is an enormous distance from Vezpro even at its closest. Right now it's not too far from conjunction on the opposite side of the sun. In other words, it's almost as far away as it can get, and the sun is obscuring it. How many Vezpronians are aware of what's happened?"

"I don't know. Wolndur told me about it."

"Every ship that arrives here will have seen it, and professional astronomers probably caught it at once. To the average layman, it's too small and far away to notice, and even when it comes closer it'll be more of a curiosity than a menace. It isn't likely to frighten anyone."

"Meaning what?"

"We're dealing with an extraordinarily considerate criminal. Instead of a demonstration with a nearby planet, which might cause riots and panic in the population, he makes it remote enough to alarm only those capable of understanding it, but close enough to scare the pants off them, if they're the kind that wears pants. In other words, he aims at frightening the government officials into paying off without alarming the world's population. I call that thoughtful of him."

"It's also possible that these demonstrations are expensive, and the bigger planets cost more," Miss Schlupe observed. "Why invest in blowing up a large planet if a small one will have the same effect?"

Darzek grinned at her. "Always the cynic, aren't you. All right— either he's considerate, or he's thrifty. Heard anything from Kernopplix?"

"Nary a whisper."

"I thought he might have stopped by to gloat. But his instructions were to wait until we came to him, and obviously he obeys instructions to the last letter as long as there's going to be a profit."

"How did your experiment go?"

"It went *ffft*. A first-rate farce. Forlan thereupon concluded that it couldn't be done, and we happily hurried back here only to find that it had been done. Forlan is crushed. When his scientific committee, which is still at the scene trying to figure out what went wrong, hears about this latest development, the members may commit harakiri, if that's the practice in galactic scientific circles. UrsNollf will never be the same again."

"What'll happen now?"

Darzek thought for a moment and then announced meditatively, "I think you'd better get some female agents ready for a ride on that ransom ship."

"I've already started," Miss Schlupe said. "I've got three hundred females in training, which gives us plenty of leeway for rejects. They're all sturdy, healthy specimens, and my Vezpronian males screened them for good looks, just in case that turns out to be a criterion. I can't tell a pretty Vezpronian girl from an ugly one."

"Neither can I," Darzek said.

"Anyway, I've got three hundred, and I'm training them, and I'll tell you this—you don't know what judo is until you've seen the three-armed variety. If the villain approaches one of these gals, he'll be slammed good."

"Glad to hear it," Darzek said. "Sorry I won't be able to see it. Heard from Raf Lolln?"

"No."

"I'll have to go see him. Too bad I couldn't take him along, but I didn't think it'd be politic. He would have laughed himself silly over that experiment and gone into convulsions when we got back and found that demonstration waiting for us. I wonder why Forlan didn't put him on his committee. Probably no orthodox scientist would work with him. I also wonder if UrsNollf is right when he says Raf Lolln and the Zarstans couldn't possibly come up with the answer. He hasn't been right about anything else."

"What do you want me to do?" Miss Schlupe asked.

"Go back to bed. Keep training your three hundred females. We may need them soon.

She retired to her bedroom, and Darzek, after meditating for a few more minutes, woke up Gud Baxak, who was startled to see him. "Does the world of Vezpro have any enemies?" Darzek demanded.

Gud Baxak regarded him sleepily. "Sire?"

"I need to know about Vezpro's competitors," Darzek said. "We've been so intent on our scientist complex that we've neglected the fact that a world is much more likely to be behind a conspiracy of these dimensions." He was mentally kicking himself—an exercise he had indulged in so frequently of late that it threatened to become habit-forming. "What world or worlds would profit most if Vezpro's industry failed?" he asked.

"Vezpro dominates twelve sectors of space," Gud Baxak said protestingly. "If its industry failed, worlds would be ruined throughout the twelve sectors and beyond. Vezpro is their market for raw materials, and it supplies them with fabricated goods."

"I see. I never thought of economics in ecological terms, but I suppose the comparison is apt. Couldn't those worlds sell their raw materials to someone else, or develop the industries to use them themselves?"

"No doubt they could, eventually. But a long period of adjustment would be required, shipping charges would be higher both on the raw materials and on the goods sent in payment for many worlds, and before all concerned could find new markets and suppliers and get their trade running smoothly again, individuals, agricombines, factories, even worlds would be ruined."

"Then Vezpro has no one major rival, or group of rivals."

"None," Gud Baxak said firmly.

"I'm sorry to hear that," Darzek said. "First thing in the morning I want you to find me an expert in transmitters. I want this to be the ultimate expert, one who can make those things turn somersaults."

"*Somersaults?*"

"Never mind. Just be sure it's the best expert available. Now go back to sleep."

Darzek returned to the living room and his meditating.

"The problem is," he muttered, "we don't know what this villain really wants. Does he actually expect to collect that impossible ransom, or is he trying to create as much mental anguish as he can before the world is destroyed? Has he intended from the beginning to make Vezpro a horrible example so other worlds will pay up instantly? In a society that has no criminals, a criminal mind is totally unfathomable."

They would have to yield at once on the spaceship. It, plus passenger and freight compartments—which Kernopplix certainly would order custom-made or with expensive custom features—and with the outfitting and provisioning, would come to a tidy sum, but not one large enough to make the most conservative world finance committee blink. Properly managed, the preparation of ship and contents could be stalled at a number of points, giving them more time, and time was critically important if only Darzek knew what to do with it.

The billion billion solvency units was another matter. Darzek had no doubt that even a wealthy world would have to mortgage its future for generations to accumulate such an amount; and there was nothing at all to prevent the blackmailer from returning next cycle, or next term, with a similar demand. Forlan had mentioned that the Mas of Finance thought they could create an illusion of solvency with phony certificates. This was not a solution; it was merely a way of buying more time.

"But the problem," Darzek said, still muttering, "is not the ransom. The problem is to catch him—and that's my specialty. So why am I worrying about solvency?"

He meditated further, and then he went out to send a message.

To E-Wusk, galactic trader of legendary fame and close friend of Darzek's, who also was TWO, the second member of the Council of Supreme.

No one could assemble a fleet of spaceships more deftly than E-Wusk. Sometimes Darzek thought the old trader maintained a mental chart upon which was positioned every trading ship in the Galactic Synthesis, along with its cargo manifests. The only method Darzek could devise for tracking a ship through its space jumps was to arrange an enormous fleet so that a ship would be waiting for it no matter where it jumped. No one but E-Wusk had the know-how to do that.

And if, sooner or later, they had to consider the logistics of evacuating a world of five billion inhabitants, plus their prized possessions, that, too, was a problem that only E-Wusk could cope with.

Kernopplix greeted Darzek with his usual excessive, oily cordiality. Darzek could imagine his faceless sensory organs contorted in a triumphant grin. "Ah!" he exclaimed. "You return. I've been expecting you."

"It was a most interesting demonstration," Darzek told him. "Please give your employer our congratulations."

"But I have no communications with my employer!" Kernopplix protested. "I have never met him. I have only his written instructions."

"Which you intend to carry out precisely."

"But of course!"

"You have lists and estimates, I believe."

"But of course!"

Kernopplix handed over a sheaf of indited sheets, and Darzek sat down to study them. He ran a practiced eye over the figures, occasionally raising his eyebrows and notching one. Then he returned the sheets.

"The finance committee will want to audit these," he said.

"The committee's caution does it credit."

"Not necessarily. That happens to be the law on Vezpro. And would you provide detailed cost appraisals for the items I've marked? If you will bring these to me as soon as the additional information is ready, I'll pass them along to the committee—through proper channels, of course. Like you, I'm only a messenger, though I have no written instructions to follow. Just a stern order to use my common sense."

"Which is highly uncommon," Kernopplix observed. "But I respectfully point out—"

Darzek raised a hand. "I have no doubt that those apparently excessive figures are there for sound reasons. We will save time if you provide the reasons along with the estimates."

"Of course."

When Darzek returned to the Trans-Star office, Gud Baxak was waiting for him with a transmitter engineer, an elderly Vezpronian. Darzek took the engineer aside and told him tersely what was needed, adding that the fate of his world might depend on his performance. Thoroughly shaken, that worthy individual listened carefully to Darzek's instructions three times, and then, sworn to secrecy, his objections casually waved aside, he left.

Darzek called after him, "If it was easy, we wouldn't need an expert."

Kernopplix delivered his estimates later that day, with the questionable items and everything else broken down into almost excessive detail. Darzek thanked him gravely and took the estimates to Wolndur, who was to pass them to Forlan, who was to pass them to the finance council. The solvency to purchase the ship was transferred to Darzek's account almost at once, and Darzek immediately transferred it to Kernopplix, promising the remainder as soon as the audit was completed and approved.

Kernopplix's spidery features were incapable of expressing elation, but when he came to thank Darzek, there was a distinct note of rapture in his voice. Darzek suspected that Kernopplix was a shoestring operator on the verge of running out of solvency.

Kernopplix handed over a solvency certificate made out to Darzek personally. "Your commission," he explained. Darzek thanked him. Kernopplix performed a sweeping gesture of generosity. "You're entitled to it. As I said before, there'll be profit enough for both of us."

"I'm sure there will be."

"Which is why some of those estimates looked high. If the council shaves them, the cut will have to come out of your share."

"Since you've provided such convincing details, I doubt that the council will alter them," Darzek said soothingly.

Kernopplix departed with a grin in his voice.

Miss Schlupe, who had watched this transaction, asked, "What are you going to do with that certificate? I'm running short—paying and training those three hundred females costs something, not to mention my other investigators—and since I'm supposed to be a nobody, it might cause comment if I start transferring solvency here. And I don't think Trans-Star's accounts should be used for my nefarious activities."

"I'll deposit this to your account," Darzek said. "Since it was extorted from Vezpro, it's entirely appropriate to use it for Vezpro. Sit down for a moment."

She dropped into her rocking chair, and Darzek made himself comfortable nearby, feet up, and kicked his shoes off. "Tell me this. What are the odds that our villain is on Forlan's blue-ribbon nuclear committee?"

"It's an interesting thought," Miss Schlupe conceded. "He'd be in an ideal position to sabòtage any experiments the committee sponsored."

"They were so certain they'd figured the thing out. Then it went *ffft.*"

"Did they really have it figured out?" Miss Schlupe asked.

"That's the rub. Only a nuclear expert could say, and—since all of them were wrong—maybe not even one of those. Forlan, who is no fool but also no nuclear specialist, said he understood what they were doing only up to a point, after which their equations became the scientist's equivalent of indecipherable hieroglyphics. Is it conceivable that our villain could be so much more knowledgeable than his most expert colleagues?"

"A scientist can discover something by accident," Miss Schlupe said.

"It's been known to happen," Darzek agreed. "Since Forlan picked the best scientists available, he may have put the villain on his committee. If he did, how could we identify him?"

"I wouldn't know. As for the 'best scientists,' you probably mean the best known. I seem to recall that great scientific discoveries can happen to obscure nonentities just as easily, and they have a devil of a time getting them accepted or even noticed, They become famous generations after they die when someone accidentally discovers that something has already been accidentally discovered. If you really think he's on the committee, why don't you put Melris Angoz to work on it? Computers are good at gulping up a million details and spitting out the one or two that don't fit."

"Good idea," Darzek said. "Go spend some solvency, and I'll have a chat with Melris."

The computer that ran the galaxy, Supreme, was the size of a world. The computer that ran the world of Vezpro was merely the size of a building, though a large one. Melris Angoz, who had unlimited access to it, was doing nothing behind her terraced banks of controls when Darzek called. She had exhausted her imagination, and she welcomed any kind of assignment. Darzek seated himself and described two projects for her.

She seemed doubtful about investigating the members of the mas's committee. They came from many worlds, and she did not know how much information the Vezpro computer might have on them. What it had, she would glean. She would ask Wolndur for the list of names and worlds of origin.

But the second assignment, while extremely complicated, obviously delighted her. What Darzek wanted was a computer study of the economics of the surrounding dozen sectors—more if she could manage it—if Vezpro suddenly ceased to exist. This was a challenge any competent computer tech could enjoy, and he left her enthusiastically laying out a program.

Darzek went to Naz Forlan's office and asked the Mas of Science and Technology for a copy of the plans and any related materials used in the ill-fated experiment. Forlan did not håve an extra one, but he promised to have a copy made for Darzek and send it to him. The scientists, he said, were on their way back to Vezpro to study the phenomenon of the eleventh planet.

"You aren't planning on making yourself a nuclear specialist, are you?" Forlan asked. "If so, I can suggest better texts—ones with experiments that work." He was smiling, but there was bitterness in his voice. He told Darzek that the solvency requested by Kernopplix for outfitting and supplying the spaceship had now been approved and transferred to Darzek's account.

"You can deliver it to Kernopplix at once," he said.

Darzek reflected. "No," he said. "Tomorrow will be soon enough. Or the day after."

Forlan gestured indifferently. "Whatever you think best." Clearly the matter of solvency transfers was of no concern to him. Darzek did not tell him that Kernopplix might as well become accustomed to delays, because he was going to encounter a lot of them. Also, Darzek wanted to go to Zarst.

But first he went to see the fabricator from whom Kernopplix had ordered custom-built cargo and passenger compartments. With him he took the elderly transmitter expert. The company's director was overwhelmed at receiving a visit from a special emissary of Supreme, and Darzek had no difficulty in arranging for his transmitter expert to make several secret modifications that Kernopplix's plans did not call for.

When he returned to the Trans-Star office, the copy of the nuclear experiment plans was waiting for him. Darzek went immediately to Zarst and had no difficulty in talking his way past the receptionist, who now knew him and regarded him with blended awe and resentment. Raf Lolln was at work in a lab with Zarstan scientists, and he greeted Darzek cordially. All of the scientists seemed astonished at the fate of the eleventh planet; and, as Darzek expected, his account of Forlan's ill-fated experiment convulsed them.

He spread his copy of the plans on a worktable. "A small job for you," he said, speaking to Raf Lolln but addressing the whole group. "Figure out where they went wrong."

He left them crowded around the table.

He waited two days before he went to see Kernopplix. He already had transferred the balance of the requested solvency, and Kernopplix cheerfully met him with a certificate for Darzek's commission. "Since you were able to obtain approval of my estimates, it's the full 10 per cent," Kernopplix pointed out. "A nice sum, but I'm sure you earned it."

"Thank you," Darzek said. "I'll put it to good use."

Kernopplix responded with an abdominal rumble that Darzek interpreted as a giggle.

"I assume that you'll want to supervise the loading of the compartments yourself, as soon as they're completed," Darzek said.

"Of course. That already has been specified."

"And I shall have to be present."

Kernopplix's suddenly rigid sensory organs registered astonishment.

"Since the compartments were financed by the government for a specific purpose, I must certify that they actually were loaded into the ship for which they were purchased. How the loading is arranged is of course your prerogative."

"I see. As long as you are merely an observer—"

"An observer with invoices," Darzek said, "checking off each item as it is placed aboard."

Kernopplix said thoughtfully, "As you say, the government paid for the compartments and everything that goes into them, and it has a proper interest in seeing that they reach their destination." Obviously he was not convinced.

"If you were to load them, or part of them, or part of the requisitioned supplies into another ship, then your employer could accuse the government of not carrying out his instructions," Darzek pointed out. "My inspection protects you as well as the government of Vezpro. I shall of course make my certifications in triplicate, so that you can have a copy."

Kernopplix's voice brightened. "That is thoughtful of you. Now I understand. Yes, it is appropriate that the loading be inspected. What are the third copies for?"

"Manufacturers and suppliers," Darzek said. "For them, it will be a receipt. Everyone concerned should be protected, and the proper fulfillment of your employer's instructions has been made my responsibility as well as yours. When all is completed, we will have to make a joint certification that the instructions have been carried out —you, for your employer, and I, for the government of Vezpro, with copies to each."

"I have no means of communicating with my employer, but such a certification could be useful in the event of some question arising later. Your caution does you credit."

"Sometimes," Darzek said, "it even surprises me."

14

Miss Schlupe had established a secret commando camp for her three hundred young Vezpronian females. She was teaching them all the techniques of unarmed mayhem that she knew, and her knowledge was considerable.

Darzek, stopping by to watch them practice, studied their bald-headed, triple-armed and -legged appearances for a time and then asked, "Who was it who selected these specimens for their beauty?"

"Some Vezpronian males. If they don't know, who does?"

"How is it going?"

"The problem is, we don't know what sort of life forms they'll have to contend with," Miss Schlupe said. "On the other hand, unarmed combat is an art that hasn't even been thought of here, so I think they'll make out all right. As a last resort, just before the balloon goes up, we might bring in an assortment of life forms for them to practice on."

"Good idea," Darzek said.

"Have you decided about weapons?"

"I'd feel better if they were armed. I think knives would be best. They're easily concealed, they're silent, and we can make them ourselves."

"That's what I was thinking. Handguns, even if we had any, require a lot of practice, and even with practice most people can't learn to shoot straight."

"I'll find someone to make the knives," Darzek said. "Carry on, you're doing fine."

He took a last look around the camp: the neat row of huts where the recruits slept, the well-trampled training grounds, the mockup spaceship—as soon as Kernopplix's ship was outfitted, the mockup would be arranged as identically as possible so Miss Schlupe's charges could practice taking it over.

Things were shaping up very well indeed, Darzek thought, and he went off to watch Kernopplix load a spaceship.

Thanks to the transmitter, ships operating in deep space were hollow hulks except for their operation and service sections. There was no need for corridors and stairs and such superfluous paraphernalia. Passenger compartments were taken aboard as they were engaged and hooked up to power and ventilation connections. Freight compartments were loaded the same way; and in weightless space, tons of freight compartments could be safely stowed atop fragile passenger compartments. Any compartment, freight or passenger, was only a step away from any other, or from the passenger lounges or the control room, by transmitter.

Since compartments could be transmitted to and from a world's surface by specially designed transmitters, all ships docked at satellite transfer stations, and there was no need for a spaceship to come close enough to any world to have to contend with its gravity. Passengers normally transmitted up to the transfer station and embarked from there. Making a ship ready—which meant guiding the compartments about and stowing them aboard under conditions of zero gravity—could be tricky and time-consuming, as well as rather unsettling to anyone inside them, and it was much easier to step through a transmitter to the transfer station and then step aboard one's reserved compartment by way of another transmitter during an announced boarding period. Since the freight was less likely to complain about delays and rough handling, its compartments frequently were transmitted up to the station and maneuvered aboard ship already loaded.

Darzek encountered Kernopplix in the passenger lounge of the ransom ship, which by his specific instructions remained nameless. He had encountered a long series of frustrating delays, mainly because—as Darzek had patiently pointed out each time one happened—his custom-designed compartments required materials not commonly used, and these were sometimes hard to obtain. Eventually Darzek decided that he could stall no longer, and now the compartments and the ship were ready.

The elongated lounge was positively baroque in its lavish furnishings, and Kernopplix was inspecting it with evident satisfaction. "Very nice," he murmured, reaching a trio of spidery arms over the service counter for a bulb of fruit juice. The artificial gravity was set at minimum, so he pressurized the container and shot a stream of its contents into his mouth with slurping satisfaction. "Something for you, Gul Darr?"

Darzek looked up from his stack of invoices. "I think," he said gravely, "that we're short one seating convenience. Oh—there it is, behind you."

Kernopplix had pirouetted in alarm. "No, no," he assured Darzek. "Everything is precisely as specified. I inspected it at the factory."

"Someone could have removed it between there and here," Darzek said. "But don't worry—I'll check everything." Then, belatedly answering Kernopplix's question, "Yes, I'll have the same. I doubt that any complications will arise if the ship is short a few servings of food."

Kernopplix regarded him uneasily. Then he filled a pressurized container and passed it to Darzek, who shot a well-measured gulp into his own mouth, swallowed, and murmured, "Thank you. When do the compartments begin to arrive?"

A thump overhead answered him.

"How do you wish to inspect them?" Kernopplix asked. "As they are stowed, or all at once, afterward?"

"As they are stowed," Darzek said. "I want to check the transmitters and then the furnishings. Why don't we inspect them together?"

"Indeed, that's a good thought," Kernopplix observed. "That should save time for both of us. We'll inspect each compartment as soon as its connections are completed."

The examination of three hundred passenger compartments, with the freight compartments and their supplies to follow, could only be a long and tedious task. Darzek's problem was to make it last as long as possible without his delaying tactics becoming obvious. He was still fighting for time, still hopeful that one of his investigations would turn up something.

As each compartment became habitable, with its air and heating connections functioning, they entered it by way of the lounge's transmitter. Darzek immediately inserted a test meter into the inspection slot to check the compartment's emergency power supply. Kernopplix had not thought of this, and he congratulated Darzek—who did not tell him what else he was testing. Darzek also located, amidst the compartment's elaborate ornamentation, a concealed number, and he entered it on his chart. Later, each of Miss Schlupe's commandos would memorize that chart. Those selected as victims would know where they were in the ship the moment they entered their compartments.

Kernopplix's enthusiasm increased as Darzek meticulously checked service transmitters, artificial gravity controls, and inventories, and noted an occasional missing item. The manufacturers had committed the minor oversights common to rush orders, and Kernopplix sent off an indignant message each time they turned up one. Darzek, pausing in his labors to contemplate the plush luxury of these compartments, found it awesome. He had traveled extensively, in all kinds of ships, but never in surroundings such as this. He wondered how Kernopplix would go about selecting occupants for these sumptuous quarters. Surely the spidery alien's eye for Vezpronian beauty was no more practiced than Darzek's.

The two of them put in a long day's work, adjourned for a rest period, and then worked again—and they were inspecting only a dozen compartments a day. Kernopplix at first complained about the slow pace, but as Darzek kept turning up missing items, the spidery trader stopped protesting and began to assist enthusiastically. In order to nurture that cooperation, Darzek returned to the transfer station at night and removed items from compartments they had not inspected, and the innocent fabricator was the recipient of daily tirades from Kernopplix on the sloppiness of his work.

Each day Darzek prolonged the inspection was precious time gained. Miss Schlupe's squad of investigators had spread around the planet, looking for clues, looking for Qwasrolk, trying to trace the whereabouts of the missing nuclear experts. Melris Angoz had exhausted the resources of the Vezpronian computer as concerned Forlan's scientific committee, but she had sent requests for information to other worlds, and while she waited for it she was reconstructing the economy of a dozen or more sectors of space without Vezpro.

And old E-Wusk had arrived. He listened to the task Darzek had for him—the probably impossible tracing of the ransom ship to its destination—and responding with a resounding, "Oh, ho! Gul Darr never asks for anything simple!" Gurgling with laughter, he established his headquarters in rooms adjoining those of the Trans-Star Trading Company that Raf Lolln had vacated when he moved to Zarst. He plastered the walls with charts of the galaxy, and with his multiple, telescoping limbs began to draw circles on them and make calculations. As fast as his circles and calculations could be resolved into coordinates, he began to dispatch ships.

It was impossible to track a ship through its transmitting leaps, when it became a transmitter that transmitted itself through space; but between leaps, secret equipment that an electronics engineer had installed for Darzek would be loudly proclaiming the ransom ship's position in a signal that could be picked up across the light-years by ships properly positioned and equipped. If all went as planned, and if E-Wusk had time to get enough ships on the stations he had selected, the ransom ship's track across the galaxy would be as clear as that of a herd of elephants stampeding through tall grass.

Days passed. Darzek, having stalled as long as was reasonably possible, turned the ship over to Kernopplix, whose bulging multiple eyes gleamed satisfaction as he thanked him with a spidery embrace.

"You have been most helpful, Gul Darr. It is easy to understand how you achieved your great reputation as a trader. Your meticulous attention to details amazes me!"

Darzek murmured a polite thanks.

"And now," Kernopplix said, with an air of apology, "there remains only the matter of the . . . ah . . . occupants for the passenger compartments and the agreed solvency certificates."

"Neither of those are my responsibility," Darzek said, "for which I am thankful."

"That I understand perfectly," Kernopplix said, affecting sympathy. "Still, someone must be responsible."

"That someone should have the necessary arrangements completed and will be in touch with you shortly. At least, I presume so."

"Splendid! Does this mean, Gul Darr, that we will not meet again?"

"Of course not. I'll look in occasionally to see how things are going, and if you encounter any kind of obstruction, please inform me immediately, and I will investigate and add my feeble powers of persuasion to yours."

"Together," Kernopplix said delightedly, "I am confident that we could move worlds."

"If we only succeed in moving the government of this one, that is a memorable accomplishment."

He left Kernopplix seized by rumbling giggles and returned to Vezpro to see how Miss Schlupe was making out. He found her instructing her students in a new three-armed judo technique that she had invented. In an adjoining room of the barnlike structure, a group of young Vezpronian females was practicing knife play on stuffed dummies shaped in a variety of life forms, some unfamiliar to Darzek. All had their most vulnerable areas clearly marked.

Darzek felt inclined to feel sorry for the villain and his cohorts. He went off to report to Wolndur that Kernopplix would soon be demanding action on the ship's passenger component and the solvency, and that he was prepared to supply three hundred females that met the blackmailer's specifications. Hopefully, Kernopplix would not reject more than one out of three. The solvency was supposed to be the problem of the finance committee, and the certificates should be ready by now.

Wolndur assented woodenly. Forlan's special committee of scientists had turned its full attention to the eleventh planet, with no better results than those achieved in studying Nifron D. It was impossible to turn a rock heap into a sun; it had occurred. The thing all of them had dedicated themselves to prevent—the ransoming of their home world—also was occurring. He had the look of utter defeat.

He expressed the government's gratitude to Darzek for handling the recruitment of the females. That part of the villain's demands had been the most difficult for the government to face. If word had got out, young, patriotic females of good families would have insisted on volunteering, to the embarrassment of everyone. The females Miss Schlupe had recruited came from anything but good families and were happy to obtain jobs with good pay, whatever the risk. It solved a touchy problem, and the masfiln's delegates had passed a resolution thanking Darzek for helping them out of an impossible situation.

A member of the finance council, Wolndur said, was responsible for the solvency transaction. Darzek wanted no last-minute complications upsetting his plans, so he went off to talk with him. He was a pompous individual named Hur Rarrl, and he seemed determined to treat the matter as an ordinary business arrangement, even if the business was highly irregular.

"A billion billion solvency units is a considerable number," he observed. "I find the entire procedure exceedingly questionable. Is it you who are accountable?"

"Hardly," Darzek said. "I thought I was assisting in carrying out a decision the finance council had already made. Am I to understand that there's anything irregular about these approved expenditures, or about the arrangements for the solvency certificates?"

"No. Nothing irregular. The finance council approved all of it. But a billion billion solvency units is a considerable number and in my opinion rashly granted."

It dawned on Darzek that the council was much more subtle than he had realized. He knew that various manipulations had provided certificates of solvency whose ultimate value was zero, though it would take the villain a number of transfer clearances—any one of which might serve to identify him—and a considerable lapse of time to find that out. But the council had turned the handling of the transaction over to a member who obviously was a fool and therefore would be presumed honest. He thought it best not to ask more questions.

At the Trans-Star office, there was a message from Kernopplix complaining that his queries about the passengers and the solvency certificates were ignored. Darzek sent a return message, explaining that Kernopplix had been querying in the wrong places and he, Darzek, would take care of it. Kernopplix could expect his passengers on the morrow; the solvency certificates would be handed to him when the ship was ready to leave.

Then he went off to tell Miss Schlupe that if her students weren't trained yet, she had the rest of the day to finish up. His next stop was to see UrsNollf at the office assigned to the committee of scientists. UrsNollf was still studying the eleventh planet, and he gloomily reported no progress. At Zarst, Raf Lolln and the priests were trying to dissect an error from the plans for the experiment that failed. Raf Lolln was of the opinion that the entire project had been an error. Darzek resignedly returned to Vezpro and called on the masfiln. He told him the ship would have to be released to Kernopplix and sent as instructed, and their only recourse now was the hope that the plans for tracing it succeeded. Min Kallof agreed reluctantly and thanked Darzek for his efforts.

Early the next morning, Darzek visited the transfer station. Kernopplix had appropriated a suite of rooms, and Miss Schlupe's students filled all but one, where a Vezpronian doctor Kernopplix had engaged was examining them. Kernopplix greeted Darzek effusively. "My friend, all difficulties vanish at your touch. How I could have managed without you, I do not know. I am forever indebted to you!"

"Why?" Darzek asked innocently. "We've both profited. I'm at least as much indebted to you."

"I have been a party to many joint enterprises," Kernopplix said soberly. "Your generosity is as rare as your competence, and I'll remember both with pleasure—and repay you in kind if the occasion presents itself."

Darzek looked about him. "How are you proceeding?"

Kernopplix gestured at the waiting females. "The selection seems to be quite good. In fact, excellent. I've rejected only two thus far. I send them one at a time to the doctor, who certifies their health. Then I take them aboard."

"Immediately?" Darzek asked.

"But of course. I see that they are settled comfortably in their private compartments and want nothing. Then I leave them, disengaging the transmitter. I have been provided with special instructions for that. No one will be able to enter their compartments until the ship reaches its destination. The service transmitters of course remain connected."

"A wise arrangement," Darzek observed. "One never knows about these space crews."

"This crew will not be Vezpronian."

"That, too, is wise," Darzek agreed. Kernopplix's screening of the young females was considerably less strict than he had expected, which pleased him; but on the world of Bbran, perhaps all of Miss Schlupe's candidates would have been considered rare beauties. Kernopplix obviously was too busy to squander time in idle talk, and Darzek said as much and took his leave.

At the other side of the space station, he entered the small room where Miss Schlupe had established her headquarters. She was seated before a block of paired lights. The moment Kernopplix disengaged a compartment's transmitter, one of a pair of lights went out, and Miss Schlupe stepped through to the same compartment—for the electronics engineer had ingeniously devised a transmitter within a transmitter, and these supposedly isolated females would have the run of the ship any time they wanted it. Miss Schlupe delivered a kit that consisted of a knife, a blackjack of her own design, a chemical spray guaranteed to render any life form unconscious for several minutes to an hour, and a roll of cord for tying up victims. This equipment, added to Miss Schlupe's arduous training in unarmed combat, made each of the ship's passengers positively lethal.

There was nothing for Darzek to do, so he sat down and watched. When the 195th passenger had been taken aboard by Kernopplix, Darzek went back to the other side of the station. He watched while Kernopplix accepted his 200th passenger and escorted her aboard. When he returned, a special messenger was waiting for him. The messenger carried a thick package—the solvency certificates—and pushed a cart on which was a cube slightly larger than a meter square on each side.

Kernopplix took the package and checked the contents carefully. Then, his manner obviously jubilant, he signed a receipt and dropped the package into a slot in the cube. The slot sealed automatically. The messenger then handed over an envelope that contained the key words for opening the safe. Kernopplix signed another receipt and added his own seal to the envelope. With the messenger's help he pushed the cart through a transmitter to one of the cargo compartments. He left the cube there and disengaged that compartment's transmitter.

The ship's crew was ready; so was that of the chartered ship that was to accompany it. Kernopplix escorted both crews aboard their ships to give them their verbal and sealed instructions. Then he returned for one more spidery embrace and a sputtering gush of thanks before he took his final leave of Darzek and stepped through a transmitter to his compartment on the chartered ship.

Darzek went to the transfer station's restaurant, from which he could watch the two ships departing. They drifted away slowly, using their maneuver rockets. Finally they reached clearance distance. Moments later they made their first jump and vanished.

Darzek returned to the Trans-Star office. He found a message from Miss Schlupe waiting for him: "Come immediately." Darzek stepped through to her training center, and there, in the large building, seated disconsolately in circles, were three hundred young Vezpronian females, two hundred of whom Darzek had recently seen put aboard a spaceship now departed.

He said, in a voice that cracked with disbelief, "Are these—"

"They are," Miss Schlupe said bitterly. "Your pal Forlan and his assistants got the bright idea of putting an army aboard and protecting the purity of Vezpronian womanhood. So they had a special transmitter built into a closet in each compartment. After I got my bunch safely installed, they invaded all the compartments and told the females they were ordered back to Vezpro. So they went. There are now three males in each compartment—including the hundred compartments that weren't used. Nine hundred males in all. Of course they don't know about our special transmitters, they wouldn't know how to use the weapons we smuggled aboard even if they knew where they're hidden, and they haven't got any plan."

"Where'd they get the males?" Darzek asked.

"From—wouldn't you guess—the planet's staff of proctors. Not only has Vezpro failed to follow the blackmailer's instructions on every point, but this shenanigan isn't going to accomplish a thing."

15

Darzek headed for the government complex, intending either to remove the roof or place the entire government under some kind of interdiction that he would invent when he got there, but before he arrived he thought better of it. The damage was done. Miss Schlupe's female commandos might be needed for some other purpose, so there was no point in publicizing their training.

He quietly asked Forlan and Min Kallof why the substitution had been made, and they explained that they wanted the captives aboard the ship to be individuals capable of capturing the blackmailer and his cohorts.

"Besides," Min Kallof said emotionally, "we could not simply give away Vezpro's innocent females like so many animals. The honor of the world was at stake. Believe me, the proctors will cope with this schemer."

"Supposing he doesn't appear?" Darzek asked. "He may have the ship picked up by an agent, such as Kernopplix, who won't know his identity or anything else about him. It'll immediately be obvious that Vezpro did not meet his demands."

They had no answer, so Darzek left them. He could count on Vezpro's inept proctors to blunder their assignment no matter what happened. Now everything depended on E-Wusk.

The old trader was at work in the communications center he had set up next to the Trans-Star office. Darzek looked in on him and saw him huddled in the corner, his telescoping limbs twitching with concentration, while assistants hovered nearby, delivering messages and waiting for instructions. Darzek decided not to bother him.

He returned to his living quarters, where a still-furious Miss Schlupe was rocking at a pace that would have got her ticketed in any residential area on Earth.

But she spoke calmly. "I've been thinking. The whole proposition was a fraud. Why would this blackguard want two hundred females

and all that solvency? He was just asking for something he knew
Vezpro couldn't or wouldn't deliver."

"You may be right."

"I know I'm right."

"But he won't know Vezpro couldn't or wouldn't deliver until he
inspects the ship, or sends someone to do it, and if things work out
for E-Wusk, no one will approach the ship without being identified."

"It's still a long time until the new cycle," Miss Schlupe said.

"True. One might almost suspect that our villain expected shenan-
igans, and he'll be back shortly with more demands."

Miss Schlupe snorted. "That's his worry. What I meant was—
there's still plenty of time to figure this thing out and nail the person
responsible. You can keep that committee of scientists at work and
maybe add a member or two. You might accidentally get one with an
iota of imagination. I've been reading the reports, and I don't understand any of it except the word 'impossible,' which gets tiresome
after the first hundred times."

"Good point."

"And I'm still working on the missing scientists. Every new name
we turn up is checked with the Zarstans, and I have lists of those that
disappeared again after joining the Order and those that disappeared
without joining it. There's got to be some kind of connection."

"There's no argument that our mad scientist couldn't have done it
all himself, even if he supplied the know-how," Darzek agreed. "He
had to have expert help."

"And then there's Qwasrolk."

"There's always Qwasrolk," Darzek said wearily. "Nothing to do
there but keep looking for him and wave good-bye when we find
him."

"We've found him," she said.

"Dead?"

"No. Very much alive."

"Strange. According to the Skarnaf doctors, he should have died
long ago. How much of a glimpse of him did you get?"

"We didn't see him, but we found someone who did. And we
found out where he's been hanging out occasionally."

"Show me," Darzek said.

They were Naz Forlan's people—the aliens, the refugees from an
exploding sun, who had received grudging charity on this world of

Vezpro—and, according to Forlan's assistants, had been discriminated against and despised ever since they arrived.

Darzek had never seen a more relaxed, happier people.

Each farm was a model of order and meticulous upkeep. Farm buildings and dwellings were circular, their sides curving outward like doughnuts, with small, circular windows. The agricultural operations were automated to a point almost beyond Darzek's comprehension. One elderly farmer and his wife ran a farm that seemed to be the size of a U.S. county. The widely separated towns were supply centers and storage depots for agricultural products. Forlan had said a million refugees arrived here; Darzek wondered what had happened to them.

The old farmer was simply a more venerable edition of Forlan—dressed in less stylish, coarser clothing, skin darkening with age, bushy hair thinner, but as quietly polite and with the same air of culture about him. "Ah—the crazy one," he said, when Miss Schlupe had introduced Gul Darr and asked about Qwasrolk. "Farmer himself, I'd guess. I've seen him four, five times. Usually he stands on the hill yonder, watching the autocultivators. Probably never saw anything like that where he farmed."

"I've never seen anything like it either," Darzek confessed. "And Qwasrolk comes from a world where the holdings are small and animals pull the machines."

"Ah, that'd account for it. Loves the land, though. Maybe it reminds him of home."

"It might," Darzek agreed. "The place where he grew up was rolling land very much like yours."

"Thought so," the old farmer said with a shy smile. "A farmer knows. Some people love machines. Some love solvency. Some love land. Me, I love my land, and I recognize others who do, no matter how alien they are."

"What was he wearing?" Darzek asked.

The farmer fingered his own clothing. "Old stuff. Something thrown out. Not his. He's only two-armed, and I could see where he'd torn the other two arms from the clothing. Got in his way, I suppose." He paused. "Had a bad accident, hadn't he? Even at a distance I could see how disfigured he was. First couple times I tried to walk up to him, but he disappeared. Funny business, that. Know how he does it?"

"No. We'd certainly like to know."

"So would I. Good trick, but a funny business all around. Suppose he's shy about meeting people, being disfigured that way. Loves the land, though. Stands there and looks at it as though he'd like to get down and dig in it with his hands. Easy to see he was a farmer."

"He grew up to it," Darzek said. "Then he went to school—to the university—and became a scientist."

"Ah. Should have stayed a farmer. One that loves the land should farm it."

He invited them in, and his elderly wife served a cool drink made from the leaves of a native plant, and small, crunchy cakes. Darzek already had lost interest in this reappearance of the unfortunate Qwasrolk. That tortured soul might or might not be able to reveal something concerning his accident, but he certainly wouldn't as long as he permitted no one to approach him.

But this farmer, this cheerful, obviously prosperous and contented member of an allegedly oppressed minority, interested Darzek immensely. Darzek bluntly asked a question: Did the refugees from Hlaswann have any difficulties with the natives of Vezpro?

The old farmer chuckled, flexing his four arms. "Refugees? Been a long time since any of us was a refugee. When we first arrived, some resented us. Natural that way, you know. But the government made us welcome, and there were plenty of Vezpronians who gave us the hand of cousinhood, and sympathy, and even financial help. And no one resents us now. They're begging us to stay. We made Vezpro agriculturally independent, you see. We brought intensive farming to Vezpro. They knew nothing about it, but we were experts. Once they saw what we were about, they helped us in every way they could. We showed them what machinery we needed, and they designed it. No one in the galaxy is better with machines than the Vezpronians. Of course once it was perfected they made a very good thing of it, building it for export. It increased the productivity of our farms, and now we sit and watch the machines work until the land is needed for something else, and then we leave."

"Leave?" Darzek echoed.

The old farmer gestured an affirmative. "Got our own world again. Way over on the other side of the galaxy. Uninhabited. Synthesis government found it for us, and our young people've been going there for years. We old ones wait and watch the machines. It's hard to leave even an adopted world when we've been here so long. The Vezpronian government would like to have us stay, because we supply the world's food. Machines are great for doing work, but they don't know the land. They're worthless without a farmer to tell them what to do and when. We said, 'Give us your young people, and we'll make farmers of them,' but the young Vezpronians want to be scientists and engineers. So we watch our machines, and the cities and factories grow and come ever closer to us, and eventually they take our land."

"Take it?" Darzek echoed. "Surely they make some compensation."

The old farmer laughed. "Surely. Ten times what it's worth. The Vezpronians have been good to us. They gave us refuge, they let us buy farms on credit, they built us machines, and now they buy the land back at far more than it's worth. And they'd like to have us stay and open up marginal land for farming, with government assistance. Some think we should. A lot of us will die here, still watching our machines, still growing food for Vezpro, still waiting for the cities and factories to grow and take our land, because Vezpro has done so much for us. But most of us want our own world—a farming world. A world without stinking factories and growing cities. So we sell our land and go there. If it wasn't so far, we'd continue to sell food to Vezpro and buy its machines. No, we have no difficulty with the natives. We love them like cousins. We always have, and we always will. The debt we owe them is beyond payment."

"One of your number has done well in another way," Darzek said. "The Mas of Science and Technology. Naz Forlan. I know him well."

"Do you? Yes, he's done well. There are others like him who have gone into science and industry and done well. We're proud of them. But they would have been happier if they'd stayed farmers. That's our people's destiny—with the land."

They left the old farmer leaning on a stone fence watching his machines. Behind him, on a low hill, was the grove where Qwasrolk had paused several times in his tortured wanderings, his pilgrimage from nowhere to nowhere, to gaze at a land that looked hauntingly like that remote plot where he was born.

Why had Qwasrolk come here, when obviously he was homesick for another world? "He surely knows he hasn't long to live," Darzek said. "If he's that homesick for Skarnaf, why didn't he stay there to die? We not only don't know why he came here, but we still haven't a clue as to how he got here, have we? Has Gud Baxak found out anything?"

"No. There may be a simple explanation, if only we knew what it was. If there isn't, then he must have teleported. And if he can

teleport from Skarnaf to Vezpro, then he could—maybe—teleport
from Nifron D to Skarnaf."

"Improbable," Darzek said. "But suggestive."

"It might be perfectly clear if we had all the facts. To Qwasrolk,
whatever he's doing must seem perfectly logical."

"He has to be living somewhere and eating something when he
isn't admiring the landscape. If he could be cornered and questioned,
could he tell us anything?"

"Of course. He could tell us where he was when the accident happened, and what he was doing there, and for whom."

"If he remembers."

"There is that," Miss Schlupe agreed. "An atomic explosion at
close range might be memory-shattering. Perhaps hypnosis—"

"When you figure out a way to make a teleport hold still to be
hypnotized, let me know." Darzek turned to look back at the grove.
It actually was a tangle of stalklike vegetation on a rocky promi-
nence that probably was unsuitable for agriculture. "I want to see
that place," Darzek announced suddenly.

They returned to the old farmer. "Sure, have a look," he said.
"But if you're thinking the poor creature is hiding there, how would
he get in? He'd have to tromp a path, and I can tell you no one has
done that."

"I think he could find a way in without a path, though I'll have to
tromp one," Darzek said. "How does it happen that you left that hill
there? Couldn't it be leveled easily and converted to productive
land?"

"Easily," the old farmer agreed. "But there're still a few wild creatures about, and that tangled grove is home to them. Every living
creature is entitled to a home. So I leave it."

They parted with him and went on up the hill. The slope was not
steep, but exertion of any kind was so unnatural after life in a transmitterized society that Darzek was breathing heavily when he
reached the top. Miss Schlupe trudged spiritedly at his side; she always was in exceptional physical condition despite her age—if not
from demonstrating self-defense tactics to her commandos, just from
bustling about.

She said severely, "You should exercise more. Come and work out
with us."

"I should," Darzek agreed. "I spend too much time in conferences
and in trying to think. Excellent exercise, but not for the body."

They circled the grove. Obviously no one had forced his way into it from the outside. "Well," Darzek said finally, "I'll give it a try. But I think I can worm my way in there without leaving a trail, and I'd like to."

"The farmer said—"

"The farmer has four arms, which is two extra ones to get tangled in things. Handy for a wrestling match but inconvenient for squirming through small holes. Watch me."

He dropped to his knees and started crawling.

Fifteen minutes later, Miss Schlupe called anxiously, "Are you getting anywhere?"

"I'm moving," Darzek said. "Where, I couldn't say."

His clothing was wet with perspiration; his knees had acquired a layer of mud. The stalks, some as large as small tree trunks and just as unyielding, grew at every angle, and it was only by constantly casting about, backtracking, trying one way and then another, that he was able to find openings he could squeeze through. He wondered what sort of wild creatures made their homes in such a place.

Then, abruptly, he found it.

He broke through into an open space where the stalks had been cut recently. The stumps were still oozing a pungent, yellow sap. The cut stalks had been fashioned into a rough lean-to. Inside, piled at the back, were containers of foodstuffs, beverages, water. Nearby was a pile of bedding. The only incongruous items were a table and chair, placed at the front where the light was best. Darzek pondered the problem of teleporting furniture, but only for a moment. Something on the table caught his eye, and he stepped closer.

It was a large sheet of the metallic parchment used as paper on Vezpro. And on the paper—

Darzek bellowed for Miss Schlupe. Her answer, since it came from directly behind him, startled him.

"I followed you," she explained. She bent over the table. "What is it?"

"It looks like a distorted drawing of the device Forlan's scientific committee tested. That hodgepodge below it no doubt is the plan for the innards of the thing. Can you get back to Klinoz in a hurry and pick up some equipment to copy it?"

"Why don't you take it?"

"I'd rather Qwasrolk doesn't know it's been found. But just in case he returns and gets suspicious and decides to move, I'd better stay here."

"All right. If it has to be brought in here, it'll have to be some kind of small camera. I'll find something." She paused. "Do you really think that Qwasrolk—"

"We won't think anything at all about Qwasrolk until we find out what he's drawn."

"Right. I'll hurry."

She turned, dropped to her knees, and started out along the tortuous, wiggling path they'd followed in.

Darzek seated himself on the edge of the table, prepared for a long wait. Fortunately every farmer had his own transmitter, and Miss Schlupe had only to walk back to the dwelling and step through to the nearest village, where a public transmitter would take her to Klinoz. How long it would take to find suitable equipment was another matter. He hoped she could make it back before dark.

He waited. Finally the light in the little clearing began to grow dim. He regretted not thinking to tell her to get a camera with some kind of lighting arrangement.

Abruptly Qwasrolk stood beside him. Darzek's sudden awareness was not of a physical presence, but of odors: unwashed clothing, decaying flesh, almost—he thought afterward—the horribly sweet, penetrating stench of death. He reacted instinctively. He grabbed the hideously disfigured form and held on.

For an awful moment Qwasrolk struggled in his grasp, the skull-like face close to Darzek's. Then Darzek's hands were empty; Qwasrolk had vanished.

Darzek had slipped from the table to his feet at the first thrust of the struggle, and now he stood motionless with the revolting feeling of having touched a corpse. Shreds of decaying flesh still adhered to one hand. He did not move until he had made up his mind. Then he rolled up the metallic parchment, tucked it inside his clothing to protect it, and started the arduous crawl out of the grove. He was walking down the slope toward the farmhouse when Miss Schlupe appeared.

She hurried to meet him, carrying a tiny, cameralike object in the palm of her hand. He explained briefly what had happened. "I decided there was no point in leaving the plan there, since he probably won't return again," Darzek said.

"Won't he return for the plan?" she asked.

"What he's drawn and worked out once, he can do again. The question is, what is it?"

16

Darzek had a reproduction made of Qwasrolk's scribblings. Then he sent for UrsNollf, who was still studying the phenomenal transformation of the eleventh planet with Forlan's committee of scientists. Darzek handed the copy to him and asked, "Does this mean anything?"

He sat down to study it. An hour later he was still silently engrossed, and Darzek quietly left him and went to see E-Wusk, who was performing the impossible task of tracking a spaceship across the galaxy and enjoying it immensely.

"Still with it?" Darzek asked him.

E-Wusk's huge body shook with merriment. "Ho! Ho! Ho! Look what they did!"

He led Darzek over to a huge wall chart and showed him the tortuous convolutions the ransom ship and its companion had followed to throw off any pursuit. They had slipped from one crowded space lane to another, looped behind solar systems to mask their changes of direction, slipped off on tangential lanes and then doubled back; and finally, having made certain that no one and nothing could follow them, they had set course for the world of Dranga. They moored at a transfer station there, and one of E-Wusk's ships moored right beside them.

"That's quite a maneuver," Darzek observed, studying the zigzagging line.

"Ho! Ho! Every way they turned, I had a ship waiting for them."

"What are they doing at Dranga?"

"Nothing. Kernopplix disembarked there. The ships topped off their supplies and left immediately. I'm waiting for the report on their first jump."

"Good work," Darzek said. "No one but you could have done it."

"But of course not!" E-Wusk exclaimed, gurgling with merriment.

Darzek returned to UrsNollf. Miss Schlupe had arrived, and they both silently watched the astrophysicist until he finally looked up at them with what Darzek had come to recognize as a scowl creasing his queerly offset head.

"It isn't finished."

"We had to grab it when we could or risk losing it," Darzek said. "What is it the beginning of?"

"It's more than a beginning," UrsNollf said. "It's almost finished. Unfortunately, the final critical steps—"

"What is it that's almost finished?" Darzek demanded.

"The detailed drawing of a device for turning a planet into a sun. Where did you get it?"

"I think the less you know about that, the better. I want you to return to Primores at once and show this to Supreme. With that beginning, could Supreme complete those final critical steps?"

"Perhaps. Is there a direct ship to Primores leaving soon?"

"Ask Gud Baxak," Darzek said.

"Yes. Of course."

"And I remind you—what that document describes may be the most dangerous thing in the universe, apart from the person who invented it. No one is to know of its existence but the three of us—and Supreme. And when you show it to Supreme, make it clear that no one but yourself and the First Councilor is to have access to it. Once Supreme has it on record, destroy the document."

"But it's only a copy!"

"I'll assume responsibility for the original."

"The person who produced the original easily could make another."

"True. But if he does, he'll probably guard it carefully. We can't safeguard what we haven't got, but we can protect this, and we'd better."

"Very well." UrsNollf carefully rolled up the scrawled drawing and its row after row of scribbled numbers and symbols. "I'll say this. The person who produced this document is the person who transformed Nifron D and this system's eleventh planet into suns. I say that because no one else, not even the finest scientists I've worked with, has been able to produce such a thing." He thrust the rolled plan inside his clothing. "I leave that problem to you, Gul Darr. I'll ask Gud Baxak to arrange passage to Primores for me."

After he had gone, Miss Schlupe seated herself in her rocking chair, rocked for a moment, and then came to a full stop. "I don't believe it. Qwasrolk is too young, and too inexperienced, and too impoverished. He couldn't have done it."

"He certainly didn't do it by himself," Darzek said. "Assembling a gadget of that complexity would require an enormous amount of time for a large number of people. On the other hand, Qwasrolk must have been a member of the organization. He certainly saw the original plans, even if he didn't produce them himself. He may have been trying to draw them from memory."

"Why?"

Darzek shrugged. "One more point. While Qwasrolk may have been involved in the Nifron D transformation, he almost certainly had nothing to do with that of the eleventh planet. His physical and mental condition wouldn't have permitted it. And though he once was a member of the organization, he isn't now. Otherwise, why would he be living in that grove and working in the open? He'd have a comfortable lab to work in."

"So why was he drawing the plan?"

"That's one of the many questions I'd love to ask him."

The ransom ship and its companion crept across the galactic charts like arthritic ants. The Galactic Synthesis had no space navy —had no need for one—but E-Wusk had outfitted three survey ships with official Synthesis credentials and borrowed some proctors from Skarnaf to reinforce their crews, and these ships were following two jumps behind.

As the line that traced their progress crept across the galaxy, Darzek became increasingly frustrated and worried. The growing communications time lag meant that their charts became more out of date with each passing day. Finally decisive news arrived. The ransom ship had been placed in orbit around a world so barren that no one had bothered to name or even number it. It was the third of three worthless planets of a sun called Klonarl. The chartered ship assumed a nearby orbit. Then, abruptly, it left.

By prior arrangement, the three survey ships intercepted it three jumps away and boarded it. A careful search turned up only the two crews—the chartered ship's and the crew that had brought the ransom ship from Vezpro. The ransom ship's crew, following the sealed orders Kernopplix had supplied, had placed the ship in orbit around the Klonarl planet and transmitted to the chartered ship. The crew members knew nothing at all about what the ransom ship contained or why they had been ordered to abandon it—or so they said.

The survey ships took both crews into custody in the name of Supreme and secured the chartered ship. Then, with other ships that

E-Wusk was rushing to the scene, they moved into positions that would convert the Klonarl system into a foolproof trap, ready to snap shut the moment the villain attempted to collect his ransom.

Darzek and E-Wusk sat back contentedly and waited. If the villain appeared, there was no possible way he could escape.

Days went by; they continued to wait. A villain as crafty as this one could be expected to exercise caution. Five ships passed closely enough to the orbiting blackmail ship to detect its presence—heavy traffic on a seldom-used shipping lane—but they were allowed to proceed unmolested. Just in case the villain, or his agent, was making a safety check, the trap remained invisible.

When thirty days had passed, Darzek stopped relaxing and began to worry. The crewless ship continued to orbit a dead world; no other ship went near it.

"Perhaps he knows that his instructions weren't followed," E-Wusk suggested.

"How could he, without boarding the ship and looking?" Darzek demanded. "Maybe the whole thing is a hoax, and he's sitting somewhere nearby watching our ships and laughing hilariously. I'd like to get this thing settled before we all die of old age."

E-Wusk gestured resignedly with a cluster of limbs. "It's a mystery. As you say, he can't know that his instructions weren't followed if he doesn't approach the ship."

"Who says so?" asked Miss Schlupe, who had just come in.

They both gazed at her blankly.

"I know at least one person who could find out easily."

"Who?" Darzek asked.

"Qwasrolk. He could teleport himself aboard, and your precious trap would never know he was there."

Darzek said thoughtfully, "In that case, he knew before the ship left. He could enter any government building and eavesdrop on any conference. He could have checked the ship before it left the transfer station. Long before it was outfitted, he could have known all about your female commandos and also the plan to substitute males and use phony solvency certificates." He turned to E-Wusk. "Shall we call this farce off?"

"I think," E-Wusk said meditatively, "that we could arrange a termination without ourselves or the world of Vezpro seeming to be involved."

E-Wusk sent an official message to Primores. The Galactic Survey investigated his report of a ship left in orbit around an uninhabited planet, found that its crew had abandoned it, and exercised the authority of the Galactic Synthesis. It supplied a crew to take it to the nearest port, where salvage claims were advertised. Darzek posted one for the world of Vezpro, got it officially sanctioned, and sent a crew to bring the ship back.

E-Wusk heaved a sigh of relief when the last step had been taken. He cleaned out his office and took down his charts. "My business is waiting," he said. "May I go home now?"

"Better stick around for a while," Darzek said. "I have a hunch that our work hasn't even started."

Kernopplix arrived at the Trans-Star office to ask if he might call on Gul Darr. It was like the spidery trader to save the fee of a messenger by running his own errands, but his presence on Vezpro shocked Darzek. Kernopplix was no more than a mercenary stooge, and he certainly would not have spent the solvency to return had he not been ordered back.

Darzek met him, invited him into his living quarters, found a hassock that would accommodate his multiple legs, and offered refreshment—a most unusual gesture on Vezpro—which Kernopplix declined in a startled manner.

"I had the impression that your work was finished," Darzek said.

"My instructions were to wait at—at my stopping place—in case there was a final message to be delivered."

"Ah! And there was such a message?"

"Yes. I brought it by the most direct ship. And since you have been my contact with the Vezpronian government, I thought I should deliver it to you. I trust that you will promptly relay it to its destination."

"The honor is mine," Darzek murmured.

Kernopplix heaved a sigh. "Excellent. Now I can go home."

He handed over the message. It was in the same form, and on the same material, as the previous messages. It bore the same seal. The address—to the government of Vezpro—was indited in the same way. It certainly looked authentic.

"Thank you," Darzek said. "I'll see that it is relayed at once."

"My thanks to you," Kernopplix said. His spidery legs found anchorage and heaved his heavy, bulging body upward.

"One question," Darzek said. "Have you received your bonus yet?"

"I trust that it will be waiting for me on Bbran. That was the agreement."

Darzek wished him a pleasant journey and a joyous arrival, and Kernopplix thanked him, delivered a farewell speech about the pleasure of their brief association, and scurried away.

As soon as he had gone, Darzek broke the seal and opened the message.

It wasted no words. It stated bluntly that the breach of faith on the part of the world of Vezpro had been total, with nine hundred males furnished instead of two hundred females, and worthless certificates of solvency tendered. Therefore, on the first day of the new cycle the world would be turned into a sun.

Darzek pursed his lips and whistled silently for a moment. Then he went directly to Naz Forlan's office.

Before the Mas of Science and Technology had a chance to greet him, Darzek handed over the message. Forlan read it carefully, read it again, and then looked up at Darzek.

"Rather final, isn't it?" Darzek remarked lightly. "No second chances. No opportunity to mend our ways."

"What do you suggest?" Forlan asked.

"I don't know. It just arrived. I intend to do some thinking, and I recommend the same course to everyone concerned."

"Is that the most the special emissary of Supreme can offer us?" Forlan asked, a touch of bitterness in his voice.

"It wasn't the special emissary of Supreme who substituted males for females. And it wasn't the special emissary of Supreme who sent phony solvency certificates."

Forlan said despondently, "Now I suppose our only hope lies in the committee of scientists, and the committee already has admitted failure. Have you no suggestions at all?"

"I have an observation. Now that we are no longer distracted by ransom demands, perhaps we can give our whole attention to the main problem—with far better effect."

Darzek left the mas pondering the letter; and he wondered whether Forlan or Min Kallof had the subtlety to grasp what the main problem was. Either Miss Schlupe was right, and Qwasrolk the teleport was the villain—or the villain himself was so highly placed and so deeply in their councils that he knew everything they were doing. A more formidable opponent could not be imagined, and his existence meant that no one on Vezpro could be trusted.

At the Trans-Star office, Darzek went immediately to see E-Wusk.

"I told you we might have more work to do," he said. "Now you can get started."

E-Wusk gestured perplexedly with a multitude of telescoping limbs. "But what is there to do?"

"Plenty," Darzek said. "You can begin making plans to evacuate five billion people."

17

Once again they sat in a transfer station restaurant, looking down on the world of Vezpro. Miss Schlupe remarked, "Well, we know for certain that we have a teleport to deal with. What if he's in cahoots with a telepath?"

"However it was done, he knew more about what we were doing than we did," Darzek said. "Obviously he had no intention of trying to collect the ransom. I have the feeling of being played with. Cat and mouse, and I'm not accustomed to being the mouse. In fact, I resent it."

"Do you know what the masfiln is going to say?"

"The truth, the whole truth, and nothing but the truth."

Min Kallof was scheduled to address the Vezpro World Assembly, which was called the Dezmas, and the speech was being viewed around the world. Darzek and Miss Schlupe had elected to hear it in more comfortable surroundings than those furnished with seats designed for three-legged life forms.

"Won't that cost him his job?" Miss Schlupe asked.

"Forlan thinks not. He believes the Vezpronian people will feel that the masfiln did the right thing in trying to trick the blackmailer. The problem will be to convince them that the threat is real."

"How much convincing do they need? The eleventh planet is getting spectacularly visible."

"The government is worried that the people will think it can't happen here. Things will be difficult enough if they cooperate completely. E-Wusk's latest calculations indicate that the evacuation of five billion of anything would take a noticeable percentage of the galaxy's spaceships. It all depends on how far we transport them, of course, and how many round trips one ship can make. But we also have to think about things like food and shelter and beds and other necessities after they arrive. Few worlds would be able to cope with millions of refugees, no matter how hospitable they may feel. This is a job no one but E-Wusk could handle. He's already got every available factory constructing a kind of prefab dormitory passenger compartment that comes in sections and can be assembled in the ship. It'll instantly turn freighters of any size into passenger ships with maximum capacity for short hauls."

"I gather that the idea is to get everyone to safety and then worry about finding permanent homes for them," Miss Schlupe said.

"If they're needed. We can always hope that the villain's gadget will go *ffft* this time, the way ours did."

"But you couldn't bring everyone back just because he failed once," Miss Schlupe protested. "He could always try again—without announcing the date."

"Right. We've got to figure out a way to stop him, or we've got to catch him, or both. In the meantime, we'll have to play it safe and evacuate the planet. Both Kallof and Forlan agree. Here he is."

The masfiln's address to the Dezmas and the world, an unprecedented event, had been well publicized. The other diners instantly fell silent, and all watched the screen intently.

Min Kallof possessed the simple dignity of sincerity and absolute integrity. He seemed, on the rostrum before the Dezmas, to be taller than he actually was, and he used his three arms to good effect as he spoke.

And he told the truth, the whole truth, and nothing but the truth as he related the history of the ransom notes, the attempts to learn the scientific secret of turning worlds into suns, the misfiring trickery of the ransom ship, and finally the pronouncement of doom.

"An emissary of Supreme is present on this world to advise us," Kallof said. "His advice is that we evacuate the world of Vezpro before the new cycle. He already is making arrangements. Your government intends to follow his advice."

The masfiln concluded quietly, thanking his colleagues for their assistance and expressing confidence that the citizens of Vezpro would meet the emergency with calm and cooperation.

He turned and seated himself in the long row of delegates—the mases who constituted his cabinet.

But the picture did not fade. Naz Forlan got to his feet, a grotesque dwarf beside the native Vezpronians. "As Mas of Science and Technology," he announced, "it was my duty to discover the source and the scientific basis for this plot against our world. I did my best, as all those who worked with me will testify, but I failed. Therefore I consider it my duty to resign, and I shall hand my formal resignation to the masfiln before we leave this room. Between now and the new year I shall dedicate myself entirely to the attempt to save Vezpro. I will not surrender what I consider my native world without a fight, and I will not leave it until the last fraction of the final moment. And when I leave, I will be the last to go."

He resumed his seat among the mases. On Earth, Darzek thought, he would have received a tumult of applause; but silence was the measure of approval on Vezpro, and the Dezmas was totally silent.

"Nice touch," Darzek said to Miss Schlupe.

"I thought it was a bit hammy," she said. "If there were anything he could do, he already would have done it."

"Perhaps he has."

"What do you mean by that?"

"There's a certain theory that this whole business is a plot against Forlan—to drive him out of office. If so, it's succeeded. If his resignation accomplishes nothing else, at least we'll find out whether there's anything to the theory."

On their return to Klinoz, Darzek went immediately to Forlan's old Department of Science and Technology. The place was funereal. Eld Wolndur and Melris Angoz were talking quietly with a host of young scientists and technicians in the office where they were supposed to be performing supersecret work for Darzek.

Darzek watched the scene for a moment, icily, before inquiring as to whether he might have his employees' private attention for a few moments. The others quickly departed.

"How long has this been going on?" Darzek demanded.

"What going on?" they asked innocently.

"Your entertaining the whole department here and discussing your work with every passerby."

"But those are all loyal employees—"

"Loyal to whom?" Darzek demanded.

They made no response, and he said nothing further to them. He returned to the Trans-Star office and had a brief conference with Gud Baxak. Later that day he went to the masfiln's office for an equally brief conference, with the result that his two assistants found their office closed and themselves instructed to move their activities at once to isolated quarters Gud Baxak found for Darzek on the outskirts of the city. Miss Schlupe's female commandos already were guarding the place when they arrived and would continue to do so, in shifts, throughout Vezpro's twenty-six hour day. Getting a computer console installed for Melris, and tied in with the world's master computer, was a considerable problem, but when an emissary of Supreme asked, and the world's masfiln said yes, speed in the most complicated operation came as a matter of course. By midafternoon the new quarters were functional, and Melris and Wolndur, now each with a private office, were gloomily contemplating their new surroundings.

Darzek summoned them to an office he had reserved for himself and spoke with a firmness that left no doubt that he meant what he said. "If I find out that either of you has discussed the work done here with any unauthorized person, I not only will dismiss you at once, but I'll see that you're evacuated from Vezpro on the next refugee ship. It'll be a far milder fate than you deserve."

Wolndur said, "Surely you don't think—"

"I think I'm coming to my senses much too late about this. When your adversary knows everything that you've been doing, it's time for drastic measures. From this moment, we trust nobody."

"But who will direct us?" Melris blurted. "In our old location, Naz Forlan—"

"He's resigned," Darzek said. "If he calls here he won't get past the reception room. The same applies to the masfiln, or any other government official, past or present. Either security is complete or it's worthless. As for directing you, I'll do that, and I direct you to go to your offices and start using your imaginations. They've been rather dormant lately."

"But surely you don't suspect the mas!" Wolndur exclaimed.

"Ex-mas. I suspect everyone, including myself."

He chased them back to their offices, gave an equally stern lecture to Miss Schlupe's commandos, and then returned to his own office, seated himself, and reflected that his own imagination also had been rather dormant lately, if not actually comatose.

In a safe in his sleeping quarters, Darzek had concealed Qwasrolk's demented scribbles. UrsNollf had taken a copy to Primores; by this time Supreme was digesting it, but Darzek was not hopeful that even a world-sized computer could tell them anything of value about it. Profound scientific knowledge combined with the highest form of creative imagination was needed, and Darzek had long been frustrated by Supreme's lack of creativity.

And if this, the Supreme Court of computers, could not render a verdict, where then could he turn? Forlan would be working with his committee of scientists, and the villain, whether or not he was one of them, would know everything they were doing. Raf Lolln, Darzek thought, was more a skeptic and a critic than a creator. Wolndur was years away from scientific maturity.

"It's almost enough to make a man wish he'd studied physics," Darzek muttered.

Finally he went to see what his assistants were doing. Wolndur was staring into space with a Vezpronian version of a pout. On his large workscreen he had placed a formula. It looked vaguely familiar to Darzek; but after having seen so many, every formula looked vaguely familiar to him. Wolndur looked at Darzek, frowned, looked away. Darzek left him.

From Melris's room came a concert of music—of an entire orchestra of computer consoles in vigorous operation, each with its own distinct pitch. The sounds stopped as Darzek entered the room, and he found Melris studying a seemingly unending strip of computer readout.

She looked up excitedly. "I had an idea. I got a list of the materials that the scientists said would be necessary to convert a world into a sun, and I've been tracing the movement of all of them, in this entire sector, looking for unusual amounts or shipments to unusual places."

"Excellent idea," Darzek said. "Found anything interesting?"

"Yes. I've found that large quantities have disappeared without a trace. And I think I know where some of them disappeared from."

Darzek pulled up a chair and seated himself. "Where?"

"Wait."

The keyboards hummed again, and the strip of readout began to pile up on the floor. Melris picked it up and began to transcribe the embossed hieroglyphics. She scribbled frantically—names of fabrication plants, addresses, dates, statistics. When she finished, she had listed more than fifty business concerns.

"That may be only a beginning," she said. "The quantities are quite small for each one. What shall we do with it? Perhaps the chief proctor—"

"Definitely not the chief proctor," Darzek said firmly. "I'll handle this myself." He took her notes. "If this is only a beginning, keep working on it. And congratulations. But don't forget what I said. This isn't to be mentioned to anyone."

He went first to the Trans-Star office, where he and Miss Schlupe studied the names of the firms and debated what should be done. Miss Schlupe wanted to have shipments watched and her investigators become acquainted with the firms' employees and see what they could learn.

Darzek shook his head. "When something is spread out over fifty firms—and we don't know how many more—someone is ingeniously covering his tracks. I'm going to call on one of these places myself. I haven't done much detecting lately. I'll see what I can find out, and then we'll decide what to do about the others."

It was one of the world's lesser urban centers, but, like the capital city of Klinoz, it had the appearance of a single sprawling building with an occasional domed park surrounded by windowless spires. The factory was in the segment devoted to light industry. It was fully automated, and Darzek entered and wandered about unhindered, wondering what kind of strange apparatus the outpouring of diffraction discs and curlicued parts was destined for. Finally he found a maintenance worker poking his three arms into a stalled machine. The worker directed Darzek to an office, which he reached by way of a repair shop where other maintenance workers were dissecting machines similar to those Darzek had seen on the assembly and fabrication lines.

The factory was so small that a single manager, perhaps its owner, ran it. Darzek introduced himself: Gul Darr, trader, of the Trans-Star Trading Company.

The elderly Vezpronian turned at his desk and regarded Darzek speculatively. A trader might be either a salesman or a potential customer.

"I'd like to talk with your procurement officer," Darzek told him.

The manager scowled and hunched his three arms. "I do my own procuring," he said.

"In that case—I have a small problem of solvency transfer to clear. No doubt there's a simple explanation. Perhaps you credited the wrong account. Eleven terms ago you received a proweight of plutonium pellets. The solvency involved amounted to—"

Staring, the manager blurted, "Plutonium pellets? What would this factory be doing with plutonium pellets? It manufactures dlarwux!"

Darzek spoke slowly, passing over the fact that he had no idea what dlarwux might be. "Are you saying that you did *not* receive a proweight of plutonium pellets eleven terms ago?"

"Not then or ever. Even if I had a use for them, I couldn't bring them here. Radioactive materials can only be used in Zone Twenty."

"I see," Darzek mused. "That would of course explain the solvency mixup. Just so I can make my report complete, would you mind showing me your materials log for that term?"

The manager minded, but he was being polite to a stranger; also, a dispute over a solvency transfer could be a nuisance. He turned to his records file, punched the relevant dates, and one after another the invoices of materials received appeared on the screen above his desk.

"Thank you," Darzek said finally. There was no question of deceit here; the computer automatically registered materials received, or the transmitter would not send the materials; and tampering with records of this type so as to leave no trace would have required skill of an order unknown to Darzek. He doubted that it was possible.

Then he had another thought. "Do you have a warehouse?"

The manager already had turned back to his work. "In Zone Seventeen," he answered indifferently. He had humored this stranger long enough.

"Can radioactive materials be stored in Zone Seventeen?"

"If they're properly shielded," the manager said. "However, why would I be ordering radioactive materials if I can't use them?"

"I'd like to inspect your warehouse and its materials log."

"Sorry. I can't take the time today."

Darzek displayed his credentials. He was prepared to threaten the manager with the chief proctor or the masfiln himself; but the manager had heard the masfiln's speech and knew that an emissary of Supreme was on Vezpro, and he knew that his world was threatened. It dawned on him abruptly that this was no piddling matter of a solvency transfer. Without a word he got to his feet, led the way to a private transmitter in the far corner of the office, and stepped through. Darzek followed.

On any world in the galaxy it would have been, unmistakably, a warehouse. Bars and sheets of metal, rolls of plasticlike materials, containers of all kinds and sizes—these were the reserve raw materials used to manufacture what the manager had called dlarwux, and they were piled in neat rows and arranged for easy access.

There was one difference. A far corner was partitioned off with crates and obviously served as an office. It contained the records file, a couple of the strangely shaped Vezpronian chairs, and a table that might have served as a desk.

On one of the chairs, Qwasrolk was seated.

He seemed to be asleep. Darzek paused, his mind groping desperately for a method of approach; but before he could so much as whisper a warning to the manager or extend a restraining hand, the manager charged forward in a rage, shouting. Qwasrolk turned his lidless eyes and horribly scarred face in their direction. For a moment he regarded the menacing manager, his lipless mouth barring his teeth, his noseless, revolting face fully exposed under bars of light that fell from an air vent. Then he vanished.

The manager halted, staring at the empty chair. "Where did he go? And how did he get in here?"

"Never mind," Darzek said. "Let's have a look at that materials log."

The manager again punched the relevant dates on the records file, which began to flash invoices of materials received during the term. Suddenly the screen went blank. A moment later another invoice appeared, and another, and then the screen went blank again.

The manager perplexedly punched the dates again and started the series over. And again the blanks appeared. The manager backed up to the chair recently vacated by Qwasrolk and sat down.

He said, protestingly, "Nothing is missing. We take regular inventories and take them carefully."

"I'm sure you do," Darzek said.

"Why would anyone go to the trouble of erasing my records?"

"Because," Darzek said, "they would have shown the delivery of materials you didn't order and that never appeared on any of your inventories."

Darzek returned to tell Miss Schlupe what had happened. They agreed that the results would probably be the same at all of the factories, but a check would have to be made, so she took Melris's list and went off to put her investigators to work. Darzek rocked in her rocking chair and tried to figure out what Qwasrolk had been doing in the warehouse.

Then Gud Baxak entered with a message from UrsNollf. Supreme had been unable to supply the final, critical steps in Qwasrolk's calculations. It had, instead, found three serious errors in the work already completed—errors that made further steps in the calculations impossible.

18

The Prime Number of the Zarstans called on Darzek—an unprecedented event, since that august and austere individual by tradition never left Zarst.

The Zarstans were highly disturbed. The threat to Vezpro could not endanger their world. At long intervals, when the worlds were in conjunction, the surface of Zarst facing the new sun might get uncomfortably warm; but at present its temperature was frigid, and neither heat nor cold could affect them in their deep tunnels. What worried them, and brought the Prime Number to see Darzek, was the economic threat. Vezpro's industry provided them with most of their business. Vital supplies—food, manufactured goods, even air and water—could be obtained on Vezpro and transmitted inexpensively to Zarst. Without Vezpro, Zarst would face a drastic loss of income and an enormous increase in expenses. The Order would have to move. It insisted on owning its own world, and it almost certainly would be unable to obtain one as conveniently located as Zarst.

"We must prevent this," the Prime Number said solemnly. "The entire talent of my Order will be dedicated to that."

Darzek's first impulse was to refer him to Naz Forlan. Then he remembered that Forlan's group of scientists was suspect—and so, probably, were the Zarstans and Raf Lolln—but one group had to be innocent. If he kept their activities separated, the innocent one might accomplish something.

He excused himself, went to his safe, and got the plan that Qwasrolk had been working on. He presented it to the Prime Number, along with Supreme's analysis and description of the three fatal errors, and explained the plan's origin, though he was cautious enough not to name Qwasrolk.

The Prime Number said slowly, "Then you believe that the person who made this was trying to reproduce the actual plan from memory?"

"Trying, and coming close," Darzek said. "Probably the calculations weren't carried to a conclusion because the errors were making the thing come out wrong."

"I see. You'd like us to correct the errors and then carry the calculations to a correct conclusion. And then what?"

"I don't know," Darzek said frankly. "This thing could be horribly dangerous in the hands of the wrong person. I don't want every scientist in the galaxy knowing about it. In fact, I'd prefer that no one knows. What we need is a means of stopping such a device, not the knowledge to build one. The question is whether we can devise a defense against it without first finding out how it works."

"I understand," the Prime Number said. "I shall set up a special group within the order, and no one but its members will know about its work—not even me. It will report directly to you. If it first has to find out how the device works, few will know, and those few will be older scientists whose loyalty to the Order is beyond question and who can be relied upon to consider this the Order's ultimate secret. Is that satisfactory?"

"Perfectly," Darzek said.

"Should Raf Lolln be included in the group?"

"If your scientists think he would be of value—and if he will agree not to leave Zarst before the new year."

The Prime Number smiled. "You have a rare wisdom, Gul Darr. It's unfortunate that you did not study science. The Order could have used you."

"Perhaps you'd change your mind when you got to know me better," Darzek murmured.

Darzek's next visitor was Eld Wolndur. The young scientist clearly was unhappy. "I can't think of anything to do," he confessed. "I was wondering—the mas, the former mas, has established a research center, and he probably could find employment for me."

"What is he researching?" Darzek asked.

"Many things. He has taken over an unused factory complex, and there will be a large staff of scientists. Some are already at work. Others will start as quickly as equipment is available. One project I saw is working on the assumption that a device that turns a world into a sun must have a trigger of some kind and probably a timing control as well. It will explore the possibility of putting artificial satellites in orbit that would keep the entire surface of the world bathed with waves to inhibit the device's operation—stop the timing control or prevent the trigger from functioning."

"What if the device is underground?" Darzek asked. "Would the waves still reach it?"

"I don't know. There are many problems. Not knowing the type of metal used is the one they were most worried about. By the way, the mas—the ex-mas—invites you to visit and observe any time you like."

"That's kind of him," Darzek said. "I trust that you didn't discuss our work with him."

"Of course not!"

"Good. At present, I think you're likely to make a more valuable contribution working with me."

"What is there for me to do?" Wolndur demanded.

Miss Schlupe had come in and stopped to listen to them. "I have a job for him," she said.

"What is it?" Wolndur asked.

"Find Qwasrolk." Before he could protest, she went on, "I have investigators looking for him, but he was a scientist, and you're a scientist, and you should be able to help. Why was he out in the country drawing a plan? What was he doing in that warehouse? Where is he likely to turn up next? We need someone who can think the way he does."

Wolndur looked at her doubtfully.

"I'll tell you this," Miss Schlupe said. "Nothing you could do for Forlan would be a tenth as important. We've simply got to find Qwasrolk."

"Well . . ." Wolndur was resigned but still doubtful. "If you think I can help, I'll try."

He left them, still looking unhappy.

"If you really think he'll be useful, fine," Darzek said. "But it isn't another scientist you need, it's another teleport."

"Look," Miss Schlupe said. "We've got to find him. Right?"

"We've certainly got to try."

"Who in the Galactic Synthesis is more expert in tracking down people than us?"

"Probably no one. But on a world like this one, where the transmitter is virtually universal, I doubt that anyone could be an expert. When you complicate the situation with a teleport, expertise isn't enough. An idiot with a rabbit's foot would probably do better."

"Have you considered how amazing it is that Qwasrolk's still alive?" Miss Schlupe asked.

"Amazing isn't the word for it, considering the massive dose of radiation he suffered, but I haven't figured out a way to use that to find him. He doesn't glow in the dark, and if a Geiger counter would detect his presence, you'd have to get into his presence to use it."

"That isn't what I meant. Hasn't it occurred to you that we aren't the only ones looking for him? And that may be why he vanishes the moment anyone sees him?"

"Why would anyone else be looking for him?" Darzek asked.

"Because Qwasrolk, if his radiation burns have anything to do with Nifron D or the experiments that led up to it, is the only person we know who can provide us with a link to the villain. He may even know who he is. Surely the villain is aware of that. So we're trying to find Qwasrolk to probe his seared memory, but the villain will be trying to find him to kill him. I'll be surprised if he hasn't done it already, because he certainly knows more about Qwasrolk than we do. With the right kind of weapon, he'll only need a glimpse of him."

"You're right, as usual," Darzek said. "But there's one thing in our favor. If the villain is looking for Qwasrolk at the same time we're looking for him, somewhere along the way we might accidentally meet. I'd enjoy that."

E-Wusk came waddling in, and for once he did not look his jovial self. "The first refugees are leaving," he said.

"Congratulations," Darzek told him. "That was fast work. I was afraid you'd have trouble getting things moving."

"This is none of my doing," E-Wusk said. "These refugees made their own arrangements. The transfer station manager says there's trouble."

"What sort of trouble?" Darzek asked.

E-Wusk delivered himself of a massive, multilimbed shrug. "I don't know. I thought you'd like to see what's happening."

"I think I'd better," Darzek agreed. He summoned Miss Schlupe, and the two of them went together.

The transfer station was crowded, and the crowd was an unruly, shouting mob. It subsided somewhat as Darzek and Miss Schlupe entered; they looked about bewilderedly and then turned toward the restaurant. A moment later a group of Naz Forlan's people, the refugees from the incinerated world of Hlaswann, entered and started across the room toward the embarkation transmitters. The uproar became deafening. The Vezpronians spat, threw objects, snatched at the personal belongings and luggage the Hlaswannians carried, aimed three-armed blows at them. The Hlaswannians finally fought their way through the room and disappeared into an embarkation transmitter.

Miss Schlupe nudged Darzek and pointed. The Vezpronian chief proctor was looking on approvingly. "I'll handle the mob," she shouted above the din. "Will you handle him?"

Darzek nodded. She pushed toward the exit transmitters, and he moved toward the chief proctor. When he got close enough to make himself heard, he announced icily, "You are suspended for gross neglect of duty. Report to the masfiln immediately."

The chief proctor turned, stared bewilderedly at Darzek, and would have protested had Darzek not pointed a stern finger toward the exits. He began to struggle through the crowd. Mercifully, no more Hlaswannians appeared before Miss Schlupe returned with a company of her commandos. All of them were armed with long staves, and it took them less than five minutes to clear the station.

"I was afraid something like this might happen," Miss Schlupe told Darzek, as they watched the last of the unruly populace being expertly herded into transmitters. "So I gave them a course in riot control."

"Good thing," Darzek agreed.

When the next Hlaswannians appeared, they walked peacefully to the embarkation transmitters through a double row of Miss Schlupe's commandos, and other commandos were checking all arrivals to make certain that their business was legitimate.

"Maybe you'd better train more commandos," Darzek told Miss Schlupe. "I have a feeling this is only the beginning."

He left her in charge of the transfer station and returned to the Trans-Star office, and there he found Min Kallof waiting for him, along with several of his mases.

"Have your seen your chief proctor?" Darzek asked him.

"No—"

"I just suspended him. I want him to receive the most severe penalty your law permits." Darzek described the scene at the transfer station.

Min Kallof heaved a long sigh; his head had acquired a multitude of new wrinkles since Darzek had last seen him. The mases were silent. Kallof strode to the viewing screen, activated it, dialed a number.

They looked down on a park filled with a different sort of screaming mob. One middle-aged Vezpronian was speaking; the screams came after every statement he made.

"Politician?" Darzek asked.

Min Kallof gestured an affirmative.

Darzek studied the crowd. The Vezpronians had spent a lifetime free from threats of war, or crime, or economic crisis, or civil disorder. Now, suddenly, everything they'd ever known or owned, along with their very existence, was threatened. They were both frightened and angry.

Min Kallof described an opposition revolt that had occurred in the Dezmas that morning. He had handled it, but now the opposing politicians were taking their case to the people. They were claiming that the threat to Vezpro was a hoax invented by the government to keep itself in power. He needed more information about the evacuation plans in order to reassure the people. Where would they be taken? And if the threat did prove to be a hoax, were there plans to return them safely and quickly? What about the solvency to pay for transportation, housing, and food for five billion refugees? And what about valuable possessions, family pets, records, historical treasures . . .

Darzek took the group next door to E-Wusk's headquarters, and the old trader, who had the talent to reduce every crisis to a matter of logistics, greeted them jovially with a multitude of waving, telescoping limbs, got all of them seated comfortably, and began an outpouring of statistics. Living quarters and supplies already were prepared for the first loads of evacuees. At each refugee encampment, materials were being stockpiled to expand it. The moment the first group arrived, its members would be put to work building quarters for the next group and storage facilities for more supplies. Skilled technicians would be assigned to each site to teach and assist. Medical facilities would be provided. Community kitchens would prepare food. Eventually the world of Skarnaf would take five million refugees; the world of Rulloz, two million; the world of Vormf, a million—he read down a long list. Solvency had been made available for all of this, as well as the transportation, by the Galactic Synthesis. The citizens who cooperated and left early would be permitted to take more personal property with them than those who left later. And, the moment scientists declared Vezpro safe, those who left early would be the first ones to return.

"But," E-Wusk declared solemnly, "if the evacuation is not started immediately, there are not enough spaceships in the galaxy to complete it in time."

He produced charts; the masfiln and his mases began to study them, and Darzek quietly withdrew. E-Wusk's management of an operation such as this one was incomparable, but neither he nor Darzek would be able to convince a rioting population that the evacuation was necessary. Darzek wondered if the politicians would be able to. He switched the viewer from one park to another, and in each one the scene was the same. Min Kallof would have to reassure his citizens in a hurry.

Melris Angoz arrived with an addition to the list of firms from which nuclear materials seemed to have disappeared. While Darzek was studying it, Miss Schlupe returned.

She looked careworn and extremely tired. He remembered, with a wrench of conscience, that she was more than seventy years old, and she had been carrying a physical burden that exceeded his.

"You need to take a day off," he announced.

She halted abruptly. "What catastrophe has struck now?"

"There are protest mobs in all the parks. Min Kallof and his delegates are with E-Wusk, getting data on the evacuation so they can quiet things. There's nothing either of us can do about it. Why don't you take a nap, or go shopping, or something?"

"I'm going to visit a mushroom farm," she said. "I need to make my mind a complete blank, and I can't think of a better way to do it than by watching mushrooms grow."

"Mushroom *farm?* Where is it?"

"No idea. In a cellar or cave or somewhere like that, I suppose. I was praising the gourmet fungus dishes to one of the native traders, and he offered to show me a farm. I suppose he hopes to sell me a ton or two. If I knew now to preserve the stuff, I'd buy it."

"Go ahead," Darzek said. "And buy enough for supper, anyway."

He turned to the viewer again, but one mob looked very much like another, and there was something decidedly artificial about their performances. He realized finally that these people were in a mood to riot but didn't know how. They had never felt this way before, never seen it done. They were like a motion picture cast awkwardly moving through a first rehearsal and waiting for a director to tell them what they were doing wrong.

Then came a special announcement: the masfiln would address the world that evening, Klinoz time. In the meantime, he asked all citizens to go home or go to work. The world's factories needed full production right up to the moment their employees were evacuated. This plea was boomed to the milling populace, which seemed not to notice it. Darzek turned off the screen and resumed his analysis of Melris's latest report.

The swirl of events was preventing his keeping things in proper perspective. Riots, evacuating a world, mushroom farms—none of these was his concern. The lists Melris had compiled constituted the only traces they'd found of the villain's activities. Every item on them should be followed up at once, even though it was virtually certain that all the records had long since been wiped out.

But Qwasrolk had sat in that warehouse, in front of the records file. Perhaps he had done the wiping out himself, a moment before they arrived.

Or was it possible that Qwasrolk was making some kind of search of his own? He could gain admittance to any factory or warehouse without an argument with the management.

Miss Schlupe had started some of her investigators on this task, but those few hadn't even reported. The matter hadn't seemed urgent. Now he would have to call her troops off the various piddling assignments that had them chasing in all directions and put them to work on a systematic search. They might find Qwasrolk in the process. They might even find the villain.

By Darzek's personal sense of time, it was two hours later. He could not break himself of thinking in terms of hours, even though lengths of days differed on different worlds, and native populations divided them to suit their own convenience, or on religious principles, or by happenstance.

In those two hours Darzek had found one of Miss Schlupe's lieutenants and told him to start all available personnel on a search of the firms Melris had listed. And then he had taken part of the list to work on himself and immediately fumbled his way into a world he had not known existed.

It was a tunneled world of small shops, crafts establishments, and food and produce marts that was located somewhere under the city. At first Darzek was amazed; then he was amazed at his amazement. On Earth, fads in handmade items, in organic foods, in imported novelties, came and went, and there was no reason why the people of Vezpro should not indulge themselves in the same way. He remembered Miss Schlupe describing a similar place, where she'd found the shop that made her rocking chair. He could understand that a handcrafted chair in some distinctive pattern might add a note of irregularity and satisfying charm to the cell-like residences most of the population occupied. As for the foods, the unvarying menu offered by the planet's food transmitters would certainly drive a portion of the population into doing its own cooking, and there were special gadgets on sale here, from crude smokeless burners to the latest forms of nuclear cookers, to enable people to do just that.

But he was looking for a particular shop, and he found it difficult to make the transmitter address coincide with its physical location. He wandered along the vast, brightly illuminated tunnel—illuminated by the entire arched ceiling, which was coated with a luminous substance that gave off a strong, slightly bluish light. Throngs of people, who evidently did not know or care about the slow-motion riots going on over their heads, swarmed in a tangle of movement along the shops on either side of the tunnel.

Darzek moved with them, searching for the address he wanted. Queries of shopkeepers and passersby netted him little information. He soon found that many of these establishments were short-lived. Sometimes a proprietor occupied a shop only long enough to dispose of a single stock of goods. A number of the shops were unoccupied.

So was the shop he was looking for when he finally found it. He had the good fortune to locate a shopkeeper who sold fresh foods and enjoyed a steady trade. He had been there for years, and he was able to identify the address Darzek wanted. He also remembered the young Vezpronian who had briefly occupied it about the date Darzek named. He had sold some kind of atomic appliance—seemed to be doing well, sold at a reasonable price, but was only there a few days. Had a limited stock, the shopkeeper supposed, and closed the moment he disposed of it. Such things happened all the time.

Darzek bought an assortment of greens for Miss Schlupe and moved on to the next address on his list. It proved to be a craft shop that made floor pieces, and its proprietor knew nothing about earlier tenants. Eventually Darzek found a witness who told a story very similar to the one he'd just heard. The same thing happened at a third shop.

Darzek located the nearest public transmitter and went directly to the governmental complex, where Min Kallof consented to see him immediately.

"I want to talk to your new Mas of Science and Technology," Darzek said.

A few minutes later an elderly Vezpronian hurried in, panting.

"Listen," Darzek said, and he described in detail the process by which nuclear materials had been illegally brought to Vezpro. "They

—or he—started using legitimate firms," Darzek said, "but it must have been a lot of trouble to erase the invoices and collect the shipments without anyone noticing anything or becoming suspicious. So they—or he—solved that problem by setting up temporary businesses. The name would suggest a legitimate use for the material. The supplier, given only the transmitter address and paid solvency in advance, would have no reason to be suspicious."

Min Kallof looked puzzled. "It's a brilliant discovery, Gul Darr, but surely it's too late to do anything about these firms now."

"It tells us how the materials were acquired to turn the eleventh planet into a sun. Perhaps Nifron D as well. If the villain hasn't already acquired what he needs to destroy Vezpro, a strict control on the acquisition of nuclear materials my frustrate him."

"That might be difficult," Min Kallof observed.

"Not as difficult as evacuating a world. Every firm using such materials should be required to take a complete inventory, place its stock under guard, and hereafter to account for every particle. And you must absolutely control the import of every item on this list."

"May I have the list?" the new mas asked.

Darzek handed it to him.

"I agree completely," he said. Then he added, with a quiet smile, "It'll be a great relief to have something to do. I've been sitting in my new office wondering. Just wondering. A crisis faced my world, it fell within my sphere of responsibility, and there seemed to be nothing I could do about it. Now there is. What you suggest is eminently logical. No matter how difficult, I'll see that it's done. I only fear that we may be too late."

"We probably are," Darzek said. "But we must try anyway."

The new mas smiled again and hurried away.

Darzek said to the masfiln, "I missed your speech. Have there been any positive results?"

"A few," Min Kallof said. "The crowds in the park are smaller, but that may be only because it's mealtime. You need have no regret about missing it. You'll have many opportunities to hear one just like it before we're finished." He paused. "You're sure this evacuation is absolutely necessary?"

"No. But I refuse to gamble with five billion lives."

Min Kallof gestured resignedly. "Better evacuate and be wrong than leave them here and be wrong. Yes. We must. But it's so difficult to persuade people to leave their homes over such an unbelievable threat, even with the eleventh planet becoming more vivid each night. This suggestion of yours, to restrict essential materials, seems promising. And of course the scientists will continue to work until the last moment. Naz Forlan is setting up a large establishment and financing it entirely himself. But I can see that the evacuation must proceed. We must not gamble with our citizens' lives." He sounded as though he were trying to convince himself.

Darzek left him and returned to the Trans-Star office. Melris Angoz was waiting for him. She asked anxiously, "Where is Eld? He hasn't been in his office today."

Darzek wearily dropped into a chair. Wolndur. He had completely forgotten him. Miss Schlupe had told him to do something—yes. Find Qwasrolk. "He has a job that'll keep him away from the office for a while," he said.

She left reassured, but Darzek was not. He checked with Gud Baxak. Wolndur had not returned. There was no reason why he should. Miss Schlupe had given him no specific instructions, and he wouldn't come to report unless he had something to report.

But Darzek had suddenly thought of the long list of nuclear scientists who had disappeared from Vezpro. Wolndur was a nuclear scientist.

Was it possible that those missing scientists had been kidnapped?

19

Darzek decided to perform his own survey of the milling mobs in the parks. As a result it was late when he returned, and Miss Schlupe already had gone to bed.

He was unable to sleep. He felt like a juggler with too many plates in the air. There were scientific plates—Forlan's group, the Zarstans, UrsNollf and Supreme; there was Qwasrolk, who had some connection not yet guessed; there were the politicians, the demonstrating citizens, and E-Wusk's evacuation plans; there was the investigation into the missing nuclear materials; there were the vanished scientists and Wolndur's possible disappearance. Every time the plates went around, he had the feeling that he'd forgotten one and there would be a crash behind him.

He got up, finally, and sat in the Trans-Star office until his calendar clock said dawn, thinking.

Melris Angoz arrived early, looking much more concerned than she had the previous day. "Eld hasn't come to his office," she said. "He's never late. And he didn't return to his dormitory last night. I asked."

Miss Schlupe walked in while she was talking, refreshed by her mushroom farm excursion and a night's sleep and looking—as she put it herself—at least six days younger. "What's that about Eld?" she asked.

"He's missing," Darzek said.

"He's probably wandering around trying to do detective work. I saw him yesterday."

"Where?" Melris asked quickly.

"On my way to the mushroom farm. There are queer stretches of shops in tunnels under the city. I think I mentioned them to you."

"I saw one yesterday," Darzek said.

"That's where the fungus is grown—in intersecting tunnels. There must be acres if not square kilometers of fungus farms—they go on and on. Anyway, on the way there I saw Eld walking along the tunnel where the shops are."

"Was he . . . all right?" Melris asked anxiously.

"He looked a little vague, as though he had something on his mind, but there certainly wasn't anything wrong with him. I didn't speak to him because he was on the other side of the tunnel and the trader I was with was in a hurry."

Melris left for the office, reassured but still concerned. After she left, Darzek remarked, "I've been sitting here wondering if Wolndur has been kidnapped."

"Why would anyone do that? There are far more competent scientists around."

"He knows what we've been doing."

"Would that help anyone?" Miss Schlupe demanded.

Darzek reflected. "No. But the kidnapper wouldn't know that."

"True enough," Miss Schlupe said. She pushed a chair forward and flopped down. "Had your viewer on lately?"

Darzek shook his head.

"Everything's about to bust loose. The political opposition is openly opposing the evacuation. The masfiln is said to be considering resigning."

Darzek quickly activated the screen.

A Vezpronian, undoubtedly a politician, was orating. "Should we leave our homes, our businesses, our factories, our farms, to escape a figment of the masfiln's imagination? There are hundreds of explanations for the transformation of the eleventh planet, whose composition was nothing like that of our beautiful world. Let us forget these demented outpourings, get on with our work, and celebrate the coming of the new cycle in our usual joyful fashion."

Darzek switched off the viewer. "Is that a universal custom—celebrating the new year?"

"I suppose. This year it may be a warm celebration. Too bad I didn't know yesterday that Wolndur was missing. I could have grabbed him for you. I thought he was just wandering around looking for Qwasrolk."

"No doubt he was," Darzek said. "What did you think he would do with him if he found him?"

"I don't know. I've been wondering how Qwasrolk would react if someone behaved friendly toward him, instead of trying to capture him, as you did, or rushing toward him shouting, as that manager did. He might not vanish instantly if he isn't threatened."

"It's a thought," Darzek agreed. "Is Wolndur bright enough to figure out something like that?"

"I don't know. I was going to speak to him about it today."

"I still think the best approach is by way of these lists Melris has compiled. I put all your investigators onto them yesterday."

"In that case, we might as well help them," Miss Schlupe said. As Darzek wearily got to his feet, she remarked, "Poor E-Wusk. He's all tooled up to evacuate five billion people, and no one wants to go. It's like giving a party when no one comes. He's listening to those opposition speeches and muttering in his own language. I think he's swearing."

"He should be," Darzek said. "Shall we go?"

After inspecting a dozen warehouses, the two of them sat down on crates and looked at each other. "I think," Miss Schlupe announced, "that one uninhabited warehouse is very much like another. Strange that there's never anyone around."

"That's why the villain had no problem in removing his materials. The owners didn't miss them, since they hadn't ordered them. The shippers had no reason to check, since the shipment had been paid for in advance. By erasing the invoices the receiving transmitter recorded, he removed all traces. If the owners found a few blank spaces in their records, they probably thought that the machines accidentally hiccuped a couple of times, which no doubt happens. It was an ingenious scheme."

"It's strange they rarely miss things when they don't even have a caretaker," Miss Schlupe observed.

"Schluppy, that's what's so thunderingly peculiar about this whole business. You and I keep forgetting we aren't on Earth. These people don't need caretakers. Nobody steals. We were talking about kidnapping scientists, but nobody commits such crimes. The traders indulge in sharp dealings, but they're of the kind where one more knowledgeable person outdoes another. One wouldn't think of lying about a deal, and if he did he'd be permanently ostracized. And no one would blackmail anyone, or threaten to turn a world into a sun. No wonder the Vezpronians can't comprehend this threat. I'm amazed that the masfiln and his cabinet had the understanding and the courage to order the evacuation. Do you realize that you and I are the only ones in the entire Galactic Synthesis who can grasp what is going on here and plan effective action?"

"Not very effective," Miss Schlupe murmured.

"Action, anyway. Maybe it'd be more effective if we had some help."

"Maybe it'd be more effective if we could figure out how there could be a master criminal in a crimeless society. I've been giving some thought to that myself."

"And?"

She shook her head. "Nothing. Are we really accomplishing anything with this tour of warehouses?"

"We might if we visited all of them."

"What are you looking for, really?"

"Qwasrolk and Wolndur."

"All right. Let's keep looking."

But they finally tired of inspecting warehouses and returned to the Trans-Star office, where a worried Gud Baxak greeted them. "The masfiln," he whispered. He led them into the presence of a grave Min Kallof, who rose to greet them.

"The Dezmas will meet tomorrow," he announced gloomily.

"And it will oppose the evacuation," Darzek suggested.

The masfiln gestured despondently. "It not only will oppose it; it will forbid it."

Darzek got the masfiln seated again and made himself comfortable. Miss Schlupe dropped into her rocking chair and began a vigorous movement that the masfiln regarded perplexedly.

"Does this rejection of your program mean that you must resign?" Darzek asked.

"For a masfiln to resign when the Dezmas opposes him is a confession of error," Min Kallof said scornfully. "I have not erred."

"My friend, you have cooperated with me fully from the moment I arrived here, with the one exception of substituting the proctors for the females on the ransom ship—and that probably wasn't your idea."

"No. Naz Forlan suggested it, but I gave it my approval."

"In any case," Darzek said, "you've cooperated when my suggestions must have seemed peculiar indeed. Believe me—I want to save Vezpro, but if I can't do that, I want to save its people. I can invoke all the power of Supreme if that is necessary, or if it would help us. Would it?"

"Supreme," Min Kallof said thoughtfully, "might seem very distant to the opposition politicians of the Dezmas."

"I can make it seem very close merely by closing the port of Vezpro."

Min Kallof echoed perplexedly, "Closing the port—"

"All ships presently at the transfer stations would be ordered to leave at once. No more ships would be permitted to dock here."

"And—the ships would obey?"

"If they didn't obey Supreme, they wouldn't be permitted to dock anywhere." Darzek didn't know how long it would take to make such an edict enforceable, but he doubted that many captains would care to disobey an emissary of Supreme.

"That would destroy Vezpro as effectively as turning it into a sun," Min Kallof protested.

"No," Darzek said. "It would destroy its trade and economy, but it would leave the world inact and its people alive—to be evacuated to safety. The question is whether this is a wise course. Are we justified in using coercion, either on your opposing politicians or on your people? Do we have the right to force the people of Vezpro to abandon their world in order to save their lives, when we ourselves are by no means certain as to what will happen?"

"The message said the new cycle."

"The author of the message is without a doubt a genius, but he also must be demented. Who knows what to expect of the insane? Perhaps we sprang the thing on your people without proper preparation. I have a suggestion. Bring your opposition leaders here, and I'll quiet them for you."

Min Kallof agreed and departed. Darzek went to the Trans-Star office for a piece of the metallic parchment the Vezpronians used for paper and began to sketch out a proclamation. Miss Schlupe continued to rock.

"Think you can change their minds?" she asked finally.

"I didn't promise to do that," Darzek said. "I just promised to quiet them."

"You're going ahead with the evacuation?"

"That depends on how much I can quiet them." He continued to write.

It took Min Kallof some time to locate the opposition leaders. Probably they were touring the parks, agitating. Eventually he arrived shepherding a group of a dozen, all of them obviously angry, and never had Darzek seen opposition politicians looking more firmly opposed than this group.

Min Kallof introduced him. Darzek took the time to give each of them his most sternly disapproving stare. "My understanding," he announced, "is that the intention of your political leadership is to defy a special emissary of Supreme—which by extension means a defiance of the Council of Supreme and Supreme itself."

That iniquity did not seem to impress them. As Min Kallof had remarked, Supreme was a long way off.

"Accordingly, I have prepared a proclamation," Darzek told them.

He read it. He made their perfidy in defying a special emissary of Supreme sound very bad indeed, and he concluded by expelling Vezpro from the Galactic Synthesis and classifying it as an Uncertified World. He had no authority to take such action without the concurrence of his fellow councilors, but the politicians would not know that.

There were howls of protest even before he finished. Darzek said sternly, "The moment the Dezmas votes against the actions proposed by Min Kallof's government, which were taken at my recommendation, I will make public this proclamation. All ships currently at the transfer stations will depart immediately, because trade or any other contact with an Uncertified World is forbidden. No more ships will visit Vezpro for any reason. I'll leave to you the problem of explaining to the people of Vezpro how your defiance of Supreme has ruined them."

The howls had subsided to silence—sullen, but no longer defiant.

"Now I'll suggest a compromise," Darzek said. "You will join with the masfiln in making the people of Vezpro aware of the impending danger to their world. For the time being, evacuation will be voluntary. Scientists and others will continue to work on the problem. It may be that they will solve it. In the meantime, nonessential population, especially females with children, should be encouraged to leave. They will be well cared for, and they will be returned the moment it seems safe to do so."

"The evacuation will be voluntary?" one politician repeated.

"As long as sufficient numbers of citizens volunteer. It will be your task to make certain that they do."

"And—if sufficient numbers don't volunteer?"

"My objective," Darzek said firmly, "is to save the population of Vezpro. That also should be your objective. Supreme has expended vast amounts of solvency and brought the galaxy's leading expert here to assist us. We have a small amount of leeway, so we can test the volunteer system. If it doesn't work, then we will reconsider. Anyone who fails to cooperate will be dealt with severely."

"How?" a politician demanded.

"He'll be left here. He can give us a firsthand report on what it feels like when the world one is standing on becomes a sun."

After a moment of silence, a politician said, "Do you actually believe—"

"Vezpronians are reputed to have brains in their heads," Darzek said. "Use yours. The author of that threat has done it twice. How much proof do you require? All of you should be ashamed of yourselves—attempting to make political capital when your world and the lives of its citizens are threatened. Your duty is to quiet the protests, not incite them. Now get to work."

They left. Min Kallof lingered behind to thank Darzek. "Did that mollify them?" Darzek asked.

"For the present," Min Kallof agreed.

"You can let it be known that I won't summon them again. If there's further obstruction from any of them, I'll simply act."

Min Kallof left looking graver than when he'd arrived. Darzek went next door to report the development to E-Wusk.

"Volunteers?" E-Wusk echoed doubtfully. "How much delay will there be?"

"We'll have to wait and see. It's a politically delicate situation."

E-Wusk heaved his tangle of limbs erect and ambled over to his charts. "Then we'll need fewer ships now and more later." He sighed and began to adjust his calculations. "All right. If we must, we'll manage somehow."

Darzek returned to the Trans-Star office. Gud Baxak was busily at work on a trading transaction. Darzek glanced at him enviously, wishing he could think of something to do.

In the living room he found a visitor waiting. UrsNollf got to his feet respectfully as Darzek entered.

"For Supreme's sake!" Darzek exclaimed. "Why didn't you let us know you were coming? Have you learned anything new?"

UrsNollf gestured apologetically. "Nothing. Or I would have sent a message."

"Apart from the errors, was there anything of value in that plan of Qwasrolk's?"

"It was theoretically ingenious, but it couldn't possibly have led to any practical application—especially not in turning a planet into a sun."

"Are you certain?" Darzek demanded.

"Positive," UrsNollf said. "Supreme worked out every possible projection and every possible application. It was ingenious, as I said, but it was nothing."

Darzek shrugged resignedly. "I thought it might give us the beginning of a solution, despite its errors. I thought Qwasrolk *must* know something about the device. And all it meant is that he is addicted to scientific doodling."

20

Eld Wolndur was still missing. Miss Schlupe's commandos and investigators worked an entire day, checking and rechecking all the warehouses and firms on Melris Angoz's list. They found no trace of either Wolndur or Qwasrolk. They produced a stack of reports of which the most interesting items were descriptions of prosaic encounters with an occasional employee who was either puzzled or angry at their intrusion.

Darzek, who had something more serious to worry about, left the search to Miss Schlupe. The first shiploads of volunteers were leaving Vezpro, and he had gone to the transfer station to watch the departure—and discovered that virtually all of the evacuees were refugees from Hlaswann, Naz Forlan's people. They had planned to leave Vezpro anyway, and obviously this seemed like a propitious moment. No doubt the fate of their native planet was a tale kept very much alive with them.

The eleventh planet now could be seen clearly in the daytime, a small, remote sun. The people of Vezpro knew all about Nifron D. And still they refused evacuation.

Darzek went to see Naz Forlan.

It was the first time Darzek had seen the former mas in a relaxed mood. His normally greenish flesh flushed a deeper green of pleasure when Darzek entered, and he greeted him heartily.

"You look much less careworn than when I last saw you," Darzek observed.

"For the first time since all this started, I feel that I'm accomplishing something," Forlan confessed.

He got Darzek seated and inquired as to Gula Schlu's health and the success of Darzek's own endeavors.

"One of them, at least, is having no success at all," Darzek said. "No doubt you saw the viewer coverage of the protests. The Vezpronians refuse to be evacuated."

Forlan said thoughtfully, "That's hardly surprising. You're asking them to believe something that even the most competent scientist can't understand. And people naturally are reluctant to leave all that they possess and disrupt their lives because of a mere phantasm."

"Your own people were the subject of a worldwide evacuation," Darzek said. "That's why I came to see you. How was it managed? An exploding sun is a concept that must seem almost as phantasmal as turning a world into a sun."

"I have no recollection of how it was managed, because I was an infant. But a known natural phenomenon, even if it happens rarely, is not phantasmal. No doubt the scientific data was available to everyone, and all scientists were in agreement as to what was about to happen. In this case there are two problems. First, why would anyone want to do such a thing, even if he could? Such a malevolent being is phantasmal. Second, how could he do it when the best scientists of the galaxy can't figure out the way? That, too, is phantasmal. So they resist a forced evacuation. Wouldn't you do the same?"

"I'm not a representative specimen," Darzek said with a grin. "I come from an Uncertified World. Evil is not phantasmal to me, and since I've seen the eleventh planet and read all the reports on Nifron D, I know that it can be done. The eleventh planet, at least, is obvious to anyone who looks up. Why can't the citizens of Vezpro accept it?"

"I don't know," Forlan said. "You have the handicap of your origin. I have the handicap of my education." He brightened—visibly, since his greenish hue, which had faded, flushed vividly again. "But your evacuation may prove unnecessary. It very much looks that way. We're finally making progress."

"You're about to figure out how it's done?"

"Turn a world into a sun? No. What good would that do us? The committee I appointed was composed of elderly idiots, and it's my fault. Now I'm using younger scientists whose imaginations haven't atrophied. We aren't worrying about how it's done. We're concerned with keeping it from being done. Right now we're concentrating on triggering mechanisms. However the device is made, there are only a certain number of ways to set it off. If we can develop techniques that will keep all of them from working, we'll save the planet. Would you like to visit our projects?"

"No, thank you," Darzek said firmly. "I wouldn't understand any of it. But UrsNollf is back, and I'll send him to see you. If you can make use of him, please do so."

"Thank you. We'll welcome his assistance. Concerning your problem—" The greenish hue deepened again. "I'm afraid I can't help you. I, too, have seen the eleventh planet and read the Nifron D reports—and I have no intention of leaving Vezpro. This is my home, and my world, and if I fail and Vezpro dies, I'll die with it."

Darzek returned to the Trans-Star office feeling both disappointed and dejected. He was disappointed that Forlan could make no positive suggestions to help with the evacuation and dejected about the research his group was doing. He refused to share Forlan's confidence that the number of trigger types was limited and ways could be found to frustrate all of them. He told UrsNollf that Forlan had a job for him and returned his attention to his own problems.

He found E-Wusk in a state of total frustration. Most of the aliens from Hlaswann had left. Vezpronian volunteers came in a trickle—individually, by twos, now and then a family. "At this rate, it'll take days to load one ship," E-Wusk protested.

"Then that's how many you'll evacuate," Darzek said. He went to the living room, sat down, and slipped his shoes off.

Miss Schlupe came in and settled herself in her rocking chair. Her report was brief. Her commandos still hadn't found Wolndur, and now Melris Angoz was missing.

Darzek said to her, "Have we ever flopped as badly on any problem as we have on this one?"

"Of course," she said. "We always flop until we get something figured out. The trouble here is that we've tried to rely on scientific experts, and naturally they've confused the real issue to a point where it isn't recognizable."

"And what is the real issue?"

"The real issue," Miss Schlupe said, "is not how a world is turned into a sun, or who knows how to do it, or who has already done it with a couple of worlds nobody cares about, or how to stop someone from doing it. The real issue is who would want to do it to Vezpro. We've been trying to solve a scientific problem, and we should have been looking for a criminal."

"We did," Darzek said, "though I must admit we didn't do it very well. So here's the situation. We have two groups of scientists that don't find out anything. We've consulted Supreme and got nothing at all, not even a Delphic pronouncement. We've arranged to evacuate the world, and the people won't go. Our attempt to use the ransom demand as a trap was thoroughly messed up by the world authorities, but there's no evidence that anyone intended to collect it anyway. We tracked down innumerable illegal shipments of nuclear materials without finding out where any of them went. The one promising lead would seem to be Qwasrolk, who vanishes before anyone can get close enough to ask a question. Now my own assistants have disappeared—perhaps kidnapped, though if they don't know any more than I do, and they don't, it was a waste of effort. What do we do next?"

"Nothing," Miss Schlupe said firmly.

"What's different about that?"

"You represent the authority of the Synthesis, and the Synthesis has done everything it could for the people of Vezpro. They don't want to be evacuated, which is the final contribution it can make, so the Synthesis is withdrawing and leaving the solution up to the people and their government. Announce that publicly, and then we'll all leave. E-Wusk can easily transfer his operations to Skarnaf and be ready just in case someone screams for help at the last minute—and he can continue to evacuate that trickle of volunteers. Gud Baxak can close the Trans-Star office and return to Primores. You can close your office and let Wolndur and Angoz go back to the government when they're found. And you and I will officially leave the planet, though actually we'll move next door and do what we should have done in the beginning—look for a criminal. What do you think?"

"I want to leave UrsNollf here," Darzek said. "He can keep us informed about what Forlan's scientists are doing. But we'll have to arrange to get him off Vezpro before the new cycle."

"My ship will be back to evacuate us and everyone who's worked with us who wants to go."

"All right. I don't see that we can lose anything. I'll notify the authorities by letter so they won't know until we've supposedly left. I'd rather avoid unpleasant confrontations."

"You can be called away by urgent business."

"Of course. And I can promise to return before the new year if my schedule permits. I like this idea. I was getting very tired of politicians and scientists."

"I've always been tired of them," Miss Schlupe remarked.

Darzek wrote an official notice to the masfiln and had Gud Baxak indite it. E-Wusk simply packed up his records; he could open a new

office on Skarnaf and be in business again as soon as his communications equipment was installed. Gud Baxak transferred his un-
completed business to another trader. Miss Schlupe sent one of her
investigators to rent a new apartment for them. In the meantime, she
rounded up her crew and had her captain apply for clearance.

The ship left the transfer station before midnight. E-Wusk and
Gud Baxak went with it, and Darzek's and Miss Schlupe's names
were on the officially filed passenger list. The announced destination
was Primores, but the actual destination was Skarnaf, where E-Wusk
would set up his new office and Gud Baxak would take passage for
Primores on another ship. Miss Schlupe's ship would wait at Skarnaf
until she ordered it back to Vezpro.

Darzek and Miss Schlupe disappeared before the ship left. They
moved to their new apartment, and the only things they took with
them were Miss Schlupe's rocking chair, which was an awkward contraption to get through a transmitter, their stock of mushrooms, and
their clothing. The new quarters came fully furnished, so they left
behind them the few gadgets and appointments they had acquired.

Before they moved, they stuck invisible pieces of tape to their
right hands over their solvency credentials. The tape contained a
new credential. It was Darzek's invention for changing his identity
when he thought he needed to. They then transmitted up to a
transfer station on Gud Baxak's credential, joined the throng of arriving passengers, presented stacks of solvency certificates for credit
to their accounts, registered the phony credentials as those of newly
arrived visitors, and returned to the planet. Now they were incognito,
with a world to operate in.

"Disguises?" Miss Schlupe suggested.

"I suppose so. Too many people know us. But all we need to do is
dress differently and wear a nocturnal's headpiece."

"And disguise our voices," Miss Schlupe suggested.

"I don't intend to talk with anyone," Darzek said. "It didn't get me
anywhere as an emissary of Supreme. Why should it when I'm
nobody?"

"What we should have done," Miss Schlupe said, "is bring someone to front for us and keep ourselves incognito from the beginning.
For all we know, the villain could be the masfiln himself. He's not a
scientist, but he could hire some."

"Or kidnap some," Darzek suggested.

"Precisely," Miss Schlupe said.

On the wall of the transfer station's restaurant was an enormous structure that looked like an abstract sculpture with moving parts. It was reported to be an ingenious chronometer that told the time anywhere in the galaxy if one knew how to read it. Darzek didn't.

Staring at it, he muttered, "World enough and time. We certainly have world enough. What we desperately need is time."

They were clothed in the flamboyant robes of their disguises along with the light shields that covered half their faces. Miss Schlupe wore a wig. Darzek had experimented with facial hair, but it was too much trouble to put on and take off. Also, it itched.

"We might as well sum up," Miss Schlupe said. They were speaking English, which was as good a way as any to encipher a conversation. It didn't even sound like a language to anyone closer than the planet Earth.

Darzek nodded. "All right. Sum up."

"Point one. Psychology. Will he or won't he? Is he just trying to stir things up and inflict wear and tear on a lot of nervous systems, or is he actually malicious enough, or nutty enough, to kill a few billion intelligent beings? I suppose we could consult an expert in alien psychology, if there is such a thing, but preserve us from another scientific expert. Also, he may be Vezpronian, which on this world isn't an alien. Will he or won't he, and I don't see any way to find out before the new cycle. Does that cover it?"

"Perfectly."

"Point two," she went on. "If he will, the question is whether he can be stopped. The scientists are working on it, and we can wish them luck, but we won't know whether they've succeeded until the new year, and if they haven't it'll be too late to try anything else."

"Very well put," Darzek said. "Is there a point three?"

"There is. We'll have to identify the villain before the new year and put him out of action. Then it won't matter whether he will or won't, or whether the scientists' gadgets actually work. Am I right?"

"Certainly. All we have to do is catch him and take his atomic contraption away from him. And maybe slap his hands."

"Points one and two are for scientists," Miss Schlupe said. "We're the experts in tracking down criminals."

"True, but when I look at the size of that world I don't feel very expert—especially when I consider that our villain may not be there, may never have been there, and may not even show up until a min-

ute before midnight on New Year's Eve and then stay just long
enough to place his gadget in a nice concealed place and run."

Being incognito had not destroyed their sources of information.
There was no Official Secrets Act on Vezpro. No documents were
stamped TOP SECRET. Miss Schlupe had spread her net of investigators widely, and they knew everything the government was doing.
They also managed to remain in contact with UrsNolff, at Forlan's
research center, and Raf Lolln, on Zarst.

Eld Wolndur had returned. He had been looking, unsuccessfully,
for Qwasrolk. Melris Angoz also had returned. She had been looking
for Wolndur. The two of them had gone together to the new Mas of
Science and Technology and asked if they could continue to work on
the projects given to them by the special emissary of Supreme before
he left, and the mas not only agreed but offered them any additional
assistance they required in the way of equipment or personnel. All of
this surprised Darzek immensely; he couldn't imagine what projects
they were referring to.

Darzek spent several days thinking about Qwasrolk, after which
he acquired a new office. He called it "Klinoz Engineering Consultants," had a computer installed, and hired the best computer specialist available to feed information into it and train a task force of Miss
Schlupe's investigators. The result was that the investigators paid sur-
reptitious visits to all those firms whose records had been tampered
with; and everywhere they found a blank where an invoice had been
erased, they inserted the phrase "Record transferred to Klinoz Engineering Consultants." In the meantime, the computer specialist was
creating fake invoices from Melris Angoz's data and feeding them
into the new computer. Darzek hoped that Qwasrolk, in his search
for information or evidence, would sooner or later happen onto one
of the notices and pay a visit to Klinoz Engineering Consultants. If
he did, carefully trained employees who staffed the office continuously might—possibly—be able to engage him in friendly conversation, offer food and comfort while he studied the phony records, and
even get the answer to a question or two.

"It's a feeble ploy, but it was the only thing I could think of," Darzek admitted.

Nothing came of it. Qwasrolk probably had found enough blank
records to know that such a search would lead nowhere.

Darzek was still mulling over this failure when Miss Schlupe asked suddenly, "What ever happened to Kernopplix?"

"He went home," Darzek said. "Rich and about to become much richer—he thought."

"Since he's completely out of it, perhaps the full authority of the Galactic Synthesis could prevail upon him to supply some information. It might even be suggested that traders around the galaxy will refuse to do business with him if he doesn't cooperate."

"I'm slowing down in my old age," Darzek said disgustedly. "We never should have let him leave."

"Do you know for a fact that he went home?"

"No."

"We'll have to send someone to Bbran," Miss Schlupe said.

"It should be a trader. We'd better let E-Wusk handle it—he'll know the right person to send."

"What if it turns out that Kernopplix didn't go home?" Miss Schlupe asked.

"What's one more complication in a case like this?"

The evacuations were continuing at a diminishing trickle. Finally Darzek received a message from E-Wusk. He read it and told Miss Schlupe, "If we haven't passed the point of no return, we're about to. From now on, there's no possibility of evacuating the entire population—just getting off as many people as we can."

"Tell the government that," she suggested.

Darzek had E-Wusk send a message, purportedly from Primores and the Council of Supreme, informing Min Kallof that if mass evacuations did not start immediately, it would be too late to complete them by the new year, and the Council would order E-Wusk to close down his rescue operation and return to Primores. This brought an instant response; the evacuation rate picked up considerably, with the government actively encouraging people to leave.

But the politicians refused to make evacuation mandatory. Darzek muttered, "The fools!" Then he added, "I hope they're right."

Miss Schlupe's employees continued to work meticulously, checking out every line of investigation that either of them could think of and piling the results on their desks each morning before starting another day's search. Inevitably it amounted to a mountain of drivel, but Darzek and Miss Schlupe had to sift it carefully on the chance that it concealed a gem. Darzek obtained sets of photos of Vezpro from space, covering more than a year, and put a special team to work with the best space photo reading equipment available to meticulously search for an excavation in a barren place that had been quickly covered over and relandscaped. They found nothing that looked remotely suspicious. It was more time and effort wasted, and time was relentlessly slipping away.

One day Miss Schlupe asked Darzek, "Are you going to stay?"

Darzek reflected. "No. I have no obligation to die here. What about your investigators and commandos? They're probably better informed about the risk than anyone on Vezpro. We can easily evacuate all of them in your ship."

"Good thought," she said. "I'll find out how many want to leave." She hesitated. "They may want to know whether we're going. I agree with you. I don't mind dying in a cause, but my death on Vezpro wouldn't accomplish a thing. Our first duty was to save the population, but the population wouldn't let us. Our second duty is to keep this bastard from doing the same thing somewhere else."

She polled all of her employees and came back to report, "They're staying. One hundred per cent."

"No wonder we couldn't evacuate the population," Darzek said. "What's the refugee total going to be?"

"The rate is still picking up. E-Wusk hopes for a rush as the new cycle approaches. If he gets it, the total may reach half a billion."

"That's still a lot of lives," Darzek said. "So we didn't exactly labor in vain."

"No. But E-Wusk feels crushed anyway. He wanted to save everyone."

"Where are you going?"

"To buy mushrooms. I get them directly from one of the farms, now. They'll sell retail if you buy large quantities, so I keep what you and I need and distribute the rest among my employees. Want to come along? Those long tunnels with acres of fungus are quite a sight."

Darzek shook his head wearily. "My mind is on matters rather remote to mushrooms. What I'd really like is some tobacco."

Miss Schlupe sniffed disdainfully. "Do you want to poison yourself?"

"Maybe that's the kind of stimulus I need," Darzek said.

21

Darzek decided to visit the rural grove and makeshift shelter where he had seen Qwasrolk and found his scribbled nuclear speculations. He wondered whether Qwasrolk had ever returned to the place. Emerging from the nearest village, he discovered to his amazement that winter had arrived. In the sprawling, transmitterized cities with their domed parks, one could forget that such a thing as weather existed. Here the fields were lightly snow-covered; the strange treelike plants in the grove were bare stems. The cold felt bitter and penetrating. Winds had blown the shelter apart.

Darzek strolled down to the farm and found it deserted. The farmer and his wife probably had sold out and gone off with the other Hlaswannian refugees. As for Qwasrolk, no one had seen him for so long that Darzek doubted that he was still alive. Certainly he should have died long ago—all the doctors agreed on that. His remains might be lying at this moment in some similar grove, beneath another improvised shelter that the winds were tearing apart, lightly snow-covered and awaiting chance and the spring for discovery.

If spring came again to this hemisphere of Vezpro.

Darzek, with the feeling that he was doing nothing, learning nothing, trudged back to the village and the nearest transmitter that would return him to Klinoz. He could see, in the gathering dusk, the eleventh planet blazing vividly above the horizon. Soon the night side of Vezpro would be bathed with a light brighter than moonlight. Perhaps at opposition Vezpro's climate would be affected—if Vezpro was not having its own distinctive effect on the climates of other planets by then.

Back at the apartment he shared with Miss Schlupe, he found her placidly rocking while a pot of mushrooms bubbled in the corner of the room that served as a kitchen when the occupants wanted to do their own cooking.

"My ship just arrived," she said. "It's parked at Transfer Station 411. Have you decided when you want to leave?"

"We don't need to hurry," Darzek said. "From what I've seen, there'll be no last-minute rush for ships. Most of the Vezpronians act as though they couldn't care less."

"Never mind. We've moved quite a few millions to safety, and the traffic is increasing a little. You didn't answer my question. Do we leave now, and pick up E-Wusk, and go back to Primores where we can pretend we wield a little influence, or do we hang around here until the last minute?"

"The evacuation should be continued until the last minute," Darzek said. "Anyone who wants to leave should be able to. Is E-Wusk prepared just in case there is a rush?"

"I don't know. I can tell him to be prepared."

"And I can send Min Kallof a message, supposedly from Primores, ordering him to announce to the entire population that it has one final chance to leave. As for us—we don't have to wait until quite the last minute. How about noon of the day before the new cycle?"

"I'll tell UrsNollf," she said. "And I'll have my crew aboard and waiting."

Darzek studied his calendar absently. He had replaced the elaborate gadget left behind at their former address with a simpler model, but it told the date just as vividly. Ten days until the new cycle.

"Tell your crew to go aboard five days from now and obtain clearance so there won't be any last-minute delay. And let E-Wusk know that we'll be prepared to haul a load of refugees, just in case there is a rush."

"Will do," Miss Schlupe agreed, with a nod of satisfaction.

Min Kallof reacted to Darzek's message with alacrity. He himself spoke to the people of Vezpro, conveying the final warning of the Galactic Synthesis. Listening to him, Darzek regretted that he hadn't handled the promotion himself. They were offering an all-expenses-paid vacation on some remote, scenic planet, with round-trip passage if there was any world to return to, and any minion of Madison Avenue could have started a stampede with an opportunity like that. Min Kallof delivered his presentation with neither urgency nor appeal, but he conveyed the facts as ordered, and a mild run on E-Wusk's ships resulted.

Even that effect was somewhat spoiled by the activities of Naz

Forlan's scientists. They chose that day to launch the artificial satellites that were to save Vezpro. Forlan did not publicize his project—in fact, he managed it as discreetly as possible. The satellites were launched on the night side of the planet by a small spaceship that towed them, one at a time, into the proper orbit, got them moving at the prescribed speed, and turned them loose.

But some of his scientists talked, or perhaps it was the spaceship crew. The news spread, and by evening the parks of Klinoz were filled with citizens watching the new, fast-moving stars.

UrsNollf came to see Darzek. There was nothing more for him to do, and he was eager to go home. "Will the things work?" Darzek asked him.

"I think they might. It isn't my field, you know, but Forlan's scientists seem very confident."

Darzek told him he wouldn't have long to wait and sent him aboard Miss Schlupe's ship.

"You don't believe it, huh?" Miss Schlupe remarked, when he had left.

"I do not. But then—science left me with Galileo. I've never been able to understand why a heavy object doesn't fall faster than a light one. It certainly falls harder—enough things have landed on my feet to convince me of that, even though they didn't drop from the Leaning Tower of Pisa. I can't understand how any kind of ray or wave, be it radio, or magnetic, or X ray, or ultraviolet, or whatever, would have much effect on a mechanical device that probably is buried ten or twenty meters deep. The scientists at Zarst can't understand, either."

"What have they accomplished at Zarst?" Miss Schlupe asked.

"Nothing. At least they admit it. Raf Lolln is heartbroken."

"Then we can write off the scientists. We can't criticize them, because we didn't do well, either. It's certain now that we're not going to catch the guy—we still haven't got a clue as to who or what or where he may be. That leaves the psychological angle. Will he or won't he? Shall we start packing?"

"What have you got to pack?"

"I'm taking a cargo compartment of dried mushrooms," Miss Schlupe said. "And my rocking chair. Otherwise, a couple of suitcases will get me back to Primores. What about you?"

"I have no rocking chair, and I can eat your mushrooms. One suitcase. But we aren't going directly to Primores. We'll park in a remote orbit and observe. If Vezpro turns into a sun, I want to see it happen. Then we'll go to Skarnaf and pick up E-Wusk."

"I think I'll make it two cargo compartments of dried mushrooms," Miss Schlupe said thoughtfully, "just in case they're no longer available after the new cycle."

On the third day before cycle's end, the leader of Miss Schlupe's commandos came to see her. She listened briefly and then summoned Darzek. "Eld Wolndur recognized one of my commandos and asked if there was any way to get a message to you. He says it's urgent."

"Since we're about to leave anyway, there's no harm in letting him know that we're still here," Darzek said. "He and Melris might want to leave with us." He turned to the commando leader. "Find out where he'll be, and when, and I'll meet him."

She returned a short time later and gave Darzek a transmitter address. He didn't recognize it, so he copied it for Miss Schlupe. "This is beginning to sound peculiar," he said. "If I vanish, follow me with your commandos."

"Delighted to," Miss Schlupe said. "All that training and no one to use it on. They'd be ecstatic if I let them perform some three-armed judo on the villain."

"Make certain they know I'm not the villain," Darzek said and stepped through the transmitter.

To his amazement, he found himself in an underground tunnel that housed a marketplace. It was not one he had seen before. These shops were narrow stalls built of rough stone, and the customers were served at a counter-type opening; but the general arrangement was the same, with vendors on either side of the brightly lighted, arched tunnel, and here and there a vacant stall, sometimes enclosed with slats.

He was looking about bewilderedly when Wolndur came hurrying toward him. "Gul Darr—"

Darzek pressed a finger to his lips. He had dashed off without his disguise—not that it mattered, but he thought it just as well not to advertise his name. "What do you want?" he asked.

Wolndur looked about nervously and then whispered. "We've found Qwasrolk."

"Alive?" Darzek asked quickly.

"Yes. Barely."

"Where?"

Wolndur turned and headed along the tunnel. Darzek followed at a discreet distance. They both wove their way through the slow-moving shoppers and occasionally became entangled with them where some shop was offering a bargain.

Up ahead, the tunnel came to an end. The stall on the right was empty and enclosed with slats. Wolndur, without looking behind him, pulled the slats aside and slipped from sight. Darzek arrived a moment later and paused to look about. No one was paying the slightest attention. He supposed that empty stalls were routinely inspected now and then by prospective tenants, though this location at the end of the tunnel wouldn't be a choice one. To a citizen of Vezpro, any kind of illegal or even improper activity would be unthinkable. Darzek pulled at the slats and struggled past them, catching his clothing on the edges.

Wolndur stood bending over a low cot of a type Vezpronians used to save space—it could be folded up like an accordion. Melris Angoz knelt beside it. On the cot was Qwasrolk. A dim light hung above them.

Darzek spoke softly. "How'd you happen to find him?"

"This was one of the addresses on that list Melris compiled," Wolndur said. "I decided to have a look at all of them. And he was lying on the floor here, unconscious. So I got Melris, and we brought a bed and blankets."

Darzek regarded the two of them respectfully. The warehouses had been checked carefully—they had records to look at. But he himself hadn't thought to give the empty shops more than a glance. "Has a doctor seen him?" he asked.

"Yes. A friend of mine. He promised not to file a report. There's nothing that can be done for him medically. We've been trying to build up his strength—he takes food tablets and water and liquid food capsules if they're placed in his mouth. We've been afraid to let anyone know he's here, because they'd try to take him to a hospital, and he'd disappear again." He paused. "I was sure you hadn't left Vezpro, but I didn't know how to find you."

"You couldn't have done any better with my help," Darzek said. "You handled things exactly right. Have you tried to talk with him?"

"Just to try to get him to eat, or to make him comfortable. We haven't tried to ask him anything. We were afraid he'd disappear."

Qwasrolk was lying on his side, his face to the wall, with a light blanket pulled over his head. Darzek was not unhappy that the grotesque mask of his face was concealed.

"He seems stronger, now," Melris said softly. "I don't think he'd eaten in a long time. He was obsessed with something. Nothing else mattered, not even food."

"And yet he refused to tell anyone," Darzek mused.

"We don't even know whether he can talk," Melris protested.

Darzek reflected. "That's right. He's certainly never said anything the few times I've seen him. We'll have to find out. It would be a help if he could just tell us what happened to him. It may have no connection with Vezpro."

"It's suggestive that he was found here and that he was seen at another location where the nuclear materials were shipped," Melris said.

" 'Suggestive' is the word for it," Darzek agreed. "But if he can't or won't talk, it'll never be anything more than that. We'll have to try to question him."

Darzek knelt beside Melris. He resisted an impulse to shake Qwasrolk awake and start firing questions. This mutilated being perhaps knew the answers to all the riddles that had plagued them, but Darzek remembered only too vividly what had happened the last time he clutched that dead flesh. A sudden move, loud speech, or a threatening manner could undo all that Melris and Wolndur had accomplished with kindness and gentle care.

"Perhaps it would be better if you questioned him," he said to Melris.

"What should I ask him?"

"What happened to him, and where, and who did it."

"All right. But I think we should wait until he wakes up."

They had been talking in whispers. All that time the shrouded form on the cot lay motionless except for irregular, deep breathing.

They waited.

The blanket heaved suddenly as a bent knee straightened. The body turned; the grotesque mask stared up at them.

Melris bent over it with a smile. "How are you feeling? Hungry?"

She offered a food pill, but there was no response. The lipless mouth did not open; the teeth remained clenched. Melris, sounding very nervous, asked, "Qwasrolk, can you tell us what happened to you?"

At least he was accustomed to them and to his surroundings. He showed no alarm, even when his gaze wandered and his eyes rested briefly on Darzek. Melris asked again, "What happened to you?"

Finally Qwasrolk spoke a word. He repeated it twice, and the third time Darzek was able to understand. He was saying, "Error."

"Where?" Melris asked.

Again Qwasrolk spoke. It sounded like no place in the galaxy that Darzek had heard of, but there were millions of worlds in the galaxy. Melris asked again, "Where?"

Then Darzek caught the answer. "Plans." Or—"In plans."

Suddenly he understood. Qwasrolk had been performing some kind of experiment, and it had gone wrong, and he was still trying to figure out why. That was the meaning of the sketch and the scribbled calculations Darzek had found in the grove.

"Is that what happened at Nifron D?" Darzek asked suddenly.

The lidless eyes rested on him. "Error—in plans—at Nifron D." It was becoming easier to understand him.

Then Qwasrolk spoke wildly and tried to sit up. "Still error in plans." He had to repeat that twice before they understood.

Then Darzek said, "Another experiment with an error? Where is it being performed?"

"Here."

"Here—on Vezpro?"

"Yes."

"Can you show us the place?"

"Yes."

And before they could move, he vanished.

22

Darzek recovered first. He went at once to the entrance and looked out. The first person he noticed was Miss Schlupe, standing in the center of the tunnel some twenty meters away and looking about her apprehensively. He motioned to her, and she started toward him.

He turned to Wolndur and Melris and pointed at the stone wall, which ended the tunneled street and also served as the side of the stall. "What's on the other side?" he asked.

They gazed at him blankly.

"This must be a remnant of an underground transportation system," he said. "Segments of it were blocked off long ago for markets and fungus farms. I'm an idiot for not having thought of it before. Move a transmitter frame into an unused part and you have a perfect place for a secret underground laboratory. How far does it go?"

They were still staring at him. Their civilization had been transmitterized for hundreds of cycles, and references to underground transportation meant nothing to them.

Miss Schlupe pulled the slats aside and stuck her head in. "Things under control?"

"Where are the commandos?" Darzek asked.

"I brought about a hundred of them. The rest will be along as soon as they're rounded up."

Darzek went outside the shop where he could study the wall in the bright light of the tunnel. It looked as though nothing less than a charge of dynamite would make a dent in it. "It'd probably take days to break through," Darzek said, "and if we just casually started using sledgehammers here, someone might ask an embarrassing question."

Miss Schlupe stood beside him and studied the wall. "You want that thing knocked down?"

"No. I just want a hole big enough to crawl through and see what's on the other side. We'd probably need a lot of handlights, though, and I haven't seen such a thing on Vezpro."

"Then you haven't looked very well. There's a shop just down the tunnel that sells them. Why do we have to do the hole-knocking in public? It's the same wall inside there, isn't it?"

"So it is. Let's have a look."

At the rear of the stall, they found a doorway leading into a small room. Some previous tenant had taken advantage of his position next to the wall to add a stockroom to his premises, rent free—and the stockroom was beyond the wall. Darzek removed a few slats with one kick. The dark tunnel stretched beyond.

He turned to Miss Schlupe. "Go buy a couple of hundred hand-lights, if they have that many. And have your commandos slip in here inconspicuously, two or three at a time."

"Right," she said. "But I'll need a few with me, to carry all those lights. And I'll have to post guides to tell the others where to go."

"Do that," Darzek said.

She hurried away, and Darzek turned and sat down on the low cot Qwasrolk had been occupying. "I think he really wanted to show us what he was talking about," he said, "but his mind's been affected to the point where he doesn't realize that others can't travel the way he does. You two did a remarkable job with him. I only hope something results from it."

"We were lucky," Melris said. "We just happened to look in the right place."

"That was because you kept on looking. And you gained his confidence—not even the doctors were able to do that." Darzek paused. "The question is whether he'll come back."

Miss Schlupe's commandos began to slip into the stall. Darzek showed them the stockroom and told them to crawl into the tunnel, sit down in the dark, and relax. He felt hopeful but not optimistic. For all he knew, the old transportation system was part of an inter-city network with thousands of kilometers of tunnels. A thorough search might take years, and they had less than three days.

He said to Wolndur, "Are there archives somewhere that would have a map of these tunnels?"

Wolndur didn't know.

Suddenly Qwasrolk stood before them. He said, sounding impatient, "Come. I'll show you."

"Wait!" Melris said quickly. "We can't go the way you do. We'll have to walk. Or use a transmitter."

Qwasrolk considered this perplexedly.

"Is there a transmitter?" Darzek asked.

Three more of Miss Schlupe's commandos slipped into the stall and moved past them toward the stockroom entrance. Their presence momentarily startled Qwasrolk, but not nearly as much as his presence startled them. They stared at him but managed to keep moving.

Darzek asked again, "Is there a transmitter?"

"Transmitter?" Qwasrolk's blurred speech echoed. Not needing one, it probably had not occurred to him to look for one.

"Is it close enough to walk?" Melris asked.

"Walk?" Qwasrolk echoed. He pondered the question as though a teleport had no concept of distance.

"Is it in a tunnel?" Darzek asked.

"Yes. Tunnel."

"This tunnel?" Darzek persisted.

Qwasrolk hesitated. "I'll see," he said, and vanished.

Miss Schlupe's commandos continued to arrive. Then she came herself, accompanied by a squad carrying boxes of handlights. "A hundred and fifty-seven was all they had," she said. "Shall I look for more?"

"No. We'll only need to use a few at a time."

"Qwasrolk?"

"He's been back. He went to see whether it's in this tunnel and how far it is."

Miss Schlupe arched her eyebrows. *"It?"*

"That," Darzek said, "is the question."

"We're beginning to arouse a bit of curiosity. At least seventy-five people have gone in here, and no one has come out, and there can't be room for that many. Shall I have them keep coming?"

Darzek reflected. "No. Have them wait outside as inconspicuously as possible. No need to bring them all in when we don't know where we're going."

She turned and spoke briefly to someone outside, and the flow of commandos stopped. Darzek returned to the cot; Wolndur paced up and down; Miss Schlupe talked quietly with Melris. They were waiting without knowing what they were waiting for.

Suddenly Qwasrolk reappeared, almost colliding with Wolndur. "Come," he said.

"Is it in this tunnel?" Darzek asked.

"Yes."

"Can we walk?"

"Yes. I think so."

"How far is it?"

Qwasrolk gestured. "Far. I think."

He vanished again, but they found him in the tunnel on the other side of the wall, gazing perplexedly at the commandos. Miss Schlupe hurriedly sent word to the group waiting outside and began to pass out handlights. Darzek gave one to Qwasrolk.

"You lead the way," he said, "and we'll follow you. And we'll see if we can get that error corrected."

"I lead," Qwasrolk said.

And promptly vanished.

It was the strangest journey Darzek had ever experienced. Qwasrolk traveled in teleporting leaps. He vanished, and eventually they would see the beam of his handlight far ahead of them where he sat waiting—if the tunnel chanced to run straight at that point and there were no obstructions. When they approached him, he vanished again.

Darzek, Miss Schlupe, Wolndur, and Melris led the way, with the commandos spread out behind them. They had no idea how long the handlights would last, or how long they would need them, so they used only a few. The footing would have been difficult even in good light. They had to examine the tunnel floor for holes and crevasses, and Darzek kept flashing his own light on the ceiling, which was riddled with cracks and sagging blocks of stone. Occasionally the ceiling had collapsed, partially or almost completely blocking the tunnel, and the debris had to be climbed over.

"How far have we walked?" Darzek asked finally.

Miss Schlupe chuckled. "If you're tired, I can have my commandos carry you. I've been working out with them. The only thing you've exercised since you arrived here is your brain."

"Not even that," Darzek said bitterly. "For all our detective work, can we honestly claim to have a suspect?"

Miss Schlupe reflected. "No. But Qwasrolk has some connection with it."

"As a dupe," Darzek said. "He must have been one of the Nifron D scientists, and he was on the planet when it blew. Do you suppose the villain left him there on purpose to make last-minute adjustments without his knowing what was going to happen? That would explain his talk about an error. He thought it was a different kind of experiment."

"Anyone who would do that—callously sacrifice a loyal employee —might very well blow up a world of five billion people."

Darzek nodded soberly. "No doubt you're right. There may be something impersonal about destroying a world of strangers, but the scientist who would deliberately destroy an assistant and perhaps a friend in the interest of an experiment certainly wouldn't hesitate to destroy Vespro, evacuated or not, if he thought he had a reason for it. I wonder how many of those missing scientists died on Nifron D and on the eleventh planet."

"Qwasrolk survived only because he could teleport."

"He must have had latent abilities he wasn't aware of himself until he experienced the pain and horror of having the world he was standing on turn into a sun. At that instant his ability stopped being latent, but an instant was enough to burn him terribly and expose him to radiation that should have killed him."

"He reacted like a hurt child," Miss Schlupe said. "He simply went home. To Skarnaf. To the place where he was born and raised. Only the old homestead was gone, so he was found lying in a ditch."

"It must have happened that way," Darzek agreed. "And Qwasrolk must know who the villain is—but he may not know him under his real name."

"That'd be a pretty problem." Miss Schlupe observed. "It wouldn't do us much good to know the person responsible is Mr. X from planet Y. What is Qwasrolk going to show us?"

"An elaborate scientific device with an error in it, I hope—the same error that made a supposedly innocent scientific experiment turn a world into a sun."

"If we find the thing, what are you going to do with it?"

"It shouldn't be difficult to make it inoperable. There must be various kinds of circuitry involved. There must be an electrical source that sets the thing off. There may even be a timing device, set to make contact one second after the new year begins. I think we can easily convert this thing to junk—if we can find it."

"And then what?"

"We leave your commandos in charge. Sooner or later our villain will show up to find out why it didn't work. He may bring some scientists with him, but I'm sure they'll be able to handle the situation."

"I guarantee that they'll handle it," Miss Schlupe said.

They rounded a curve in the tunnel, clambered over another fall of ceiling debris, and saw Qwasrolk's light waiting for them in the distance. As they approached, he vanished once more. Squinting into the darkness, Darzek could make out his own light reflected far ahead. That wasn't unusual. Previously, it had meant that there was another fall to climb over, or that the tunnel curved.

This time it meant neither. They marched straight ahead, on level ground, until suddenly a wall loomed in front of them. It was constructed of a concretelike material, and it stretched from one side of the tunnel to the other, and from floor to ceiling. Darzek kicked it and hurt his foot.

He studied it for a long time. Finally he said to Miss Schlupe, "You carry a lot of odds and ends in that bag of yours. I don't suppose you have a sledgehammer. Or a stick of dynamite."

"Neither," Miss Schlupe said regretfully.

"Even if Qwasrolk comes back to find out what happened to us, he won't be able to help. We might go back and try to get into the tunnel from the surface on the other side of the wall, but that assumes that we could find the tunnel and that there wouldn't be any embarrassing obstacle on the surface, like Min Kallof's office. Also, it would take a long time without any guarantee that Qwasrolk would wait for us, and even if we succeeded we might walk twenty kilometers and end up at another wall."

While the commandos waited uncertainly behind them, Darzek, Miss Schlupe, Wolndur, and Melris all found themselves chunks of ceiling debris and sat down to look disconsolately at the wall.

23

They had been seated for some minutes when Darzek suddenly announced, "That wall is new."

He walked over to it and examined it with his handlight. Wolndur performed his own examination and agreed.

"Who on Vezpro has the skill to build such a wall?" Darzek asked. "No machine did that. You can see the marks of the trowel—the tool used to smooth the cement or mortar."

"Alien workers," Wolndur said. "Sometimes a few are brought in for special projects—historical restoration, or a country dwelling built in the old manner for some wealthy person."

"So someone brought in a few alien workers—a couple of them could have done a job like this in a short time—and had a wall built across the tunnel. Why?"

Wolndur gestured bewilderedly.

Miss Schlupe had come up behind them to perform her own inspection. "I'm betting that there's not one wall, but two," she said. "The two of them would form a nicely hidden, inaccessible underground retreat. Or a laboratory for secret research projects."

"Or perhaps a place to hide the device that will turn a world into a sun," Darzek suggested grimly. "There must be other entrances to this tunnel. All that was required was to bring a transmitter frame far enough into it so no one would be likely to discover the thing. Then alien workers and materials could be passed through the transmitter. Once the two walls were built, the place would be accessible only by transmitter—which of course would be personalized at once to limit access to the scientists working there. That's how Qwasrolk happened to know about it. Even a teleport wouldn't stumble onto an underground laboratory by accident."

Some of Miss Schlupe's commandos had come up behind them. When they grasped the fact that their destination was beyond the wall, they began chattering in their own language. Several of them started back down the tunnel. After a time they called out, and the whole group followed after them. When it returned, some twenty of them were laboriously carrying a long slab of concrete in their three-handed grasps. It must have been enormously heavy, and—strong as they obviously were—they staggered under its weight.

As they approached the wall they began to move faster—a shuffle, a trot, a stumbling run. The concrete crashed into the wall.

They lowered it carefully and stood panting while others closed in with handlights to examine the damage. All they had accomplished was to chip off a few flakes of the wall and convert a millimeter or two of the slab to dust.

Without comment, another group of commandos picked up the slab, backed off from the wall, and repeated the performance. More chips and dust resulted.

"The alien workers seem to have been highly competent," Darzek observed dryly. "They'll wear out the concrete before they break through."

"There's plenty more around," Miss Schlupe said.

There also were plenty of commandos. A third group took the place of the second, and a fourth group followed it. Miss Schlupe and Darzek seated themselves and watched while the concrete was repeatedly smashed into the wall.

"Why didn't we think of a setup like this?" Darzek asked. "The moment I first saw an underground mart, I should have known. Me, from New York, not recognizing a subway!"

"Your excuse is better than mine," Miss Schlupe said. "You didn't visit a mushroom farm. Now that I think about it, looking down that long bed of fungus, I should have been able to see a train coming."

The concrete crashed again. Darzek said reproachfully to Wolndur, "You're the scientist. How do we get through the wall? Tools? Is there such a thing as an explosive on this planet?"

Wolndur's face instantly became a blank study. He was a theoretical physicist. He probably knew what tools were, but he certainly had never seen a sledgehammer or a pneumatic drill, and Darzek wouldn't have trusted him to set off an explosive charge if one had been available.

"I don't suppose we could get a vehicle in here," Darzek said. "Those falls we had to climb over—"

"You couldn't get one through that storeroom anyway," Miss Schlupe pointed out.

"Right. It'd delay things a bit if we had to start by knocking down the other wall. I don't recall seeing a vehicle on this world anyway."

He sighed. "This isn't one of my better days. Since I came to Vezpro, I haven't had any better days."

The concrete crashed again.

Darzek got to his feet. "I might as well go back. I'll see if the plans for the subway system still exist and what government assistance I can get in a hurry. You wait here—"

Qwasrolk stood before them. He seemed less timid in the dim reflection of a few handlight beams. His hideousness was blurred; there was no glow for his lidless and probably damaged eyes to wince from.

Before he could speak, Melris said, "We can't get through the wall, Qwasrolk."

"What we need," Darzek said thoughtfully, "is a couple of matched, portable transmitter frames with their own power supply. One here, and one where this error has to be corrected. Is it just beyond the wall?"

"Yes," Qwasrolk said. He gestured. "There."

"Since we can't break through the wall, and since we can't travel the way you do—"

Qwasrolk had vanished.

"I think he's trying to help us," Darzek said. "But what can he do now?"

No one answered.

"The error thing is his idée fixe. Once we showed an interest in that, he was no longer apprehensive about us. We were on his side. Strange."

"The poor, pathetic creature," Miss Schlupe murmured. "If you'd been through what he's been through, you'd have an idée fixe, too."

"Mine would be to idée fixe the person responsible. Do you think I should go back and try to get help?"

"Wait," Miss Schlupe said. "Qwasrolk knows where we are, and he thinks we're on his side, and he really must want to show us something or he wouldn't have led us here. Maybe there's machinery in the laboratory, and he can punch a hole in the wall from the other side. Let's see what he does next."

"If he doesn't die first. He may, you know. Any minute."

"He acted lively enough," Miss Schlupe said. "Having a job to do seems to have revived him."

"Very well," Darzek said. "We'll sit here and see what happens."

They hadn't long to wait. Qwasrolk appeared suddenly, carrying a transmitter frame. He set it down, moved it about to find a level surface it could stand upright on, and vanished again. Darzek strolled over to examine it.

It was new, with the control still sealed.

"He stole this!" Darzek exclaimed.

"What would he pay for it with?" Miss Schlupe asked. "His solvency credential was burned away."

"This would fascinate students of parapsychology. It's possible to teleport with freight. We should have thought of that—remember all the stuff he'd accumulated in the grove? Strange that he should steal, though. In this society, theft—"

"Idée fixe," Miss Schlupe said. "Turn the thing on. Has he gone to get the other one, or did he steal them both at once?"

The transmitter was the simplest model made. It was matched only to its mate, and it operated over a limited distance. Such models were in great demand for use in factories or multiple-storied buildings where there was a great deal of traffic between two specific points.

Darzek turned it on. There was no answering light, so the mate was not operating.

Then the signal flashed and Qwasrolk stepped through the transmitter frame. "Come," he said.

He turned, walked back through the frame, vanished. Darzek and Miss Schlupe exchanged glances. Then Darzek stepped to the frame and followed.

He emerged in a long room formed by the two walls across the tunnel. Here the tunnel was in excellent repair. The walls had been refinished with white mortar over the stones. The floor had been rebuilt expertly with inlaid flat stones. The ceiling was luminous like those in the markets. Darzek was momentarily blinded by the bright light.

He kept walking, conscious of the fact that Miss Schlupe and her commandos were stepping through the transmitter after him. He heard an increasing volume of footsteps on the stone floor, but he did not look back. Neither did he look at Qwasrolk, who was walking a short distance ahead of him.

In the center of the room, extending from floor almost to the ceiling, was an enormous, pear-shaped object. The lower section could have been a huge, oddly designed generator. The humped top bristled with strangely shaped protrusions, like an insect with a multitude of mutated antennae. It even looked menacing.

At the side of the room were workbenches with banks of instruments and controls. Wolndur hurried ahead of Darzek, walked in a circle around the looming structure, and then unerringly followed a cable to one of the instrument panels.

"This must control it," he said. "The others will be test panels. With anything this complicated, a multitude of things can go wrong. Each functioning component would have to be tested before anyone could be certain that it would work."

"Is there a timer?" Darzek asked.

"I don't see one. It could be built into the mechanism."

"Can you make the thing harmless without setting it off?"

"Easily." Wolndur went to one of the workbenches and returned with a set of peculiar-looking tools. Darzek remembered what he'd thought about theoretical physicists and made a mental apology. Wolndur wouldn't know anything about knocking down walls, but he could tackle a complicated enormity like this with ease.

Miss Schlupe spoke up. "If you're going to fuss with this thing, shouldn't I send my commandos back through the transmitter?"

"If this goes off," Darzek said dryly, "it won't matter which side of the wall they're standing on. And we may need them. Once Wolndur starts dismantling it—and that's what I want him to do, first make sure it's turned off, and then disassemble as much as he can as fast as possible—it may send out a signal. If it does, someone may come to see what's happening."

He pointed to a transmitter frame that stood at the far end of the room. It obviously was a design that provided the ultimate in security. "It may be personalized," Darzek said, "but I don't know why anyone would bother. It's people getting in here that he'd worry about, not people getting out, and personalization on both ends would be a nuisance. Later, we'll try it and see—but not until this gadget is taken care of. So I think your commandos had better stay. You can arrange them on either side of the transmitter, but out of sight. That way they can grab off any visitors one at a time, as they arrive, which is much neater than waiting until they look the situation over and decide to leave."

"Agreed," Miss Schlupe said. She led her commandos over to the distant transmitter frame and gave them her instructions. Wolndur was still studying the monstrous pear-shaped edifice when she returned. Darzek and Melris were watching him. Qwasrolk, now that others had assumed responsibility for the error, the idée fixe that had haunted him, seemed to have lost interest. He had slumped to the floor in exhaustion, leaning against the wall with his arm across his face to shield his eyes.

Wolndur went to have a look at the control panel. He called Melris and spoke tersely to her for a moment before he pushed a low platform up to the menacing structure. The platform moved on rollers, and when he got it positioned, he locked them. He stepped onto it, and the top of the platform rose slowly, carrying him toward the roof. Finally he stopped his ascent and reached out to snap off a large plate. Then, for a long, tense moment, he peered through the opening with a handlight.

"All right," he announced suddenly. "I think I see the main solenoid, and I'll remove it first. Then I'll take out everything else I can reach."

"Will that make it safe?" Darzek asked.

"Maybe not to us. This thing undoubtedly contains an enormous amount of radioactive material, and I have no idea how well it's shielded. But it can't go off with the control assembly removed. At least, it shouldn't."

"Go ahead," Darzek said. "Toss down the parts as fast as you can get them out, and I'll stomp them into unrecognizable junk. At the very least, we can make certain that a lot of replacements have to be ordered before the thing can be used."

Wolndur began to apply his tools. For a time there was an occasional clinking. Then he tossed down a strange-looking coil. Darzek flattened it with one stomp. He did the same with the next part. The third was large and heavy and enclosed in an oblong shield. Darzek carried it over to one of the workbenches, found a tool that looked something like a massive wrench, and pounded the object into unrecognizability.

While he was working on it, Miss Schlupe crushed several delicately constructed items that Wolndur dropped to her. When Darzek returned, Wolndur paused and looked down doubtfully. "Maybe we're doing the wrong thing. We're destroying scientific knowledge."

"This knowledge," Darzek said firmly, "is best buried right here."

Wolndur threw down more parts. Some of them obviously contained intricate electrical pathways and represented fantastically complex custom designing. When Darzek could not smash them with his foot, he took them to a bench and used a tool.

Finally Wolndur called, "Melris?"

Melris, still at the control panel, threw a switch. A few yellow lights came on; most of the panels remained dark. "Got most of the circuits," Wolndur said with satisfaction and went back to work.

Miss Schlupe's commandos were finding the whole procedure perplexing. The deliberate destruction of property was both comic and tragic to Vezpronian psychology. They regarded Darzek's antics as acts of puzzling hilarity. Eventually all of them were watching him, and the figure that suddenly stepped from the transmitter they surrounded took them by surprise.

It was Naz Forlan.

He strode into the room, taking several steps before he noticed the small army of commandos clustered about him. That brought him to an abrupt and bewildered halt. Then his expression changed to amazement as he recognized Darzek, recognized Melris Angoz, recognized Miss Schlupe, and finally lifted his gaze from the debris that littered the floor to Wolndur, still working near the ceiling. Wolndur had not seen him enter, and he casually tossed down one more complicated element from the innards he was probing.

No one touched Forlan. He arrived, he took his steps into the room, he looked about, he finally grasped what was happening, and he spun around and leaped for the transmitter. And Miss Schlupe's commandos were still too surprised to react.

But as Forlan's foot started the final step that would take him to safety, Qwasrolk stood beside him and gripped him firmly. Forlan struggled, but the mutilated creature's strength was irresistible.

"I've been looking for you," he said, elation in his voice. "It's the same experiment, and it has the same error. It doesn't work like you said it would, and the last time I didn't know what to do. I want to show you where the error is. It must be corrected, or what happened on Nifron D will happen here. If you'll let me explain—"

Forlan said nothing. He continued to struggle.

Then Qwasrolk was gone. So was Forlan, and all of them, including the commandos who had been poised to capture anyone who came through the transmitter, stood staring at emptiness.

24

As Darzek had deduced, the exit transmitter was not personalized.

He waited until Wolndur assured him that the entire activating apparatus of the nuclear monster would have to be rebuilt before it could harm anyone. Then, after telling him to carry on, he took Miss Schlupe aside for a conference.

The result was that a squad of Miss Schlupe's commandos returned to the tunnel by way of Qwasrolk's stolen transmitter frames. They would carry one of the frames along the tunnel to the limit of its range, leave a guard with it, and return to Klinoz by way of the underground shopping center with a message for the masfiln.

Darzek, because he did not know what he would find on the other end, took two squads of commandos with him to investigate Naz Forlan's transmitter. He knew that the trip would be one-way, because the matched transmitter they emerged from would certainly be personalized. He told Miss Schlupe to guard the place well, be alert in case Forlan returned with an army, and let no one else use the transmitter until she heard from him.

Signaling his commandos to follow at regular intervals, he turned and stepped through. He emerged in darkness, reached forward blindly, found a door, opened it.

The transmitter frame had been concealed in one of several small storage rooms adjacent to a long, bare room that looked like a primitive scientific research laboratory. As he expected, it was personalized. And it had two destination settings.

The laboratory proved to be an annex to a rustic-looking country dwelling. The commandos quickly secured the place, and it took Darzek only a few minutes to confirm that the dwelling belonged to Naz Forlan. Finding out where it was would take him considerably longer.

There was no road. There were no other habitations in sight. Darzek went back inside the dwelling and thoughtfully considered the destination board on the transmitter that stood in a small foyer. He probably could step through it to any address he knew on the world of Vezpro, or even to the transfer stations; but it certainly would be personalized for arrivals, so he could not return and he still would have no notion of where he had been.

He discussed the problem with his commandos. Finally he sent six of them, with the same message for the masfiln, through the transmitter to their own headquarters. One of them was to return immediately if she could. She did not, which confirmed that the transmitter was personalized. Darzek resignedly chose another six to accompany him, told those left behind to guard the place well, and started off in search of someone who could tell him where he was.

He chose a route that led toward a distant hill, and they struggled across the tangled landscape for kilometers before they made the perspiring ascent and looked down on a small, typically Vezpronian town—a single sprawling building with a central park. Descending the hill they broke into a run, and they dashed panting along a tunneled street oblivious to the stares of passersby.

They used the first public transmitter they came to, and moments later Darzek was in Klinoz, in the government complex, being embraced by the masfiln.

"I have done everything you asked," Min Kallof said. "Is it really over? And was it really Naz Forlan?"

"It must have been."

"I can't believe it."

"As to whether it's over, he has at least one other secret laboratory, and there may be more. We can't be certain that there's only one nuclear gadget until we've searched all of them. I need six of the best transmitter technicians available. At once."

Miss Schlupe's commandos already had established a transmitter link with the underground lab they'd discovered. Wolndur had nuclear specialists in protective clothing completing the disassembly of Forlan's device and carefully encasing radioactive material in shielded containers. Miss Schlupe, finally exhausted by the long trek through the tunnel and the excitement that followed, had gone home for a nap. Darzek sent Melris with a message to tell her what he'd found.

Darzek's continuous exertions now had overlapped two days, and he felt exhausted. When he stepped through the laboratory transmitter to Naz Forlan's country estate a second time, he was wondering whether Forlan's storage rooms contained anything resembling food. The six transmitter technicians trailed after him.

Three of them went to work on the transmitter in the foyer, and the other three concentrated on the one in the laboratory, first moving the frame out of the storage room so they could have access to it.

Forlan had engineered the personalizing himself, with a system of his own devising that completely befuddled them. Those working in the dwelling succeeded first, and the place soon was crowded with more technicians, with scientists, with government officials, and with the new chief proctor, who thought that he should take charge. Disgusted, Darzek chased out all except those he had a use for.

The technicians working in the laboratory had a much more difficult task. The transmitter was an unfamiliar model Forlan had imported or built himself. Hours passed. Another shift of technicians took over, with the same lack of success. Min Kallof came to see if they were making progress and anxiously reminded Darzek of the date. Darzek was unable to reassure him. Miss Schlupe arrived, with Melris and Wolndur, irritated because Darzek's order to keep people away had been so strictly enforced that she'd had to appeal to the masfiln in order to find him.

She looked sternly at Darzek and asked, "Do you know how long it's been since you slept? You should see yourself."

"No, thank you." Darzek said. "I'll wait. I think they're getting it."

They were. A technician heaved a sigh, stepped back, turned on the transmitter, and got an acceptance light. Darzek stepped through right behind him, and they found themselves in the walled-off tunnel Qwasrolk had led them to. The nuclear specialists were still at work, but Forlan's capacious monster was now almost empty.

Darzek and the technician exchanged shrugs. "Wrong guess," Darzek said philosophically. "Now you can try the other setting."

Having solved the problem once, it did not take the technicians long to solve it a second time. Darzek followed one of them through the transmitter and emerged in another section of walled-off tunnel. This was much longer than the other and was equipped as a complex research laboratory where many scientists could work and live together. Probably the components of Forlan's nuclear devices had been built here.

And here a strange and terrible drama had been enacted. Qwasrolk, intent on demonstrating the "error" that had caused the Nifron D tragedy and was about to cause another, had started a diagram on one of Forlan's workscreens. Forlan had tried to escape to the transmitter, but Qwasrolk—who could block any dash Forlan made by teleporting himself—had seized Forlan and dragged him back. The scuff marks and twin lines left by Forlan's feet after each escape attempt told their own eloquent story. Eventually Forlan must have tried to attack Qwasrolk physically, and the maimed creature had reacted with rage.

Forlan lay near the transmitter, strangled.

Qwasrolk lay before the computer screen. After killing Forlan, he had returned to his diagram, his mind still intent on demonstrating the error he thought his employer had made. His weakened condition and his sustained exertion had finally completed his tortuous process of dying.

Darzek left the technician by the transmitter while he made a careful inspection of the laboratory. Then, carefully avoiding the bodies, he returned to the transmitter. The search would have to continue, but he was convinced, now, that there were no more secret laboratories. And no more nuclear devices.

"What do we do next?" the technician asked.

"We go home," Darzek answered. "Our work—both yours and mine—is finished."

Min Kallof had only one word. "Why?"

"Wolndur and Melris can tell you," Darzek said.

Wolndur said sadly, "He was an alien, and Vezpro treated him like one."

"But we made his people welcome here!" the masfiln protested. "They had every opportunity available to natives. Forlan became the most wealthy and successful scientist on the planet!"

"You let them do your farming," Darzek said, "but when one of them tried to do something that took him into competition with natives, he was ridiculed and discriminated against. Forlan was particularly resented because he was so brilliant. He inspired jealousy and political maneuvering that kept him from recognition and promotions he deserved."

"But he received wealth and honors!" Min Kallof protested.

"He received wealth because on an industrial world the technological expert's skill is worth money, no matter what his species is. The honors came too late and seemed more like a mockery than a deserved reward."

The masfiln still refused to believe. "Was he really going to do it?"

"I don't know," Darzek said. "I think his plans were upset because your people refused to be evacuated. He wanted them to lose this world—to become despised refugees the way his people had. But whether he actually would have destroyed Vezpro even then, I don't know. I'm sure he gloated over his power to do so. I hope that gave him satisfaction enough."

Darzek took his leave of them, expressing regret that he could not stay for the mating ceremony of Wolndur and Melris. "I have to go back and see what crises the galaxy has thought up in my absence," he said. They parted warmly.

But as he stepped into the transmitter, he still could hear Min Kallof muttering, "Why?"

Miss Schlupe was rocking comfortably and knitting. She looked up as Darzek entered and asked, "Finished?"

"I think so. Wolndur has pledged to go through all of Forlan's possessions and destroy anything that remotely looks like the plan for a device to turn a world into a sun."

Miss Schlupe accelerated her rocking. "It seems to me that it could be a useful thing to know if it were controlled properly. Converting a small satellite might make a remote world habitable."

"True enough. That's why I copped a complete set of Forlan's plans. I'll feed them to Supreme, with a lot of built-in precautions concerning who will have access to them."

Miss Schlupe nodded. She kept her eyes on her knitting; her rocking speed did not slacken. "We should have spotted him, you know. He gave himself away repeatedly."

"I know. He displayed his villainy right under our noses, but because you and I come from Earth, where villainy is commonplace, we didn't notice. And the Vezpronians, never having experienced any, didn't recognize it either."

"The first time you met, his insisting that you identify yourself—"

"Exactly. No ordinary citizen of the Galactic Synthesis would have suspected that I might be lying about my identity. That would occur only to a person who was abnormally devious himself. And I should have been suspicious when Qwasrolk vanished from the hospital. In his delirium and pain he feared the person responsible. He looked at all of us without really seeing us, and then his eyes fixed on Forlan and he vanished. I saw it, it was obvious, and it didn't register."

"Then Qwasrolk didn't decide that he was the victim of an error until later," Miss Schlupe observed.

Darzek nodded. "Probably because he thought he'd found it. And there were other clues: Forlan's giving me two youngsters as assistants so I'd get as little help as possible. And his setting up a scientific committee of dotards with reputations based on the work they did when they were young. And his horror when I asked whether Kernopplix was present at the government's trade fair symposium—what could one more trader have mattered when so many were present? He must have known Kernopplix, even though Kernopplix didn't know him."

Miss Schlupe nodded. "Abnormal deviousness is right. He was the one who suggested that an alien might ask for Vezpronian females to make us think he was Vezpronian! And when you went to Skarnaf supposedly to identify Qwasrolk, he took along nuclear personnel experts Qwasrolk had never had contact with. I checked. Abnormal deviousness—"

"We should have noticed," Darzek agreed. "Well—everyone knew he was brilliant, but he was far more brilliant than anyone suspected. He ranged through every field of science, and he must have made that basic nuclear discovery himself. And he inspired loyalty in his subordinates. Loyalty and devotion. Young scientists disappeared, changed identities, and entered into obviously illegal nuclear research to perfect his plans and build his machines and conduct his experiments. Even Qwasrolk could rationalize the destruction of a world by calling it an error."

"It didn't even occur to Wolndur and Melris to include his name on the list of people with a grievance against Vezpro," Miss Schlupe said. "How many of his assistants did he murder?"

"Probably all of them. He wouldn't want any witnesses left alive. It must have been a shock to him to learn that Qwasrolk somehow survived, but even in a state of shock he kept his poise and cleverly let someone else suggest the trip to Skarnaf. Once he saw Qwasrolk's condition, he probably decided that he had nothing to fear from him —though it must have unnerved him a bit when Qwasrolk turned up on Vezpro."

"Have we learned anything?" Miss Schlupe asked.

"Always suspect the person who possesses an unnatural excess of virtue," Darzek said. "Especially when he persists in displaying it. Forlan was an excellent actor, and his act was nauseous."

"I thought we already knew that. The thing that surprises me is the xenophobia. That's only supposed to happen on uncivilized planets like Earth, but here we have a healthy, prosperous, friendly people, and Forlan *was* mistreated by them, though no doubt he tried to pretend that he wasn't."

"He did," Darzek said. "He told Melris he'd been offered an appointment as mas several times when he was younger, but he hadn't wanted to get involved in politics. It wasn't true."

"Have the people of Vezpro learned anything?"

"They should have learned never to confine anyone in a ghetto—because of race or species or anything else."

"Ghetto? Those prosperous farms and farming communities?"

"There are spiritual ghettos," Darzek said. "If you confine a person's spirit, letting him live in marble halls doesn't compensate. He's just as much a prisoner as he'd be in a hovel. If the spirit is great enough, and the confinement severe enough, all of the civilizing influences of the galaxy can't contain the result."

"Then the people of Vezpro did this to themselves. Would it do any good to tell them?"

"No. As you said, they're healthy, prosperous, and friendly. They're also generous, kindly, and helpful. They'd never be able to accept the fact that their own petty hatred created a master criminal who came within an eyelash of destroying them. Hatred is the most dangerous emotion in the universe—to the person who hates. Hate anyone long enough and your hatred is certain to be returned. With interest. Got your mushrooms packed?"

"I decided to take four cargo compartments. I have an idea for a new kind of burger with chopped meat and mushrooms and—"

"Schluppy!"

"Bring my rocking chair," she said.

Darzek picked it up and followed her to the transmitter.